MAIDSTONE

KT-479-512

20. OCT 07
Fellowes

14. J

18. MAR 08.
11. AUG 08

03 APR 08
14.
4/11/08

7.7.08

28. MAY 08
2. MAR 09.

04. JUN 08
0 5 MAY 2009
1 1 NOV 2009

2 1 APR 2010
9th June 2010
30 June 2010
11/4/11
- 3 MAY 2012
22.2.16
26/5/21
Simmons

MAI

Please return on or before the latest date above.
You can renew online at *www.kent.gov.uk/libs*
or by telephone 08458 247 200

Winde

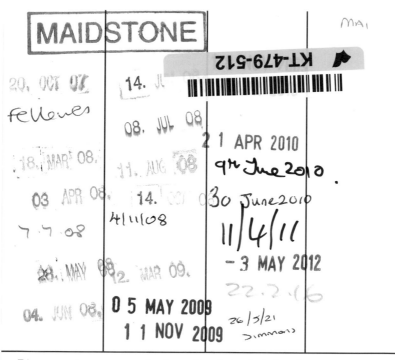

CHARTER MARK
CUSTOMER SERVICE EXCELLENCE

Libraries & Archives

Kent
County
Council

00884\DTP\RN\07.07   LIB 7

C153181568

MURDER IN THE BASTILLE

MURDER
IN THE BASTILLE

CARA BLACK

WHEELER
CHIVERS

This Large Print edition is published by Wheeler Publishing, Waterville, Maine, USA and by BBC Audiobooks Ltd, Bath, England.
Wheeler Publishing is an imprint of Thomson Gale, a part of The Thomson Corporation.
Wheeler is a trademark and used herein under license.
Copyright © by Cara Black.
The moral right of the author has been asserted.
An Aimée Leduc Investigation Series

ALL RIGHTS RESERVED
The text of this Large Print edition is unabridged.
Other aspects of the book may vary from the original edition.
Set in 16 pt. Plantin.

LIBRARY OF CONGRESS CATALOGING-IN-PUBLICATION DATA

Black, Cara, 1951–
    Murder in the Bastille / by Cara Black.
      p. cm.
    ISBN-13: 978-1-59722-433-8 (lg. print : pbk. : alk. paper)
    ISBN-10: 1-59722-433-2 (lg. print : pbk. : alk. paper)
    1. Leduc, Aimee (Fictitious character) — Fiction. 2. Women private
investigators — France — Paris — Fiction. 3. Paris (France) — Fiction. 4.
Bastille — Fiction. 5. Large type books. I. Title.
PS3552.L297M795 2007
813'.6—dc22   2007003907

BRITISH LIBRARY CATALOGUING-IN-PUBLICATION DATA AVAILABLE

Published in 2007 in the U.S. by arrangement with Soho Press, Inc.
Published in 2007 in the U.K. by arrangement with Soho Press, Inc.

U.K. Hardcover: 978 1 405 64150 0 (Chivers Large Print)
U.K. Softcover: 978 1 405 64151 7 (Camden Large Print)

Printed in the United States of America on permanent paper
10 9 8 7 6 5 4 3 2 1

KENT
ARTS & LIBRARIES

C153181568

Dedicated to all the ghosts,
past and present.

Thanks to so many generous people who shared their knowledge and themselves: savvy Kathleen Knox and her seeing-eye dog Thai; Ron Hideshima, invaluable Access Technology Instructor, of the Living Skills Center for the Visually Impaired; Bill Simpson, Donna and the caring staff at Rose Resnick Lighthouse; the Tuesday group; Steven Platzman; Grace Loh, her insight, Jean Satzer, above and beyond, Dot Edwards who lived it and shared, *toujours* James N. Frey, Ron Huberman, San Francisco DA's office, Dr. Eddie Tamura, his expertise, Mike Hakershaw, soul *soeur* Marion Nowak, Dr. Terri Haddix, and all bookseller *amies.*

In Paris: *mercis* to Anne-Françoise Delbegue, her wit, warmth and Bastille guidance; the Residence St. Louis, Carla, Kathleen and Marcus Haddock *et* Sarah, Martine, Gilles, Lesley, Gala; Brentano's on

Avenue de l'Opera; Isabelle *et* Andi; officer Cathy Etilé and Commandant Michel Bruno of the Commissariat Central du 12ème arrondissement who answer *toutes* and more.

Linda Allen for her support; deep thanks to Laura Hruska who encourages risks . . . big ones; Shuchan, my son, and Jun who puts up with it all.

You are not alive unless you know you are living

— graffiti on a Paris wall

In the country of the blind, the one-eyed man is king

— Desiderius Erasmus, *Adagia*

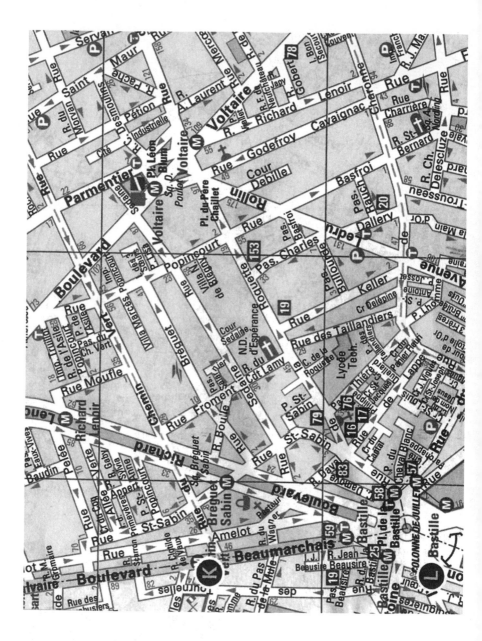

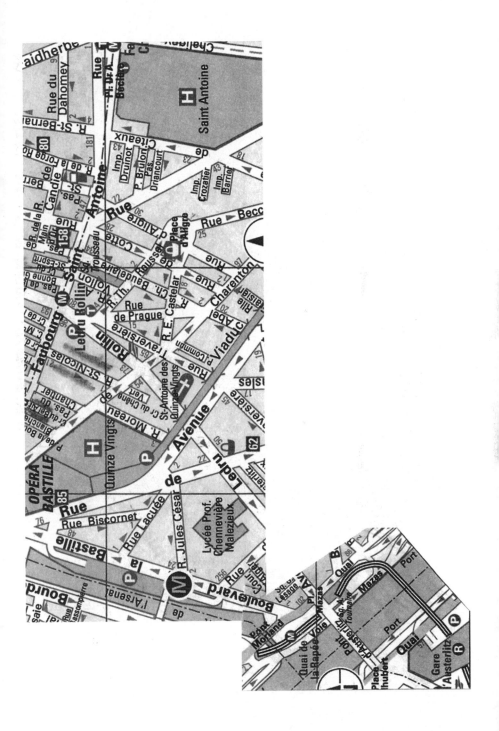

■ ■ ■ ■

PARIS
OCTOBER, 1994

■ ■ ■ ■

MONDAY EVENING

Aimée Leduc felt the air shift, the floating candles waver, as a woman murmuring into a cell phone, wearing a black silk Chinese jacket identical to Aimée's, sat down on the restaurant banquette next to her.

Great. Just Aimée's luck someone showed up in *her* jacket tonight. For a moment Aimée made eye contact with the woman. Blunt blonde shocks of hair framed her face. She favored Aimée with an intense stare. The vein in her temple stood out in her otherwise perfectly made-up face.

"Wouldn't you know it!" Aimée said to her.

"Things could get worse." The woman shrugged, as if wearing the same outfit as her neighbor were the least of her worries. Aimée noticed the frightened look in her eyes before she averted her face.

Around them, illuminated by red glass Etruscan-style sconces, Parisiens drank, dined, and smoked. This upscale *resto,* formerly a meat market, with its exposed beams and rusted meathooks, was booked weeks ahead. But her client, Vincent Csarda, head of Populax, an *agence de publicité,* never had trouble getting a table.

Tinkling glasses and the waiters' shouts made it difficult for Aimée to hear Vincent's words. Vincent, the brains behind his advertising agency, who was sitting across from her, stabbed his slithering *ziti con vongole* as he spoke.

"But I'm just the *mec* stuck in the middle. My agency subcontracted this Incandescent campaign only two weeks ago," he said. His short coifed hair and red bow tie were out of place in this fashionably dressed late evening dinner crowd. He was not quite Aimée's height. Vincent, who was in his mid-thirties, was a nervous type. She figured he was gaunt from overwork and espresso. She wished it worked that way for her.

Aimée knew she should be home preparing her apartment for the construction crew and packing her bags. She was torn between bolting for a taxi or listening to more of Vincent's excuses as he sat across from her.

"Tiens," Vincent said, "was it my fault Incandescent was a front and laundered money for gun runners?"

"Vincent, the courts see it differently," Aimée said, wishing he would accept the facts. But Vincent demanded control. Total control. Didn't they all? "E-mail and downloaded documents constitute judicial evidence. We have to turn over your Opera marketing campaign file for the domestic and Russian tour."

"But my Opera marketing campaign doesn't relate to them. I refuse to let this investigation tarnish my firm's reputation."

She mustered a small smile. After all, he was a paying client. "My connection at the Judiciare says a subpoena's imminent," she said. "Count on it. It would be better to give them your hard drive voluntarily."

It wasn't the first time she'd regretted her best friend Martine's referral. Martine and Vincent were partners in *Diva,* a new magazine. Martine, former *Madame Figaro* editor, savvy and connected, did the work and Vincent was the financial backer. Martine had been crazed, getting ready for the launch this week.

The woman next to them ground out her cigarette. She drummed her long purple fingernails on the table, then lit another and set it in the ashtray.

Aimée recognized the nail color — Violet Vamp, advertised as urban armor for girls

17

on the go — as one she'd been meaning to buy herself. She tried to ignore the curling smoke. She'd quit smoking four days ago.

Again.

Aimée's chipped nails, Gigabyte Green, needed a manicure. At least her sun-streaked hair and tan, from a week in Sardinia, helped her fit in with the sophisticated crowd.

Had everyone found the same boutique on rue Charonne? And coughed up the equivalent of the boutique's rent for the supposed "one-of-a-kind" clinging side-buttoned dress with matching jacket? Aimée had only been able to afford the jacket with mahjong buttons, unlike her neighbor who wore the knockout matching sheath as well.

Scents of fresh basil and roasted garlic drifted from the next table. When Aimée looked over again, the woman had propped her menu against an ashtray and disappeared.

Laughter erupted from the bar. Nearby, chairs scraped over the floor tiles. Time to work out this agreement, smooth Vincent's feathers, and get him to cooperate, Aimée concluded. Then she could leave.

"Dragging in my firm will give rise to rumors," said Vincent. "Damaging rumors."

Mentally, she agreed. Why be an appetizer

served up before the main course in a foreign arms investigation? But once *la Procuratrice* got something on her court docket, it stayed there.

"Vincent, be calm. We hand over the hard drive. . . ."

"I'm paid to deal with my client's information," he interrupted. "Not you. Not the Judiciare. They have no right to see my records or client database."

She wanted to deflect his anger, focus on the ongoing computer security issues. "Here's good news. We set up new firewalls so Hacktivistes pose no threat to Populax," she said, pouring sparkling Badoit mineral water into his glass. He worried about hackers constantly.

"That's what we pay you for at Leduc Detective." He stood up. Short as he was, even in his rumpled seersucker blazer, he commanded attention. "My lawyer will stop this. Why can't you encrypt the Incandescent file? It would save everyone needless trouble?"

"Too late. Look, René and I installed your system," Aimée said, "but we're following the law. Encryption is illegal. I know *la Proc,* she's reasonable."

He glared. "We *paid* you for security!" Vincent took the agency's contract with Leduc

Detective out of his attaché case, tore it up, and sprinkled the pieces, like parmesan cheese, over her pasta.

He edged past the waiter holding the second course, *artichauts aux citron.* She got to her feet to stop him. But he'd darted out the door, disappearing into the warren of passages threading the Bastille *quartier.*

Aimée's appetite vanished. Why had things gone so wrong? A multimillion franc corporation looked better volunteering its hard drive data to the Judiciare, not concealing it. No one would welcome being drawn into a money laundering case, but did Vincent, a self-made *chef d'operations,* have something to hide?

Beside her, the woman's cigarette with the Violet Vamp lip imprint — matching her nail polish — smoldered in the ashtray. Instead of lighting a cigarette of her own from it, Aimée popped a piece of Nicorette gum.

She dreaded calling René, her partner, and telling him of Vincent's outburst. René was better with difficult clients. As he often pointed out, her level of tact left something to be desired. But the bottom line was, if they didn't furnish the subpoenaed e-mail and data, they'd be disobeying the law. Even if Vincent had torn up their contract.

And then she noticed the cell phone on the banquette table. The one the woman had been using. She must have forgotten it.

Losing a phone was a pain; she'd misplaced hers and had to replace it, only last month. On her way out, she'd leave the phone with the maitre d'.

The waiter slipped her the check. A perfect ending to a perfect meal! She'd deduct it from Populax's retainer when she sent their bill.

Then the maitre d' returned to the table and handed back her card with a shrug. "No credit cards, *désolé*." So she had to dredge up her last bit of cash. No taxi tonight. She was left with just enough change for the Métro.

While she was working out how to break the news of the failed meeting to René, waiting by the register for a few francs change, the cell phone rang.

She answered it automatically, cupping the phone between her chin and shoulder as she took her change, balancing her heavy bag.

"For the love of God . . . forget your pride," said a male voice, barely audible over the hum of conversation and strains of accordion music in the background. "Meet me in Passage de la Boule Blanche, give me one more chance, listen to reason. . . ."

"But. . . ."

A familiar tune wafted over the line in the background. Like a song her grandmother had played on her accordion. But Aimée couldn't quite place it.

"Don't argue, I won't listen to a refusal." The phone clicked off.

Aimée stared at it. The cover bore the initials J. D. She looked out the window and saw the woman disappearing into the square outside.

"This belongs to that woman, the one wearing the same jacket as mine. Do you know her name?"

The maitre d' shrugged again. "I'm sorry, mademoiselle," he said. "This is a busy night."

"My receipt?" But the flustered maitre d' had turned to seat a bevy of waiting customers.

Aimée grabbed her receipt which was by the register. She hit the phone's callback button. A flat buzz. Odd. What should she do?

The corner resto faced the dark Place Trousseau. Turn-of-the-century baroque apartment buildings with filigree ironwork balconies bordered the quiet square. Leafy plane trees canopied the black iron fence that surrounded it. The woman had vanished.

She was familiar with the nearby Passage de la Boule Blanche; she often used it as a shortcut. The *Cahiers du Cinéma,* a film journal whose office was located mid-passage off a leafy courtyard, had been a client last year. She'd also joined their film club. Since the passage was en route to the Métro, she decided to return the phone to the man who had called. . . . Let *them* work it out.

She dreaded the packing that still awaited her in her apartment on Île St-Louis. And she still had to dig out the laptop cable adaptors. They were somewhere in the only closet, which was 20 feet high and full of rolled up, threadbare Savonnerie carpets.

Martine's brother, in Shanghai on assignment, had sublet his apartment to her, until the remodeling — long overdue — of her own apartment's bathroom and kitchen was finished.

At the passage entrance, streetlights from rue du Faubourg Saint Antoine illuminated peeling notices and a *Meubles décoratifs* sign affixed to the stone wall. A waist-high metal barricade, a *Piétons barrés* notice, and construction materials blocked the way. Inhabitants must have ignored the sign, since it was pushed to the side and a path had been beaten through the rubble.

Further along, the flat roof of the covered passage opened to the sky. The threadlike passage lined with narrow, looming buildings seemed to end in distant mottled shadows.

"Allô?"

The echo of her voice and faint meow of a cat reached her ears. Water dripped from somewhere. In the late evening, unseasonably warm for October, dampness from lichen encrusted water pipes chilled her.

"Monsieur?"

Why didn't the man who'd telephoned answer? He'd said he was waiting.

She stepped past the barricade, scanning the dark passage, waiting in the shadowed stillness for a reply. Had he given up?

Cellophane wrappers crackled under her black Prada mules, a Porte de Vanves flea market find. Worn once. Or so the vendor said before she'd bargained him down to 300 francs.

The scent of night-flowering jasmine floated from a hidden garden behind the damp wall. Was the man playing games? She didn't have time for this.

One of the phones in her handbag rang.

She picked it up.

"Look, monsieur, a woman forgot her phone and I picked it up. I'd like to return it, I'm in the passage."

"What are you talking about?" her partner asked. "I thought you were dining with Vincent?"

"I'm in the Passage de la Boule Blanche. A woman left her cell phone in the resto and I was trying to return it to her."

"What happened with Vincent?"

Now she'd have to admit the awful truth. She'd wanted to tell René in person.

"We were in the resto until Vincent tore up our contract," she said, "Then he stomped out, leaving me with the bill."

"*Tiens!* Aimée, you should have let me handle him," he said. She heard the sigh in René's voice.

"I won't lie or cheat for clients."

"There's always a first time!" René snorted.

"At least not for conglomerates like Populax."

"*Quel méli-melo!* What a mess!" René said. "The Judiciare's getting nasty about this. I've been warned there may be a charge of obstructing justice in our future."

The phone clicked.

"Hold on, I'm at the office," René said. "I have another call."

Aimée picked her way over the uneven path toward a widening of the passage. No windows here. Just wet cobblestones underfoot with shimmers of fluorescent graffiti catching licks of light. Further on, she knew it intersected with the dimly lit rue de Charenton.

She'd already left her dog, Miles Davis, with René's neighbor, a female impersonator who performed in a club in Les Halles. *Bon,* she'd catch the Metro home and throw stuff in her suitcase and ask René to pick her up and drive her to the flat where she would stay during her apartment's renovation. They could discuss strategies en route.

She smelled something tangy and tart. Cloth rustled. Aimée hitched up her leather backpack and grabbed her sharp keys in her fist as a defense. Before she could turn, vise-like hands clamped around her neck, squeezing and choking her. She screamed but no sound came out.

Slammed into the wall, her face scraped the moss-speckled stone. Pain exploded in her skull. Then she was pulled back and slammed again. She grabbed at her throat, struggling to pull off those hands, to summon help.

Air. She had to get air.

Panic flooded her. She couldn't breathe.

Twisting, turning, trying to bite and scratch those hands.

In the distance she heard a dropped bottle shatter, then a disgusted *"Merde,"* then laughter. Were other people coming down the passage? She saw a light, heard an intake of breath behind her. The hands let go.

Something wet seeped over her dress. She heard a ringing sound echoing off the dark walls. The last things she saw before she lost consciousness were stars peeking between the jagged roof tiles in the Paris sky.

Monday Night

René Friant stretched his short legs, adjusting the tight headset while scanning the computer screen at his desk. Shadows filled the corners of the office. He wished he were home, not on the phone with a furious Vincent Csarda, who had spoken without taking a breath for at least two minutes.

"This Incandescent fiasco could lose me the Opera Bastille marketing campaign," said Vincent. "We're trying to revitalize the *quartier*," he said, "I cannot have it."

"Of course, Vincent. You know that, I know that," René said, his tone soothing. Revitalizing took on different meanings depending on the person, René thought.

Areas of the *quartier* had become *á la page,* trendy. Decaying factories with southern exposure had become pieds-à-terre and lofts for the *gauche caviar.* These limousine liberals of the left had followed the designer Kenzo who'd purchased a huge crumbling warehouse for his atelier, a fantastic bargain.

"Aimée and I will work it out with the Judiciare," he said, hoping to placate Vincent.

From his custom orthopedic chair René noticed cobwebs on the high ceiling over the map of Paris which was sectioned into *arrondissements.* Where was Passage de la Boule Blanche?

Outside, the dark shapes of the trees on rue du Louvre brushed the tall windows. In the distance, streetlights along the Seine glittered. "Vincent, Incandescent's scandal touches each firm who's worked with them. Guilt by association, unless proven otherwise. Your Populax is no exception. Let's just let *la Procuratrice* take a look, let her see for herself."

"Don't you understand . . ."

"Vincent," René interrupted, with a sigh. "Let me speak with the Judiciare's assistant first thing tomorrow, see what I can do."

Silence. Vincent had hung up.

René rubbed his eyes, cranked down his chair and realized he had several security backup tapes to record. And today's data to monitor.

Then he remembered.

He'd left Aimée on the line.

He clicked back to her on the phone. And heard the sounds of someone choking.

LATER MONDAY NIGHT

Searing bursts of pain, a flashing staccato of agony and light hit Aimée. Then a heavy, hideous compression jammed her skull. Spread across her cranium, leveled her. Like nothing she'd ever felt.

She opened her mouth with a cry that took all the air from her. Her universe, cliffs and peaks of hurt, throbbed. A shimmery cold spiked her spine. Everything folded into dark; all was furry and fuzzy.

And then she threw up. Everywhere. All down her Chinese silk jacket. She reached out to what felt like leaves, wet with clingy bits of vomit. Then she fell over, her nails scraping the stone. Night starlings tittered above her.

René's voice sounded faraway. "Aimée, Aimée! What happened? Are you hurt? Are you still there?"

René was on the phone . . . but he was so far away. She tried to speak but her mouth

29

wouldn't work. No words came out. No rescue plea. No sound.

TUESDAY, 1:00 A.M.

A monotonous beeping slowly penetrated Aimée's consciousness, layer by layer. It was as though her head was stuffed with cotton and her mouth full of dry gauze. Her head felt fat, smashed, swollen. Constant aching, jarring, and then a distant thudding.

Voices boomed over a static-laced loud-speaker and something wet rubbed Aimée's cheek. She swatted it.

"We've stabilized the bleeding in your brain, mademoiselle," a voice said.

"What do you mean?" At least that's what she *meant* to say, but her words slurred. She couldn't focus. Everything seemed steamy and gray, blanketed by fog.

"Good thing your friend brought you in. Any longer and you wouldn't have made it."

"But where am I?"

"L'hôpital Saint Antoine. *Alors!* The neurosurgeon repaired the nasty vein wall in your brain that had collapsed."

His words faded and blurred.

"You have a venous malformation," he was saying. "Congenital, not something you'd

30

ever know you had. But pressure on your neck caused the vein to blow."

She'd dropped out of pre-med at the Ecole des Médecins but remembered brain hemorrhages. "What do you mean. . . . I've had brain surgery?"

"It's all done by threading the catheter up to the collapsed vein and embolizing it. No cutting. Count yourself more than lucky on this one!"

"But doctor. . . ."

"Shhh . . . take a little nap," he said. "This will help the pain."

She felt a prick in her arm, then icy cold.

LATER

"Stop it or you'll throw up again."

The dense grey fog shifted. "René?" Aimée asked.

"Who else?" he said.

She had to get up, get out from under this dark heavy thing.

"Take the blanket off me, René," she said. "Please, it's too dark."

No answer. She reached out to pull it off, but all she felt was skin, arms . . . short arms.

"René!"

"Quit moving," he said. "You've puked your guts out on the linoleum, which deserves it, and on me, who doesn't."

"*Desolée,* but I can't see where you are," she said.

A pause.

"Take it easy," he said.

"What's the matter?" she asked. Her fingers traveled his arm to his shoulders.

"You're on a gurney. Stay still."

"Where are we?"

She felt his large, warm hands grip hers.

"In the clinic at l'hôpital des Quinze-Vingts, Aimée."

"But that's . . . that's," she said, struggling to sit up, "the eye hospital. . . ." It was too dark. She couldn't see. "Take these bandages off my eyes, René."

Silence.

She felt her eyes. No bandages.

Footsteps stopped in front of them. "Monsieur Friant, is this Mademoiselle Leduc?"

René must have nodded. "Please help us escort her to Dr. Lambert in Examination."

That would be hard since she towered over René, a stocky dwarf of four feet. "I don't need anyone's help," she said. "I can walk!"

"Stay still."

But she sat up, then didn't know where to turn, not even where her feet were when she thought she'd stood up. All she knew was she'd landed on something hard and slippery and then she threw up again.

When they'd cleaned her up, she promised herself she wouldn't cry. In the dark fog where all she knew were sounds and textures, at least, she resolved, she wouldn't let them see her cry.

TUESDAY

"Mademoiselle Leduc," said Doctor Lambert, "there's a knot on your head the size of . . ."

Aimée reached and missed. Felt her spiky hair, then air. Then tried again. This time she hit it and winced. "A large grapefruit?"

"Close enough," he said. She felt the examining table shift with the weight of someone. A smell of antibacterial soap, the crinkle of what she imagined was a starched lab coat. Then a cold, metal disk on her chest. She shivered.

"Doctor, I can breathe," she said, pushing it away. "Please, do something about the darkness."

She felt air on her cheeks, heard the slight tinkle of a loose metal watchband. The room seemed filled with gray light. She saw nothing but little static swirls on the inside of her lids that made her dizzy.

"Any shadows?" he asked.

She felt a breeze in front of her.

"No. But you're waving your hand in front of my face, aren't you?"

"Don't treat this like a quiz, mademoiselle," he said. "You must feel angry. I would, too."

She wanted to say that anger didn't quite cover it. But after all, he was just doing his job.

"When will I see again?" She hoped her panic didn't come across in her voice. "Why can't I see?"

"We'll run tests, analyze the fluid buildup, see if the pressure on your optic nerve dissipates."

Aimée took a deep breath. "And if the pressure continues?"

"Complications occurred after the procedure in l'hôpital Saint Antoine," he said. "Let's talk after the tests."

Complications? He sounded young. . . . What if he was an intern? Or some *médicastre,* a quack?

Would she ever see? Or would she be stuck, depending on others, the rest of her life? She tamped her fear down, tried to make sense of the future.

Her business was at stake. Not to mention her life, her dog, and her apartment. She'd lose everything if she couldn't pay her bills. The little windfall she'd gotten in the Sentier had been eaten up by the contractor and plumber. Every time they opened a seventeenth-century wall, they'd shaken their heads and held out their hands.

"Doctor, no offense, but I'd like more explanation. Perhaps I could talk with the specialist or department head?"

She felt a distinct pinch on her arm. Hard. From the level of where René's arm would rest.

"No offense taken, Mademoiselle Leduc," the doctor said. "But that's me."

Was that a glimmer of amusement in his tone?

"We specialize in trauma-related optic injuries. I manage the department," he said. "Your partner specifically requested me. Had you brought over from surgery in Saint Antoine. Highly unusual, but I consented."

"But Doctor, will I be blind . . . ?" She couldn't say it. Couldn't say *forever.* Not as a prognosis. She'd never even used the word *forever* in the same breath with a relationship.

"Let's get you back on the gurney for an MRI and CAT scan." He must have leaned forward, because she smelled espresso on his breath. "Anger's essential to your recov-

35

ery, mademoiselle. Don't let up."

His warm hands helped her onto a gurney.

"I'll meet you there," said the doctor.

She felt helpless all the way through the echoing corridors and during the elevator ride. The rubber wheels squeaked on what sounded like freshly waxed linoleum. "René?"

"Right here," he said, from somewhere near her elbow.

"You should have told me if the doctor was a geek, René," she said. "What does he look like, eh . . . glasses and overweight? Is he really any good?"

René made a sound she'd heard when he'd choked on a chicken bone once. "Look, Aimée . . ."

"Well, you're right about the glasses," said Dr. Lambert.

Why couldn't the earth open up and swallow her?

"Sorry, my big mouth . . ."

"Excuse me, sir," a deep voice interrupted. "Only hospital staff allowed from here on. You can return to see the patient in a few hours."

Then she heard the ping of the swinging doors, felt the wheels wobbling. No more René.

Fear took over. She sat up, struggling to get off the gurney. They had to tie her down to the CAT scan table.

TUESDAY NIGHT

"A *flic's* waiting to speak with you," the nurse said to Aimée. The nice nurse who rolled her r's and tried to hide her Burgundian accent. Typical of new arrivals in Paris. "He's waited a while. Do you feel up to it?"

Aimée fingered the bandages on her neck. She didn't want anyone seeing her like this. How could she speak with someone she didn't know and couldn't see? She wanted to burrow into a hole and die.

"I told Sergeant Bellan you might be up to it," the nurse said. "He mentioned he was a family friend."

Loïc Bellan . . . a family friend! That low-down snake who had accused her and her father of graft. Calling them dirty and accusing them of being on the take!

Before she could answer, the nurse's footsteps clattered away.

"We meet again, Mademoiselle Leduc," Loïc Bellan said, his steps on the linoleum accompanying his words. His voice sounded low and gravelly, as usual. He'd been a protégé of her father's, until her father left the force. Once, Bellan had idolized him.

The last time she'd come across Bellan, he'd been reeling drunk and abusive, in front of the Commissariat. But she'd turned the tables in the Sentier, proving him and the others wrong. She learned his wife had given birth to a baby with Down Syndrome. Last month she'd heard from her godfather that Bellan was falling apart.

"Care for a Gauloise?"

"I quit. Smoking's not allowed anyway," she said. "But I'm sure you know that."

She smelled a stale whiff of Paco Rabanne cologne and tobacco on his clothes. He must have lit up in the hallway.

"There are just a few questions I need to ask you about the attack."

No mention of the baby, just born when he'd last seen her, nor any word of sympathy for Aimée's condition. And no apology for the drunken abuse he'd heaped on her the last time they'd met.

She wished she knew where he was standing. Most of all she wished she could see him, fix him with a steely stare. And then she had a semblance of coherent thought.

"Wait a minute, Bellan, you're stationed in the second *arrondissement,* not the Bastille," she said. "Off your turf, aren't you?"

"Good memory," he said. "I'm racking up overtime. But I appreciate your concern. Now, tell me what happened," he said, his voice businesslike.

"You must be on special assignment if you're out of your *arrondissement.*"

"I can't say anything about it," he said. "But if you cooperate, I'll take your statement."

Flics didn't travel between *arrondissements.* At least they hadn't before.

"Something else going on, Bellan?"

Silence again.

"Or does it have to do with my father? Guilt by association." He must enjoy seeing her blind and squirming.

"Like I said, take it easy," Bellan said.

Feet shifted on the linoleum. Good, she made him uncomfortable.

"You don't believe anything I say. My father crumbled from the pedestal you put him on. But he wasn't dirty, I proved it. The rest is in your head, Bellan."

"I'm harsh sometimes," he said, "That was a bad time for me."

"You mean when your baby was born," she said. Tactless again. "Sorry . . ."

"Can it," he interrupted, his voice rising. "I am on special detail, if you need to know. Feel better?"

"Concerning what?"

"I'm not at liberty to discuss that," he said. "Tell me what happened."

And she did for the most part. Even her stupidity in going down a dim passage. But this was Paris, and it was a passage she'd walked a hundred times. She'd never felt afraid before. Not like now.

"So would you say someone might have followed you from the resto?"

"If so, I didn't hear him."

"This client, Vincent Csarda, did he know where you were going?"

"Csarda left before me," she said.

Though vindictive in business, she doubted Vincent would physically attack her. He'd coerce her and René in other ways.

"The person behind me was tall; Vincent's shorter than I am."

"Just checking all leads," he said.

A slow throbbing achiness filled her head. All this thinking and concentrating hurt. At least it took her mind off the stinging bruises ringing her swollen neck.

"Someone strangled me and smashed my head against the wall. But I'm no retard, Bellan." As soon as she'd said that, hot shame flushed over her. She remembered the baby.

Silence.

"Look, I didn't mean. . . . That woman was the target, not me," she said.

"Want to explain that to me?"

"I was meeting a man . . . to give him a woman's cell phone. She'd left it behind and I answered it. . . . It's too complicated."

"Take it easy; you've been hit on the head," he said. "Hard."

From Bellan's tone she sensed mockery. But she couldn't be sure. If only she could see his face.

"Well, we could tell more if we had this phone," he said. "Check the numbers."

Of course, her bag . . . she'd forgotten about that. What happened to her laptop and the Populax file?

"Where are my things?"

"The nurse said your papers showed you were admitted with no personal belongings," said Bellan.

So the attacker had stolen her bag. Everything was gone. Thorough, Bellan was a thorough *flic*. That's what she remembered her father saying about him. He and some young Turks had been brought in to fight corruption in the department.

She felt something being wedged into her clutched fist. "My number's on here," said Bellan. "Have the nurse help you call me if you think of anything else."

Long after he'd gone, she fought back tears of frustration.

Loïc Bellan went to the parking lot, his head down.

"I'll walk," Bellan said to the driver in the dented police Peugeot awaiting him. He walked down the narrow rue Charenton hoping his mind would empty. But it didn't.

Why did Aimée's words make it all come back? All the past; how her father, Jean-Claude Leduc, left the force and later received a pardon. But the rumors in the Commissariat were never silenced. How Jean-Claude had called one day, asking to meet for coffee, "For old time's sake," he'd said. Loïc had spit into the phone and refused. Two days later Jean-Claude had died in a terrorist explosion in Place Vendôme. Sometimes, at night, he'd lay awake imagining what Jean-Claude had wanted to say. And all the things he could have said.

He pushed it away. And all the questions he couldn't answer about the attack on Aimée. Yet his gut feeling bothered him. He'd check the file at the Commissariat once more, even though the Préfet wanted to close it. Somehow he felt he owed that to

Jean-Claude.

But he couldn't push away Marie. No matter how he'd tried.

He remembered his wife Marie's blonde hair on the pillow, hearing his older daughter Danielle's snoring from her room and the rumble of the hot water heater while he shaved.

That terrible day. And he asked himself why it had happened like it had. Why he hadn't controlled himself.

But it all came back. Vivid. And his fault.

How he'd tried squirting Teracyl tooth gel on his toothbrush. Not even a dribble. He'd squeezed again. Nothing. Why hadn't Marie gone shopping? He'd worked overtime every night that week.

Funny how small things could build up, cause an explosion.

It cried from the bassinet . . . the blot of life they'd made that wasn't right, stained with its need for constant care. Their *trisomique* Down Syndrome baby. Its mewling, a feeble demand for help. More of an aberration than a baby.

Loïc's first son. His only son.

He always noticed the flattened back of the baby's head, the slanting of his eyelids, and the gap between the baby's first and second toes. Such tiny pink toes. Like perfect small rose pearls.

"Marie," he'd said, "*Alors!* The stakeout took half the night, I've got piles of work on my desk and the Commissaire wants a meeting first thing. Can't you at least get toothpaste?"

Marie stirred and batted an eye open. Small cries continued from the bassinet.

"*Cheri* . . . didn't even hear you come in last night," she said, her voice groggy.

The baby's cries mounted.

"Pass me Guillaume," she said.

She called it Guillaume, after his English relative, William. Insisted they christen it in church with the family, invite some men from the force and their close friends. Loïc noticed the single, deep transverse crease on the tiny palms.

"Guillaume had a rough day yesterday," she said cradling the baby who quieted immediately. "We went to the *médecin,* but he said it was just a cold."

Loïc bristled. He'd put in a twelve-hour shift. Half of it wasted in a dank abandoned warehouse on a stakeout, aggravating back pain from his old injury. These days, it seemed Guillaume was all she focused on. Surely she could have stopped for tooth gel? Marie's gaze never lifted. All she had eyes for was the bundle in her arms.

"But Marie . . ."

"Shhhh," she whispered, pointing to the closed eyes of the baby.

Loïc had thrown the toothpaste, and then a dresser, against the wall. Danielle and Monique had run from their rooms, rubbing their eyes. The baby wailed. Loïc's mind had blanked out the hateful things he'd screamed.

But it was the look in Marie's tired brown eyes that warned him. Fool that he was, he'd ignored it. That night he'd come home to an empty apartment. She'd packed up, hauled the children to her parents in Brittany, and told him to get therapy if he wanted to see them again.

He'd tried. She'd come once to Paris. But no matter how much they discussed it, Marie refused to put Guillaume in an institution. She'd chosen her mongoloid son over *him.* Though she told him, over and over, the opposite.

Now he was back in his apartment. His bloodshot eyes took in the packed boxes in the bare rooms. He needed to move to a smaller place, so he could send them more money.

He thought back to when he and Marie were happy here. He remembered Danielle's first steps in the kitchen one Sunday. The yellow parakeet from the quai de la Mégisserie he'd bought late Christmas Eve, rushing home from the Commissariat, and how Danielle and Monique's eyes sparkled. For once, Daddy's coming home late brought magic. They'd hung the cage in their bedroom, now empty except for the pink-bordered wallpaper.

He thought back to Marie's excitement about his promotion; her proud smile and the fancy bottle of St. Émilion they shared on the roof after Danielle and Monique finally fell asleep. The wonderful time they'd had making a son. Marie's warm skin and how her hair curled over the sheets.

The son who emerged, wrong, nine months later. Loïc couldn't stomach it. The psychologist said he suffered from guilt for chromosomes he had no control over, and grief for passing on the defect. Loïc had told the psychologist to stuff his psychobabble up his ass where it might do him some good.

In Loïc's village, there'd been Hubert the Mongoloid, as they'd called him. Harmless, he'd worked in the laundry. Worked hard. The mongoloid's father, an out-of-work prize-fighter, drank away his winnings and beat Hubert up regularly on Saturday nights. And after the village mill closed, others beat him, too.

Loïc knelt down and found a broken pink barrette in his daughter's room. The movers found him sobbing, cross-legged on the floor, the barrette clutched in one hand and a bottle of cheap whiskey in the other.

TUESDAY EVENING

Aimée heard France 2 news blaring from somewhere in the ward. A hoarse voice declared: "The Beast of Bastille may have claimed another victim late Monday night in a Bastille passage. Confusion reigned as investigators discovered Patric Vaduz, the twenty-eight-year-old alleged serial killer awaiting charges in the Commissariat, had been released due to incorrect procedure in the Procès-Verbal. Vaduz, rumored to be attending his mother's funeral, has not been located."

Stunned, Aimée grabbed for the bed rail. Where was the télé? Disoriented and dizzy, she pulled the hospital robe around her. When she located the source of the sound, she slid her feet onto the cold floor. She heard coughing, then a request for medication from somewhere behind her.

Was she in a ward or a room? She bumped into something, got caught on what felt like a plastic tube . . . an IV hookup?

Merde!

Or maybe it was a radio cord. Somehow she disentangled herself. She groped her way along the bed rail, barefoot, toward the source of the broadcast.

The newscaster continued.

"France 2's informant close to the investigation revealed that the female victim, discovered mid-afternoon rolled up in an old carpet in a courtyard, appeared to have been murdered in circumstances similar to those surrounding other victims of the Beast of Bastille. Though the particulars have not been released, rumor has it another victim was attacked in nearby Passage de la Boule Blanche. This victim remains in stable condition in the hospital. Names will not be released pending investigation and until next of kin are notified. Police offer no comment at this time other than that the investigation is proceeding."

Conversation at the nurse's station, interrupted by the pinging of bells, obscured the rest of the broadcast.

Aimée froze, terrified. Could that be her? She had to hear more. "Please could someone help me. . . ."

Her arm was gripped and someone steered her forward. "I'm a volunteer. Like to hear the evening news, eh? I'll help you to the

TV lobby."

By the time Aimée reached the *télé* she'd controlled her shaking. The announcer continued: "Our correspondent spoke with an inhabitant of the passage who said 'I saw this bloody shoe behind my neighbor's old rug,' said a quavering voice, 'near my cat's dish . . . bothered me, but then I saw the twisted leg of a woman sprawled in the corner. I thought she was Chinese. But it was just her bloodied jacket.' "

"I'm wanted downstairs, but if you need help, clap your hands to get the nurse's attention," the volunteer said. "Looks like you're new here. The staff's run off their feet with patients, but I'm sure rehab will organize an orientation."

"An orientation?"

"To help you navigate the ward on your own."

Of course. But she really didn't want one, or a white cane or a guide-dog. She wanted to *see*.

She pushed that out of her mind. Time enough to worry. Maybe she could find someone with a newspaper who'd read it to her.

The woman mentioned in the broadcast had to be her! So Bellan had questioned her because the Beast of Bastille had murdered a woman in the next passage.

She clapped her hands.

No answer. She stood. What sounded like the ding of an elevator came from behind her. She edged forward, bumped into a wall, and felt her way along it to what sounded like the nurse's station. The smooth counter and rustling papers seemed familiar. She'd made some progress. Maybe she was getting better at this. A loud beeping came from near her.

"Excuse me, but can a nurse help me read a newspaper . . ."

"Doctor's on rounds, mademoiselle," said a brisk voice. "And two new admits must be processed. Can it wait?"

"Of course." Now she was stuck.

"I'll find the volunteer coordinator," the nurse said, guiding Aimée to a hard plastic chair with sticky armrests. "Have a seat. It might take some time."

"Where's my room?"

"Second door on the left. But wait until we can show you, mademoiselle. We follow rules in this ward. It's for your safety."

Footsteps slapped over the linoleum.

No way would she wait, it could take hours. Might as well find her own way back.

She stood, felt her way along the smooth wood hall railing, guiding herself by the low drone of the TV from rooms and the muffled beep of machines. *So far so good,* she thought. But as she rounded a corner and felt the second door, she smelled bleach and soap.

Then she ran into something with ridges that crinkled like cellophane. She stepped on a soft foamlike substance that yielded. Something hard whacked her cheek. Clanging noises came from her feet and then they were cold and wet. She grabbed what felt like a pole. Her feet stung.

Great.

She'd walked smack into a mop, upsetting a pail of soapy ammonia by the stink and the burning of her toes. Or something worse. She'd stumbled into a broom closet.

A total liability! She couldn't even find her room. Useless! She fought back tears welling in her useless eyes.

What was that other smell . . . familiar and jarring? And it came back. That awful odor as hands gripped her neck from behind, squeezing tighter and tighter. Her choking gasps for air. She trembled.

Tar.

"Found something interesting, mademoiselle?" asked a voice she recognized.

Why had he sneaked up on her?

"Dr. Lambert," she said, taking a deep

gulp, "what's tar used for in the hospital?"

"Besides tarring the roof?" he said. "Who knows?"

"That wouldn't be kept in a closet, would it?"

"Mademoiselle Leduc, I planned to run more tests on you," he said, before she could ask more. "But now I need to finish my rounds."

"Go ahead, Dr. Lambert."

"First, you need help."

Strong arms grasped and lifted her up. A stethoscope hit her arm. Her wet, bare feet dangled in the air. She felt frightened and disoriented.

"Look I can walk . . . put me down.

"Not if you've got a chemical burn."

Her feet stung and a big lump wedged in her throat. Hugging her to his warm chest, the doctor carried her back to her room, sat her down, stuck her feet in a tub of water, and paged the nurse. "Do me a favor," he said, an edge in his voice. "Try to stay out of trouble until I get back."

"*Zut!* This looks like a nice mess," said a nurse with a soft Provençal accent. Embarrassed, Aimée let the nurse clean her up. The doctor hadn't answered her question about the tar. The nurse remained silent when Aimée asked, and scurried off before she could press the question.

In the hospital bed, Aimée fumbled for the room phone. After two tries she got the operator. But Leduc Detective had the message machine on. She tried René's apartment. No answer. Then she tried his cell phone, and got his voice mail.

"Please René, I'm sorry, but can you bring me clothes?" she said. "Makeup. My boots. Everything's gone. Unless it's scattered in the passage. And can you check on Miles Davis?"

She knew how to do two things well, smoke and park at an impossible angle. Now she could do only one. If only she could have a smoke!

What was she thinking? How could she apply makeup? And her apartment, she'd have to reach the contractor and put the work on hold.

All she got was their answering machine. She left a message to call her at the hospital. Would they have started the work?

She dialed the operator again and had him try Commissaire Morbier, her godfather, at the Préfecture.

"Groupe R," said an unfamiliar voice.

"Commissaire Morbier, please."

"What's this regarding?"

"I'm his goddaughter, Aimée Leduc."

"He's working out of the Commissariat in Bastille. Hold on, I'll transfer your call."

For someone approaching retirement, she thought, Morbier moved around the force a lot. He'd cut back his hours to spend more time with his grandson Marc . . . or so he said. But she wondered if his back gave him more trouble than he let on.

"Commissariat Principal at Place Léon Blum," he answered.

"Back on the beat, Morbier? Hitting the cobblestones again?"

She heard him suck in his breath. In her mind she saw him — his mismatched socks, suspenders, and shock of thick salt-and-pepper hair. She wondered if he'd kept off the weight he'd lost over the summer and if he still wore patches to help him stop smoking.

"They call it special detail, Leduc."

That meant several things. Damage control was one of them. Since he was working out of the Bastille area, was he involved with the serial killer . . . had she found what she was looking for?

"Look Morbier, I need to know about the victims and anything else you feel like sharing about the Bastille serial murders."

"Leduc, I'm busy."

Maybe he didn't know she'd been attacked.

"Something tells me you have the information I need."

"What's it to you if I do, Leduc?" he said. She heard a metallic ratcheting, as if he had turned in an unoiled swivel chair.

Something in his voice told her he knew.

"Leduc, I just got in," he said. "I haven't had time to read the update file. Or finish my espresso."

She sensed another presence in her hospital room. Something she couldn't explain. The hair stood on the back of her neck. Wariness overtook her; she covered the phone with her hand.

"Who's there?"

No answer. And then footsteps moved away. Was it a nurse, the doctor, or a volunteer?

Or . . . ? That tar smell near the broom closet? For an awful moment she was struck by the thought of the attacker, lurking, waiting to finish his task. It would be so easy to don a uniform, wear a mask, and search the corridors. Her heart clenched with fear. She took a deep breath.

"Call me curious, Morbier," she said. "Please, we need to talk."

"I'm tied up," he said. "Staff meeting in

five minutes. The unit has to come up with some answers. And I still haven't read the file."

"Answers to why Patrick Vaduz was released due to incorrect procedure? And why a woman got murdered in the passage? Well France 2 news put it together and blamed the bungling on . . ."

"Got to go," Morbier interrupted. In the background, chairs scraped the floor, murmuring voices rose.

"But they're wrong. I don't think Vaduz killed that woman," she said. "Meet me in room 312, l'hôpital Quinzes-Vingts."

"Investigating something?" he said. "Leave the serial killers to us, Leduc. Stick to computers."

"I can't, it's personal." She wanted to confront him face to face.

Morbier's voice betrayed no surprise. "Leduc, you know hospitals bother me."

True. He hadn't even come to see her after the terrorist bombing in Place Vendôme, the one that killed her father and put her in the burn unit. She'd been lucky; the skin graft on her palm was the only visible scar.

"I can help you," she said, lowering her voice. "But not over the phone."

"*Tiens!* We know Patric Vaduz did it."

She had to make Morbier interested enough to come. This needed to be said in person. "Well, there's a witness who thinks otherwise."

A siren wailed below Aimée's window as an ambulance pulled into the hospital courtyard.

"So this witness has proof?"

She heard an edge of interest in his voice.

"You might say living proof."

WEDNESDAY NOON

"Attention, petit!" shouted a perspiring delivery man wheeling a dolly loaded with beer crates. "Didn't see you."

René, carrying Aimée's bag, sidestepped the man on the pavement. He ignored the stares from passersby in rue Faubourg St-Antoine. Born a dwarf, now just four feet tall, he was used to people staring. Most of the time.

He'd heard Aimée's message on his voice mail and gathered things from her apartment. Now he turned into the Passage de la Boule Blanche, a narrow half-covered alleyway lined with old storefronts and doorways to courtyards housing craftsmen, upholsterers, and furniture makers. Wide enough for a small car. Once the site of the crimes of the notorious poet-criminal, Lacenaire, guillotined in 1836.

René retraced his steps to the place where he'd found Aimée sprawled on the cobbles. Not far from the metal waist-high barricade with a *Piétons barrés* sign. He wondered if there was anything he hadn't found last night.

Green garbage bins, emptied and waiting, hugged the narrow stone wall. Too bad, anything left behind would have been cleaned up by the *ébouers.* Nothing there to indicate the horror of Aimée's attack last night. What had she said . . . she remembered a light?

He looked around and in the October sunshine saw the imposing entrance of the Quinze-Vingts hospital at the end of the passage. The Quinze-Vingts — fifteen times twenty — was the number of beds the hospital's founder, Louis XV, had needed for his knights blinded by Saracens on the Ninth Crusade; the name had endured. Had she meant a light from the hospital?

The Passage de la Boule Blanche, in the throes of construction, lay deserted. The young designer's shop was closed. Ahead on the right lay the courtyard of the *Cahiers du Cinéma,* their former client. He walked over but the gate was chained. On it hung a sign saying CLOSED FOR REMODELING. Too bad, he would have felt comfortable asking questions of people he knew there. He could have ferreted out whether anyone had been in the office late.

He gazed up. A mossy stone wall lined a good part of the passage. The network of passages in the Bastille once connected the wood shipped down the Seine and the woodworkers and furniture makers in the faubourg's courtyards. After Louis XI licensed craftsmen in the fifteenth century, this Bastille *quartier* grew into a working-class area; cradle of revolutions, mother of street-fighters and artisans, home of the Bastille prison.

Later tinsmiths, blacksmiths, mirror-makers, gilders, and coal merchants joined them, occupying the small glass-roofed factories and warehouses. Now, many of these were gentrified, and the rest had been bulldozed.

Then he heard hammering from the niche-like entrance on his left.

René didn't feel much like a detective even though the sign where he worked read LEDUC DETECTIVE. They shared the computer security jobs, but only Aimée had a criminal investigation background.

Now he had to take up the slack. Help

figure this out. Aimée, his best friend, had suffered a brutal attack outside this atelier; maybe someone inside had seen or heard something.

He walked into a small, damp courtyard. A sign, styled like a coat of arms, read CAVOUR MASTER WOODWORKERS, EST. 1794. Low strains of a Vivaldi concerto floated through the doorway.

"Pardon," René said, raising his voice. He walked through a narrow entrance opening into a large atelier illumined by skylights. The sharp tang of turpentine reached him. "Anyone here?"

A middle-aged man, wearing a blue work-coat, glasses pushed up on his bald head, stood at a work table. With delicate strokes he rubbed the gilded legs of an antique lacquered chair. Small and exquisite, it looked to René as if anyone sitting on it would snap it in pieces. In the middle of the large room stood a heater, its flue leading to the roof, a water cooler, and more work-tables filled with furniture in various stages of repair. From the walls hung every type of antique wooden chair René had ever seen — and many he hadn't.

"Forgive me, monsieur," René said, "for disturbing your work."

The man looked up, took in René's stature, but showed no surprise. He had dark pouches under his eyes and a sallow complexion. His pursed mouth gave him a harried look.

"*Tiens!* I've done all I can with this," the man said, setting down a mustard-colored chamois cloth. "I'm Mathieu Cavour. How may I help you?" he asked René, picking up several cracked Sèvres porcelain drawer knobs, and slipping them into his pocket. "My showroom's in the front, off the other courtyard, if you'd like to see our finished work."

Should he show him the detective badge, the one Aimée left in the drawer, that he'd slipped in his pocket?

"Monsieur Cavour," he said, flashing the badge. "A woman, my friend, was attacked outside your shop last night. Were you here?"

René thought Cavour cringed. But maybe it was just his silhouette shifting under the skylight as René looked up.

"Attacked . . . here?"

"I found her outside in the passage," René said. "Did you see or hear anything unusual?"

"I live above the shop. I have trouble sleeping," Cavour said. "Music helps me. I wouldn't have heard anything outside."

"So your light was on?"

Cavour's brow creased. "Is this woman, your friend, all right?"

Why didn't Cavour answer his questions?

"The attack was so vicious it blinded her," said René.

"Je regrette . . ." he said.

René saw sadness in Cavour's eyes.

"Do you remember if you had your light on?" he asked again.

Cavour rubbed his brow with the back of his hand, "Sorry, I drift in and out of sleep, I can't remember."

Did he have some medical condition?

"Lived here long, Monsieur Cavour?"

"Long? I was born upstairs. But the *quartier* has changed. The conniving developers want to take over."

"More and more," said René, nodding in sympathy.

The telephone rang. No one answered and Cavour looked flustered, as he ignored it.

"Here's my card. In case you think of something that might help," René said. On his way out, he saw a broom and rusted dust pan by a full garbage bin. Might Cavour have found something of Aimée's?

"Did you sweep this morning?"

"As always. The shop, the courtyard. Some of these people don't care if the *quar-*

tier's run down, no pride."

He stood, René thought, like a stubborn island in sea of slick renovation.

In Cavour's waste bin, topped off by sawdust and Malabar candy wrappers, René saw a crumpled sheet of music, the black notes faded on the yellowed page.

"Look at what they leave in the passage, even in my courtyard," he said, following René's gaze. "That's not the half of it. Condoms. Once a broken guitar."

And René heard voices, a chorus. Then a lone soprano. Their timbre softened by the stone. Timeless.

"Where's that coming from?" René asked.

"Opera rehearsal," said Cavour. "We're behind the Opera, you know. A chorus from *Le Barbier de Seville,* would be my guess."

Cavour was an interesting mix, René thought. A blue collar craftsman with a knowledge of opera who worked on antique furniture. He liked Cavour, and yet, without knowing why, he felt uneasy about him.

As he walked down the passage, he realized this detective business was harder than he'd imagined. He'd gotten no real information from Cavour. Cavour hadn't answered his questions. Would Cavour have told him if he had seen anything? He wished he had Aimée's knack for getting information out of people.

And then René realized he'd forgotten to pack all of Aimée's things. The cell phone.

WEDNESDAY AFTERNOON

Mathieu Cavour latched the door behind the dwarf. His hands shook. Shook so much he dropped the old-fashioned key and had to get on his knees to find it between the stones. The pressure, the hiding, running a business . . . he couldn't take it.

And now this.

His anxiety of last night came back.

He'd awakened in his chair in the atelier, startled by a noise, and shot bolt upright. Sweat had dripped down his shoulder blades. Slanted moonlight had made patterned rectangles on the courtyard's uneven cobbles.

Then he had heard the scrape of the gate, like before. Fine, he'd get the furniture piece ready. Ignore the guilt he felt. The less he knew or thought about it, the better.

Then the sounds of a struggle had come from the passage, like in his nightmares. The last time he'd heard that sound the serial killer, the Beast of Bastille, had claimed another victim. What should he do? He couldn't very well call the *flics* and risk exposure.

His restoration work paid the bills and kept the timbered roof over the shop. Barely. Never mind where the pieces of furniture came from or who they'd once belonged to.

When would his contact come? He'd left the metal gate open . . . but one never knew. He paused near the half-open window, his undershirt damp. The struggle had come from the small, paved inner courtyard.

He had held his breath. His hand had quivered as he tugged the limp lace curtain. He had taken a deep breath and parted the lace.

In the courtyard, a man stood in his bathrobe rocking a crying infant. Mathieu had heard cooing as the man soothed the bundle in his arms under the honeysuckle. So the screams had wakened the baby, too.

It must have been teenagers fighting, he told himself. Those sulky ones who hung around the pizza place, an upholsterer's before the old boss died and Mirador Development had snapped up the building.

He had wanted to go down and check the *cave.* Make sure the piece was safe. But the old stairs creaked and the doors were rusty and stiff. The years had taken their toll. His knees had protested. And the shadowy cobwebbed basement corners, damp stone and crumbling brickwork, were things he avoided even on sunny, warm days.

He had found a Lizst piano concerto on the transistor radio on his work table. Had kept the volume low, hoping he'd fall asleep. But his eyes had stayed glued to the window until long after the baby's cries quieted and a rosy dawn had painted the jagged Bastille rooftops.

How would telling the dwarf about it help the woman now?

Mathieu should have known, he realized later, that it was a warning. A foretaste of the next day. When the past opened like a fresh wound.

WEDNESDAY

"Bonjour," said a voice from the shop interior.

In the workshop, Mathieu paused, stretching the band of ash to fit in the grooved notch. He lifted his foot from the foot pedal, halting the rotor blade saw. Sawdust and the smell of freshly sawed wood filled the dusty space.

"Suzanne . . . Suzanne, someone's in front," he said, as the metal saw teeth ground to a stop.

But no answering footsteps came from his assistant's desk.

Where was that girl? She'd gone on an errand more than an hour ago.

"A moment please, and someone will help you," he called out. He dabbed glue mixed with wood resin in the crack, stretched the wood taut, and slid it gently in place. After wiping off the excess, he sanded the rough edge until no distinction could be felt, as though it were one piece with the wood.

"Delivery!" Another voice shouted. "I need a signature."

Where was Suzanne? He had an art nouveau rosewood desk drawer to repair and the façade of a console to finish filing. . . . He couldn't do that and run the shop too. He'd gotten behind since his apprentice Yvon had gone on vacation.

"*Oui,*" he said, wiping his hands on his stained apron and peering over the reading glasses perched on his nose.

"Shall I deliver at the rear as usual, monsieur?"

Mathieu went to the front shop, signed the receipt and stuck it on the counter. He dimmed the chandelier, a remnant from his grandfather's day, and assumed the customer had left.

But when he looked up he saw a slender older woman, wearing a tailored black suit, her blunt-cut steel grey hair brushing her shoulders. She watched him from behind the marble-topped mahogany commode.

"Exquisite!" she said.

Her fingers traveled over the marquetry wood decorated sides.

Though she spoke French well, he detected a slide in her sibilants. She stood, sleek and stylish, carrying a designer tote bag over her arm.

The delivery truck's brake squealed in the rear cobbled passage. Over the open skylight, a flurry of blackbirds fluttered from the flowering honeysuckle. "My assistant's disappeared, but if you'll look at our catalogue while I deal . . ."

"Please, go ahead."

By the time Mathieu guided the chestnut planks to the rough pine pallets, Suzanne, breathless and red-faced, appeared.

Mathieu's lips turned down in disapproval. "Suzanne, clients, deliveries and how I can work when . . ."

"Monsieur . . . the police line," she said, hanging up her jean jacket, scooping up the mail, and hitting the answering machine playback in one swoop.

Suzanne had a head for figures, unlike Mathieu. And when she appeared, she smoothed the office into routine and organization with an effortless charm. He ignored her bare midriff-tops, pierced navel, and penchant for Bastille club DJs who picked her up after work.

"Another strike?" Mathieu sighed. "Who is it this time?"

"*Mais* . . . they're setting up police barricades," she said, her eyes wide. "Didn't you hear?"

Mathieu gripped the desk. His mind flew to the furniture.

"A woman murdered in the next passage; they say it's the Beast of Bastille."

The serial killer? Was that what the dwarf had been asking about?

"I had to prove I work here before they would let me into the passage," Suzanne said. "They've started questioning everyone."

What if they searched . . . found the furniture?

"Monsieur . . . excuse me," the woman said.

Mathieu looked up. He'd forgotten about the elegant woman in the showroom.

She stared at the commode taking up most of the window space. Her hair fell across her face, and she flicked it away with a graceful movement of her long fingers. Her other hand rested on a black wooden cane.

"My great-great-grandfather's work, the last one left," Mathieu said. "I like to display the family's tradition. It's on loan from a client. My great-great grandfather kept the business going after the Revolution. Figured tradesmen needed furniture even if *aristos* didn't."

"A smart move, yes?" the woman said.

Or, as he remembered the saying attributed to his great-great grandfather, "They needed to park their rears to count the money."

Was she a client?

"Suzanne, my assistant, can show you samples."

"Perhaps this is a bad time . . ." An unsure look crossed her face as she reached for something in her bag.

Honor your clientele. Hadn't his father drummed that into their heads? *Artisans must respect clients.* Mathieu preferred to stay in back and work, but he knew craftsmanship wasn't the only thing that kept the shop door open.

He smiled and stuck his ruler in his blue work coat. "Madame, I welcome special orders. Please sit down."

She ended many of her sentences in the old style with a questioning *yes.* She must be in her seventies, but her complexion could be that of a woman half her age. Wherever she came from, they took care of themselves.

He gestured toward a rosewood chair, brushed a speck of sawdust from the seat.

"For just a moment, but I'm afraid it's not what you think. I feel guilty taking you away from your work, monsieur," she said, sitting, resting the cane against her leg. "People tell me I'm chasing what is long gone, but my lawyer gave this to me."

She pulled an envelope from her bag. "This list came to us from the Comte de Breuve's estate. Evidently he'd gone bankrupt and the state took it over upon his death. On it, Monsieur Cavour, were some pieces owned by my family: paintings, sculpture, and furniture. Some of these had been in my family for generations. But they disappeared years ago, during the war. They've never been seen or heard of again. Now this list has come to light."

Cold fear rooted Mathieu to the spot. His mouth felt as dry as the sawdust beneath him.

"Rumor had it, Goering liked my father's collection. So much so, that he appropriated it for the Reich. Between the Reich and Goering's coffers there was little distinction. According to other rumors, there is some question as to whether the collection ever made it to Germany, on a specially built freight train. Many think the pieces never left France, yes?"

"Madame, why do you come to me?" Mathieu asked, gripping the edge of the work table.

"Yes, of course, I'm bothering you with this old story. Please hear me out. In the account books we saw the Cavour shop name, and know you are respected *ébénistes*. The Comte's files went back to when your grandfather, then your father, and perhaps even you, worked on his pieces."

Bile stuck in Mathieu's throat. If he told her the truth, or what he knew of the truth, he'd lose everything; the atelier, the building where he'd been born, and his business: the business he struggled to keep open and out of the tax man and developers' reach.

"I'm so sorry to hear of the Comte's passing," said Mathieu, trying to keep his expression neutral. "He was a patron and good client for us. What about the other craftsmen required by his large collection?"

"I'm an old woman," she said. "And foolish to have hope. So many have told me. But one piece was special. The pieta dura commode."

Mathieu stiffened.

"This was my father's favorite. He'd recognized it in some pawn shop. Furniture from Versailles, lost in the Revolution. Papa had an eye. He said what caught him was the marble 'the color of his little girl's eyes.' My eyes. And he had to have it. They say it's worth a lot now, but it's not the money, you see. It's that papa thought of me when he bought it. And that's all that's left. They took my father and family and everything else."

The old woman's large eyes brightened. Still beautiful, and a curious topaz amber color. Remarkable.

"The lawyer says I'm foolish but if I found it again, I wouldn't keep it. Those things aren't meant to be kept by one person, one family . . . something this beautiful belongs to all. I just want to see it again. Feel the marble, oil it, like papa taught me. That's all."

She leaned forward, emitting a delicate floral scent. "I had to come to your *atelier*, yes? See for myself the pieces you work on. Smell again that furniture oil odor I remember from childhood; yes, it's the same. Our house was filled with it, too. Funny, the things that stick in your memory. I remember it as a time when the sun seemed like a big lemon and it shone every day."

Mathieu was torn. "I wish I could help you."

"I'm sorry, I'm taking your time and rambling," she said, with a small shrug. She handed him her card. Dr. Roswitha Schell, University of Strasbourg, Professor of Art History. "I'm semi-retired and teach part-time. But I'm boring you, yes?"

"Non," Mathieu said, averting his gaze. He knew the pieta dura commode, better than she could imagine.

He couldn't remember when he'd last had a conversation with a cultured woman. These days he rarely left the *quartier.* Too much to do. His niece berated him for working so hard and he'd reply "That's how we were raised. I was born over the shop, measured chair rungs from when I could count."

But the Cavour name, the skill and secrets handed down from father to son since 1794, would end with him if he didn't continue with his plan. He wouldn't let it happen.

And Mathieu realized those eyes had shifted . . . perplexed. She'd thrust something at him, her cool fingers brushing his arm. Soft like a butterfly's wing.

"Forgive me," he said, trying to look away. But he couldn't.

"But these photos . . . perhaps they could

jog your memory. Maybe you'd seen the piece before at the Comte's, yes?"

But Mathieu turned away.

"Monsieur?"

Elegant and cultured and kind. Like the Comte.

"Art's not cerebral, there's more than that," she was saying. Her voice rose, lyrical. "The indefinable something from the soul that most of us strive for. Few achieve it, much less describe it."

Why wouldn't she stop talking? And then, quiet. He looked around, afraid of her accusing glances. But admiration and something like awe shone in her face.

"You must think me a blathering fool!" she said. "But I see, you're an artist. You, of all people, must realize how much it means to me."

A pang of guilt pierced him.

She lifted a small folder. Inside were photos from a lost time; black and white images of a young boy in a sailor suit, a serious-looking girl with long braids holding his hand. They stood in a room surrounded by museum-quality furniture, Impressionist paintings on the wall.

Conflicted, he turned away. "I'm sorry, I wish I could help you. But I don't know how."

"Monsieur, forgive me, I've offended you," she said, "I'm sorry this came out all wrong. I'm grabbing at a thread from more than fifty years ago."

He saw her to the door and watched her make her way through the courtyard.

Nothing must threaten his arrangement. Nothing. Even though the pieta dura commode sat in his cellar, refinished and ready for the auction house.

WEDNESDAY LATE AFTERNOON

Aimée fiddled with the bandages around her neck. The stiff awkward bulk bothered her. Her hair clumped in sticky strands from the gel she'd combed through it. Or thought she had. She never realized combing hair could be such an art. And how hard it was without sight.

She heard a familiar gait cross the linoleum: Morbier's slight shuffle. His right foot was half a size larger than his left, so even though he wore an extra sock on it, one shoe flapped.

The breeze had stopped flowing through the window. He must be crossing on her left and have taken in her hospital gown and seen the chart at the foot of the bed.

"There's food on your tie, Morbier," she

said, facing the window.

The footsteps stopped. "Can you see?"

"You always have food on your tie," she said. "Grab a chair."

"I spoke with the nurse. She didn't say much," he said. "How bad is it?"

Was that concern in his voice?

She let a big silence fill the space. Morbier, a master interrogator, knew how to wait.

So did she.

Trolley cart wheels wobbled and squeaked in the hallway. Lunch was over; maybe it was medication time.

"That bad?" he asked finally.

"You mean, can I see anything?"

"That's a start," he said.

He wasn't one to deal well with emotion. If at all.

"Or will I ever see again?" She threw her leg over the bed, reached for what she thought was her comb on the tray. It clattered to the floor.

She heard him grunt as he bent down for the comb.

"The neurosurgeon's procedure saved my life, but the lack of oxygen or the bleeding from the blows to my skull obscure where a weak vein ruptured."

"Say it so I can understand, Leduc."

"They call it complications of treatment."

"Aha . . . clear as Seine mud."

She agreed.

"Someone attacked me in the passage," she said. "The force of the blow caused a weak vein wall in my brain to burst."

"And the prognosis?"

She heard him rifling through his pocket, the crinkle of paper.

"The doctor's becoming repetitive. 'Just wait and see.' 'No pun intended,' he says."

She wished her relationship with Morbier was different. For a moment, she wanted Morbier to throw his big arms around her. Hold her. Tell her it would be all right and that he would make things better. Like he had once when she was little and her father was away on stakeout. After school, she'd tripped and split open her knee on the Commissariat's marble step. He'd scooped her up, held her to his scratchy wool jacket, dried her tears with his sleeve and cleaned her knee while telling her stories about his old dog who loved strawberries and would fall asleep standing up.

She wasn't a child anymore. And she might not ever be all right. What if the blindness didn't go away?

"Got a cigarette, Morbier?"

"Didn't you quit?"

"I'm always quitting," she said. "There's one in your pocket, isn't there?"

"Why do you think the Beast of Bastille attacked you?"

"Did I say that?" She lay back and stared into the blankness, imagining what he looked like; the pouches under his alert brown eyes, his jowly cheeks, the socialist party pin worn in his lapel, a used handkerchief . . . she felt a thin stick wedged in her hand, then heard the sound of crinkling.

"Suck."

"Morbier!" She smelled lemon. She aimed and hit her lip, then tasted a sour Malabar lollipop.

"Better than coffin nails," he said. "So talk to me."

"Sergeant Bellan questioned me already. I might feel like sharing, if I knew the murder victim's name."

"This case belongs to the special detail for the 11ième." That's what Bellan had said. But Morbier must know something since he'd answered the phone there. However, as always, he'd make her pay for his information. "Not my fiefdom," he said.

If only she could see his face!

She'd give him an edited version.

"Look Morbier, here's what I know, maybe you can open your mouth after you listen to me," she said. "In that trendy resto, Violette, I incurred the wrath of my big client, Vincent. Next to us sat a woman, wearing the same Chinese jacket I'd paid the moon for, talking on her phone."

She told him the rest.

"Now tell me. Who was the woman killed on Monday night? Which passage was she found in?"

Morbier hesitated. "Like I said, this isn't my case."

"I heard the old woman who found her interviewed on the *télé,*" Aimée said. "The old woman gave out more details than you."

She heard tapping on the linoleum.

"Keep this to yourself. The victim was found in the cour de Bel Air," he said. "The courtyard next door to where you were attacked."

"Those passages and courtyards all connect somehow, don't they?"

"Nice theory," he said. "But who knows?"

Since she couldn't see his face or body language she had to listen more closely to his words. "They'll find Vaduz. Don't worry," he said.

"What worries me, Morbier, is that it's not him."

"Leduc, he's killed five women," said Morbier. "This case and the attack on you both fit the victim profile."

"Which is . . . ?"

He yawned. She heard a slight snapping. He broke toothpicks when he was nervous or deep in thought.

"Why not tell me, Morbier?" Frustrated, she twisted the sheets between her palms. "Early thirties, currently blond-streaked, single . . ."

"Wrong," interrupted Morbier. "Single like you, but all living in the Bastille area. The victims were in their late twenties, thirties, and one was a woman in her forties. Dirty blonde, tall like you. Usually a party girl. Some hung out in the Spanish tapas places, the clubs. A certain type. Showy."

She hesitated. "I planned on staying in Bastille, in Martine's brother's place, while he's working in Shanghai."

"Since when?"

"Remodeling a kitchen and bathrooms takes forever. And fixing the electric wiring will take until the next century. René's neighbor's taking care of Miles Davis now . . ."

"Won the Lotto, have you?"

Why did she always forget how quick Morbier was?

"You could say that," she said, wondering whether to tell him how she'd justified finally updating her apartment's electric wiring and plumbing.

"Non," he said. "Don't tell me. I don't want to know."

She visualized his thick hands held up, as she'd often seen them if she teased him.

"Tell me, Morbier, did this latest victim match the profile?"

Silence. What she wouldn't give to see the expression crossing Morbier's face right now!

"So I take it she didn't," Aimée said. "Or the fit isn't close."

"This victim was in her early forties. Like one of the others. Close enough," he said, his voice tired. "Vaduz was released Monday afternoon on a technicality. Let's give a big round of thanks to his *salope* of a supposed socialist lawyer! One of those *gauche-caviar* elite who give socialism a bad name. So Vaduz suffered a hurry-up urge to kill after his mother's funeral. Maybe the woman reminded him of his mother. Or maybe you did."

So Vaduz was still out of jail.

"The woman in the resto had long Purple Vamp nails, thick blonde hair." She hoped Morbier would finish for her.

He didn't.

"Black Chinese silk jacket . . . it's her, isn't

it?" said Aimée. "Tell me, Morbier. I'm stuck in a hospital bed."

And she couldn't say it . . . *blind and scared.*

"*Alors,* Leduc, the victim lived above Marché d'Aligre. Next of kin haven't even been notified, so I can't give her name out. You know the rules. Like I said, I'm en route elsewhere."

A chair scraped on the linoleum; Morbier must have stood in his odd-sized shoes.

"However, Vaduz was seen in the Bastille area," he said. "So there's location and the window of time. Let's say he knows the victim, phones her, but gets you. It shows malice, forethought."

No matter how he added it up, she knew it didn't compute.

"What happened to the cell phone he rang?" he said. "We could trace the call."

"Gone," she said.

"The victim fits the type Vaduz chose: Close enough in looks, the right location, and method of murder."

It couldn't be.

"But the man on the telephone insisted she 'forget her pride and meet him.' He knew her, Morbier."

"Vaduz knew some of his victims. And when he was released, he said he was going to visit his dentist in the Bastille. He had a mouthful of rotten teeth."

"The file would show if they were acquainted," she said.

"It's not my case," he said. "Right now, it's a botched-up job from when they let Vaduz out. A real *pétard*."

Of course, releasing a serial killer to kill again wouldn't restore public confidence in the police.

"This sexual predator is supposed to have killed several women in the Bastille area. How come no one connected them until last year?" Aimée asked.

"Not you, too," Morbier said. "You sound like the parents. The one this morning harangued me for an hour; why didn't we do DNA testing, compare samples?"

"Good question," she said. "But that would be hard, since you have no DNA repository to check it against, much less . . ."

"No funding from the Police Judiciare," he interrupted. "You know how that is . . . half of Brigade Criminelle don't even have computers at their desks."

He let out a big sigh.

"That's why they called me in," he said. "Last minute."

Damage control. He'd been doing more and more of that recently.

"Like I said, it's not my case," said Morbier. "Bellan's in charge. I'm supposed to be en route to Créteil."

"Créteil?"

" 'Law enforcement in the new millennium' seminar," he said, expelling a loud breath. "Spare me. But that's up in the air now."

"Why?"

Silence. She hated it when he dribbled out bits of information then clamped shut.

"Talk to me, Morbier," she said.

"They don't have enough staff to handle the explosives scare," he said. "The ministry's pulling Commissaires and men from the arrondissements."

She took a last lick of the lollipop and wound the damp stick around her finger.

"An explosives scare? Sounds big."

"Huge, Leduc," he said, a tone of finality in his voice. "You're out of commission. So stay out of this. Don't think about asking any more."

Bigger than huge. Gigantic, if Morbier talked like this.

"I'm interested in Vaduz's teeth," she said.

"Not a pretty sight. Seems Vaduz opened his mouth, pointed to his rotting fillings," Morbier said, "moaned about needing the dentist's drill."

"What about the jealous husband angle?"

"She wasn't married," he said. "The Préfet keeps reminding me he's got another five days to retirement," Morbier said. "After a stellar twenty-five year career, the Préfet wants to depart with full honors from the Mayor. So he'd like the blame for the Vaduz mess to rest elsewhere. Too bad he can't think of where else to put it. Right now, the Gendarmerie looks like the next candidate."

"Why?" she said. "They're not responsible."

"Tell that to the public," he said. "All us uniforms look alike, and we're all to blame. The victims' families want justice or vengeance."

Morbier's pager beeped and she heard him fumble in his pockets.

"May I borrow your hospital phone, Leduc?"

She nodded. Then her aching neck protested in response.

From the brusque tone of Morbier's conversation, she knew something had gone wrong. He hung up.

"What happened?"

She heard Morbier's long sigh.

"Some problem in the Place du Trône," he said, using the old name, the King's throne, for Place de la Nation. Aimée found it ironic, since he was a dyed-in-the-wool socialist.

"But Morbier, the caller who spoke to me knew the woman he was phoning. He sounded intimate with her."

"You told me. I've got to go," he said. "The Préfet wants the case closed, clean and neat. Let's agree on this, Leduc. Vaduz thought you were the victim. He was scared off when passersby came down the passage. Lots of nightlife in the Bastille quartier. He'd been stalking the other woman before he encountered you. Then he found her."

Morbier continued. "This isn't my turf, Leduc." He let out a tired sigh. "The powers that be are trying to nail Vaduz. He's brutally killed five women. And they're salivating now, talking about the 'special accomodation' they've prepared for him at the Quai des Orfèvres — a wire and iron cage for his interrogation." Another tired sigh. "The victims' parents are angry and tired. And five bodies later, they're demanding blood. Vaduz's blood, and strong police action. So unless you've got something concrete, Leduc, I'll recommend they tie this up with a nice bow."

She leaned back against the large pillows. What Morbier said was likely true. But the man who had attacked *her* wasn't Vaduz.

"Look, you know my hunches are good," she said. "Papa trained me. I don't agree. No serial stalker like Vaduz has such finesse. You said he has rotten teeth, right? But I don't remember bad breath. It doesn't make sense."

"Heard of breath mints?" said Morbier. "Didn't you suffer a concussion and black out?"

"Morbier, what aren't you telling me?"

Silence.

"Spit it out, Morbier."

"What your father would have told you," said Morbier. "Get the hell out of what you're doing and stick to computers."

His remark made her angry.

"After dining with a client, I was attacked, blinded. But it sounds like you think I invited it," she said. She wanted to throw the phone at him but she didn't know where it was. "It wasn't the Beast of Bastille, that much I know."

A sob caught in her throat. But she stifled it.

"I just worry you're not safe. Sorry . . . don't do well . . . it's this hospital. . . ." his voice broke. "*Alors,* I'll keep my ears open."

And with that Morbier was gone.

He'd never apologized to her or anyone in

his life, that she knew of. What a first . . . a hollow victory.

The room felt chilly. Cold drafts licked her feet. She got in bed and pulled up the covers. She couldn't count on Morbier. Or the *flics*. If any investigating were to take place, it was up to her.

She felt caught between a rock and a hard place . . . wasn't that the saying? Until the police caught Vaduz, how could she prove he wasn't the one who attacked her?

The nurse came in. "Time to draw some blood, won't take a minute. Looks like you dropped a toothbrush."

After the nurse left, Aimée lay back and put the brush to her cheek, rolled it, then held it in front of her eyes. But no matter how hard she tried, even though it was right there, she couldn't see it. She'd probably never see it again.

Fatigue tugged at her. Concentrating on Morbier's words — and on what he hadn't said — exhausted her. Listening to him, she'd worked harder than if she'd had her sight and still she felt she'd missed something: a nuance, the way his stubby fingers worried his jacket sleeve or how he looked away when she brought up uncomfortable subjects. Like her American mother's abandoning them when she was eight or her father's *flic* record. All the little clues she'd learned unconsciously to depend on to read him, to decipher his meaning.

And what was all that about the explosives and pulling staff off . . . ? He'd never tell her now. She was out of the loop. Useless.

Most of the time, she could tell when he had more to say. Of course he knew, he had full access to the fat dossier on the serial killer Vaduz and he'd shared but a fraction. And now she wasn't sure she'd ever be able to figure him out — or anyone else — again.

She hooked her arm around the metal bedframe, cold and smooth, then sank back into the pillows. Deep down, the realization that she might never be able to see again loomed.

The aroma of espresso, rich and dark, encompassed her. Had it all been a bad dream?

Of course it was. She'd wake up in bed in her apartment on Île St. Louis with the Seine flowing below her window, Miles Davis, her bichon frisée, perched in the sunlight on her duvet. She'd be cuddled against that tan hunk she'd met in Sardinia, muscular and with such a flat stomach and . . .

"Aimée, how about coffee?" René said. "Or do you want to sleep more?"

She kept her eyes closed. Kept the image

of Miles Davis's wet black nose and fur that needed a trim. Then she opened her eyes.

Darkness. Only darkness. And the crisp feel of laundered hospital sheets. It wasn't a dream: she'd woken up dumped back into reality.

"With two sugar lumps, René?"

"Just how you like," he said.

"*Merci,* you're wonderful, René." She sat up, felt behind her and propped up her pillows. She tried not to think about how she must look.

Her torched brain welcomed a warm, sweet java jolt. She opened her hands to clutch the hot cup, inched her fingers to find the spoon.

She told him about Sergeant Bellan's questioning and Morbier's comments about Vaduz.

"René, any more noises from the Judiciare about Populax?"

"If Vincent doesn't release the hard drive, expect a subpoena," René said.

She chewed her lip. "Hasn't he reconsidered?"

"Not so far."

Vincent's attitude was outrageous. His veiled threat in the resto came back to her. And his arrogant denial. Either he felt he was above the law, or he was hiding something.

She circled the spoon slowly against the wall of the cup, but felt hot droplets on her chest. How could it be so hard to stir with a spoon?

"We should expect to appear at the Palais de Justice," René said. "You know the drill."

She gulped the espresso then felt the cup lifted from her hands. "Me . . . testify?" she asked.

"We're in this together," René said.

"We need Martine's help to convince Vincent to cooperate."

"I have your bag. Let me look up Martine's number."

Startled, she turned, banging her shoulder on the metal bedframe — the shoulder she dislocated with annoying regularity.

"My bag . . . I thought it was stolen."

"Who said so? It was next to you in the passage when I found you," he said, "under muck and grime."

"You're a genius!"

What would be left inside?

She felt the zipper and ridges of her leather backpack, then the contents of her bag tumbling over the sheet. She ran her finger over a phone, a dog-eared software manual, the Populax file, her Ultralash mascara, the hard-edged laptop, a key ring, what was left of her stubby Chanel lip-liner, a small tube of superglue that worked miracles on broken high-heels, alligator clips, cord to hook into the phone line, screwdriver, Nicorette gum, Miles Davis's calcium biscuit, and her father's grainy holy medal.

All the familiar things of her work and her life.

Her old life.

Aimée shivered. She ran her hands through her spiky, matted hair to cover the trembling. Not only did she need a decent cut and shampoo from Dessange and a body scrub in the steamy Hammam, she needed her Beretta, for protection. And her sight, to use it.

"Let's get Martine's help. She'll convince him. Punch in 12 on my phone, René," she said. "That's my speed dial for Martine."

René handed her the phone.

No sound.

She clicked off.

"Odd, René . . . ?"

Then it hit her.

"Wait a minute, René," she said, feeling around. "There are two phones in this bag. But only one's mine." Her voice rose with excitement.

"Isn't the other . . ."

"I was trying to return the woman's phone."

"You mean . . . the attacker didn't get either of the phones?"

She scrabbled for the instrument on the tray table and held both in her hands. "It's like mine, isn't it?"

Silence.

"René . . . are you nodding yes?"

"Sorry."

"Now we can trace the dead woman's calls!"

"He must have been in a hurry when he found out," said René.

"Found out what?"

"That he'd got the wrong woman," he said.

That was what Morbier had said. But this would be almost too easy — they'd just check the last call and find the killer's number!

"I know what you're thinking, Aimée," said René. "But when I press call back, the last number received comes up invalid."

"Invalid? Try again."

She heard René take a deep breath. "She's got the cheap version, no such features offered. No real features at all."

"So that means we can't trace who called

her," she said, disappointed.

A dead end?

Then she brightened up. "But René, it must have speed dial, *non?* Don't they all have that?"

Silence.

"Are you nodding yes?"

"I see three numbers listed."

"*Parfait,* we trace her phone's speed dial numbers," she said.

"Seems the attacker's not too smart if his number's on the phone."

"You're right," she said.

Could he be that careless?

"We have to check, René. We have to find her name, the phone number of this phone, then who she called."

"It's easy to buy a prepaid in a store without security cameras," said René. "She could have paid cash and bought airtime without leaving a trace. But why would she do that?"

Aimée thought of the burgeoning cheap second phone business for people who'd lost theirs. "Say the woman lost hers a lot. What if she wanted a cheap phone for work," she said. "Like I did until I got this one. Still, everyone has to show ID to activate a phone."

"Show ID?" asked René. "Now that makes

it simple."

"How?"

"My RAM's revved up. I crack into a few databanks," he said. "Run a program to check lists of purchases of cell phones by cash or charge. Takes about twenty minutes."

He was a master of his métier.

"You're a genius, René!"

Aimée briefly struggled with the idea of calling Morbier to tell him her bag had been found. But first she needed to find out the victim's identity. Find out if she was the woman from the resto.

She had to make sure. Get concrete proof.

"Try 12 on my phone."

René dialed and thrust it into her hand.

"*Allô?*" said Martine, her voice low and out of breath.

"Martine, don't tell me you're exercising?"

"Feels like it," she said. "Climbing in heels on this spiral metal staircase seems like my own personal Stair-master hell."

"Where are you?"

"About to meet Vincent for *Diva*'s cocktail preview, our biggest night. *Cherie,* you were invited, too. Aren't you coming?"

Of course, with everything that had happened, she'd forgotten.

"Alas, no. I'm in l'hôpital des Quinze-Vingts."

"Visiting someone sick?" She heard Martine's sharp intake of breath. *Ça va?*

"You could say that."

"What's wrong?"

Should she tell her best friend? On her biggest night? Ruin it for her? Not now, not when Martine was about to launch her new venture. She could tell her tomorrow.

"I'd feel better if you persuade Vincent to turn over his hard-drive," she said. "Besides, how could I come, I've got nothing to wear."

"All you think about is work, Aimée," she said. "Can't this wait until . . ."

"Please Martine, *la Procuratrice* will subpoena Vincent's firm."

"For what? He's not guilty. It's the *salopes* he did business with!"

"So tell him to cooperate, Martine."

Again, doubt assailed her about Vincent. An unease floated over her.

Aimée heard a low hum of conversation, strains of a chamber orchestra in the background. She visualized the fashionable crowd, smelled the wax dripping from the candles and tasted the bubbling champagne. And it came home to her that she was talking to her best friend since the *lycée,* as she'd done so many times, but it felt differ-

97

ent. Like she was speaking in a vacuum.

"Aimée, right now, it's impossible . . . *tiens,* there's Catherine Deneuve . . ."

Aimée heard the smack of lips near cheeks as *bisous* were exchanged. In the background she overheard part of a conversation, ". . . she's chic, she's fierce and there's something fresh about her. A *Belle de Jour* punk."

"Big night here," Martine said.

The background conversation continued, ". . . a facility for accents and for sliding up and down the social scale to play classy or crass, posh or punk. A little glam. A little raw."

"If Vincent doesn't act voluntarily," Aimée said, raising her voice, "that makes him look bad."

"I'll try, got to go," she said, and hung up.

"What did Martine say?"

"Besides gushing over Deneuve? She's rushing to interview fashionistas, do profiles on glamour queens not afraid to get dirt under their fingernails, get sidebar tidbits on hot new authors. If only I could see or . . ."

She reached for his hand and found his arm.

"René, remember the article we read in the Japanese software magazine about technology for the blind?"

Silence. She heard René take a deep breath. "You mean the screen reader software that converts text into speech?"

"Exactly," she said. "And the speech recognition software that converts speech into text for the laptop?"

"We make a deal," he said. "You let me help find who attacked you, and I'll get you these software programs. Even if I have go to Japan to do it."

"Deal."

But René didn't have to go that far. A few phone calls and he found several programs via a hacker friend in the Sentier.

"He's leaving," said René. "If I don't go now, I won't get it installed . . ."

"But first I have to make sure the victim was the woman in the resto," she interrupted, "and check the speed dial numbers on this woman's phone."

"There's time for that," René said. "The Judiciare problem can't wait and I need your help."

And with that, René left.

She must have drifted off. Aimée heard the metal rings on the top of the curtain beside her slide across the rod. Footsteps hurried across the linoleum.

"Mademoiselle Leduc, we're evacuating

the ward," said the nurse from Burgundy, the nice one. She broke Aimée's reverie of a gloom-filled future: her apartment sold to pay debts, creditors hounding René at Leduc Detective.

"Evacuating? There's a fire . . . ?"

No smell of smoke.

"A train disaster . . . the TGV crashed coming into Gare de Lyon," the nurse said, her words rushed, breathing hard. "Two hundred people have been injured. We're the closest facility, so we're taking the overflow. L'hôpital Saint Antoine, too."

Aimée felt her blanket pulled back.

"All the area hospitals are Code Red," the nurse from Burgundy continued. "Your condition's stabilized so we'll move you to the résidence Saint Louis around the corner. A place for the unsighted to learn how to function."

So they were moving her to a blind people's home.

"You don't understand, I have a home. . . ." She wanted to shout "I'm not like them!"

But she was.

"Before you return to your own home, it's best to learn to navigate in the world of the sighted, mademoiselle," she was told. "Chantal, our volunteer, will guide you.

She's a resident there."

A musty lilac scent accompanied the click of heels on linoleum. "Don't worry," said a quavering voice, "You can take care of yourself. I did."

"But how can you help me if you can't see?"

A cackle of dry laughter. "You've got a lot to learn."

Aimée felt the nurse tying her hospital gown and draping a robe over her. Her bag was thrust in her arms. But how would René find her?

"I have to tell my friend . . ."

"Don't worry, there's time for that. Chantal's a pro," the nurse said. "Stand up."

Aimée fought the dizzying sensation as she slid her feet to the floor. Sirens hee-hawed outside her window.

"Now, stretch out your arm and find my shoulder."

Aimée gingerly extended her arm, felt smooth material, and gripped Chantal's bony shoulder.

"*Parfait!* Let yourself see shapes with your fingers, read textures and angles. We will teach you tricks. *Vite,* eh . . . let's make way for the real unfortunates!"

Aimée hesitated.

"*Allons-y!*"

Aimée shuffled forward, a baby step at a time.

"I'm only legally blind, you know," Chantal said, her tone confiding. Her shoulder moved forward. "I distinguish light and dark, large shapes. That's our little secret, eh? The doctor said you had spirit, he recommended you for the résidence. Not everyone gets sent there . . . God forbid, you could be shipped off to St. Nazaire or some provincial backwater! Saint Louis only takes the quick learners, don't forget that."

WEDNESDAY

Vincent Csarda was born on the wrong side of the blanket. He knew he wasn't unique in that. A lot of the world was, and would continue to be. As a child, once a year at Christmas, his mother would take him for lunch with a "gentleman friend." Always at the posh Ladurée, famous for thick hot chocolate, in Place de la Madeleine. This was all kept a secret from his stepfather, an injured tram conductor with a meager disability pension.

Vincent, scrubbed clean and wearing his best, had hated the long ride at the back of the bus on the outside platform. And his mother's nervous picking of lint from his wool jacket. This "friend," with his wiry, amber mustache and red watery eyes, would ceremoniously give Vincent a gift. Odd or old-fashioned toys. Once, a much-thumbed book about steam engines.

Vincent would thank him and spoon up the hot chocolate. "Growing a mustache?" the man would joke about the chocolate swipe on Vincent's upper lip. Vincent would nod, aware of his mother's scrutiny.

The gifts had sat in a pile in his armoire. One Christmas his mother told him they wouldn't see the "friend" anymore but they mustn't be sad. He'd taken care of Vincent. His mother had never told him outright, but from what she left unsaid, Vincent figured this man was his father and he'd died.

Later Vincent found out he'd inherited a lot of money from his mother's "friend." A natural in business and promotion, Vincent started his *agence de publicité,* expanded, and never looked back. His father hadn't given him his name or birthright, but, as Vincent rationalized, something more important: the means to get it.

Vincent waved to his secretary, who applied makeup with a deft hand at her desk while talking on her speakerphone, indicating he needed five minutes. He shut the door of his Bastille office and checked his e-mail. Opened the one from "popstar." The subject read "Marmalade tea." The message:

Call 92 23 80 29 for a good time.

He wrote down the number on his palm. More secure. Then he deleted the e-mail. This was the last time. No more messages; he'd wash his hands of it now.

He adjusted the white dress shirt, spritzed Le Mâle by Gaultier, and checked for lint on his tailored black tuxedo, the trousers of which hid his platform shoes. He'd be going to the Bastille Opéra's Salle de Reception later for a press conference launch. The Arsenal Pavillon might have been more chic. But Monsieur Malraux, the art appraiser, had offered his *hôtel particulier,* a detached mansion in the faubourg that carried *cachet.* And *cachet* counted with the *gauche-caviar.*

A soft, blurred blue shone from the high-paned windows overlooking the courtyard in the Faubourg Saint-Antoine. The pilasters and sculpted frieze on the façade reflected the glow. The bluish star Vega, in the Lyre constellation, hung in the sky. Inside, myriads of tiny blue lights blanketed the balustrades, giving a gleaming otherworldly luster to the foyer.

Blue like *Diva,* their new magazine. Perfect for the pre-launch gala, Vincent thought, tenting his fingers. A mix of elegance and freshness.

One of the Bourbon monarchs had installed his mistress, a well-known actress, here. The monarch built the *petit théâtre,* a gem complete with a foyer hung with Gobelin tapestries, for her performances. He liked to show her off to court intimates, to keep her happy. Rumor had it, he was so enamored of her that he had an underground passage to the Bastille dug to permit impromptu visits.

Vincent doubted that part of the story. Why hide a liaison? Few at court had.

The theatre, perfect for the pre-launch gala, had a gilded stage scalloped by cherubs under a painted ceiling. It seated 200 at most in the frayed maroon velvet seats. The theatre had an *élan* that money couldn't buy. Vincent hungered for it. Something he'd wanted all his life . . . an entrée into a world that excluded him.

But not for long. He would obtain his backers' and the arbiters of fashion's approval at this pre-launch event for the élite of society.

Vincent lifted up the first issue of *Diva,* a glossy four-color magazine. On the cover were three Bastille divas representing trag-edy, wisdom, and glamour. Martine's first issue profiled women spearheading the arts; the designer Jean Paul Gaultier; and a fer-ment of young filmmakers, architects, instal-lation artists, dancers, and singers in the "new" Opéra.

A winner. He felt it in his bones. A bit of flash, glamour, and *luxe* tempered by con-science; interviews with activists, writers, and the editors of the *Cahiers du Cinéma*. A smattering of locals as a guide to the *branché* clubs and bistros. A French rapper and a Chinese teahouse and its owner in the *Arts et Chic* section.

With the success of *Diva* Vincent would truly join the *gauche-caviar*. Not just pre-tend from the sidelines. Money did not guarantee entry; he had plenty of that. He needed the *cachet* of owning a politically conscious, avant-garde and quasi-*intello* fashion magazine.

A sprinkling of socialist ministers, human rights activists, prominent left-wing lawyers, trust fund hippies, and *aristos* glossed the guest list. Vincent noted every detail: the lobster and truffle *hors d'oeuvres,* bowls of glittering Petrossian caviar, the magnums of chilled Champagne, handmade chocolate favors shaped like the Bastille columns. No matter how politically diverse the guests' views, Vincent was savvy enough to know their preferences.

The best.

Like the Prime Minister or President, they might be very "left" but they dined on caviar. On a regular basis.

They would launch *Diva* for the public in a media circus at the Opéra's Salle de Reception. Vincent knew *Diva* would shake the élite, the wannabes, the *bon chic bon genre* . . . but in a fresh way, the way they liked. And they would beg to be featured in it. The participation of the former editor of *Madame Figaro* guaranteed it.

"Monsieur Csarda?"

Vincent spun around. A waiter, his long white apron brushing his ankles, towered over him.

"Oui?"

No one crept up on him like that. Ever. He must focus, concentrate on the larger picture. Not become lost in minutiae.

"Pardon, monsieur, the organizer needs your approval for the orchids. A last minute change, only purple ones arrived."

"Merci." Vincent smiled. He could afford to appear gracious.

By the time he resolved the crisis with the orchids — Malraux, the Bastille Opéra patron, detested purple — he realized Malraux was late. A no-show? Impossible . . . Malraux owed him. In more ways than he could repay.

WEDNESDAY NOON

Downstairs at the Commissariat, in sunlight dappled Place Léon Blum, Sergeant Loïc Bellan thumbed the fat Beast of Bastille dossier. As he had so many times. But this would be the final run-through. After this, he'd sign off on the compilation, then turn it over to the *frigo,* slang for the archives . . . to be frozen cold and deep in the police vault's repository under the Seine.

Bellan hunched over the long wooden table in the deserted operations room. Outside in the square, named for the Socialist Prime Minister of France between world wars, early morning buses, taxis and bicycles passed the grilled windows.

Nearby, embedded in the pavement, were five stones which had once supported the wood scaffold of the guillotine. Lacenaire, the poet, had referred to them as the "flagstones of death." Today they were part of the white-striped crosswalk pedestrians used daily.

Bellan knuckled down to what he did best,

putting the perp under his own brand of microscope. Rereading and combing the information one more time, sifting the loose ends, arranging and rearranging items. Searching for loose threads and ways to knot them. Maybe then he could let go.

He pored over the notes made by the quai des Orfèvres' psychological profiler, the photos of the victims, details from the forensic lab reports, the few witnesses' and neighbors' accounts. Then he looked at the map of the Bastille *quartier* . . . at the location of the attacks.

No question remained in his mind. Vaduz had committed the murders described in the dossier. But this last one, of Josiane Dolet, smelled off. Like an overripe Brie.

His conscience had to be clear . . . his nights were bad enough without Marie and his daughters. Whiskey deadened the pain for only so long. He'd wake in the middle of the night, thinking he had to get the girls up for school. But a yellow pool of light on the bare wooden floor was his only companion.

Jean-Claude Leduc's aphorisms from Loïc's rookie year echoed in his head: "If you smell something, follow your nose. . . . When it pecks at your shoulder night and day, pay attention."

What had he missed?

With the combination of his huge case-load, the few of hours of restless sleep, the endless espresso on prolonged stakeouts, and the flask of whiskey he'd taken to keeping in his vest pocket . . . he couldn't be sure.

Something nagged at him. Was it the remark Aimée had made about the passage . . . its narrowness? Loïc chewed the end of his pen. He stood back and surveyed the enlarged bus and Métro map on the wall.

Vaduz's victims' trails aligned themselves in the few blocks where the #86 and #91 bus routes merged. This corresponded with the Bastille, Ledru Rollin and Faidherbe Chaligny stops along the purple Métro line. Loïc studied the detective's notes verifying that the suspect and victims had taken the same bus to work; his customary bars, cafés, and laundromats in the *quartier* which were also frequented by the victims. This commonality had led them to Vaduz, a seasonal prop mover at the new Opéra.

Bellan reread the file notes. Vaduz picked the same type, over and over again. All the women resembled his cousin: blonde, curvaceous, glamorous. The cousin had ignored the introverted Vaduz since childhood, refusing to introduce him to her friends.

110

But he'd fixated on her, covered his walls with obsessive poems and drawings reflecting the fantasies he'd had about her. On weekends when he'd visited the family, she'd had boys with her in her room. Though she belittled and rebuffed him, he claimed he loved her.

But Josiane Dolet was rail-thin, stylish, and reserved in appearance. Wealthy and left-leaning, she'd followed her family's tradition and joined the family newspaper. When the paper merged with *Libération,* she went freelance, writing investigative exposés and garnering respect for solid reporting.

Josiane Dolet seemed an unusual choice of victim for Vaduz. She was the most intellectual of them all. Had that made her the most threatening? But when he attacked women, they had no time for discussion.

Yet, Bellan reasoned, his selection of victims showed premeditation and a pattern. Methodical, though sick, he'd taken his time. His victims either lived in a passage or walked through one to their apartments. But Josiane Dolet's apartment overlooked the glass-roofed market in Place d'Aligré; she would walk through the open square to reach it.

The Préfet was breathing down his neck; the report had to be submitted by noon.

How did Aimée figure in this? Loïc couldn't put his finger on it, but something troubled him.

"Bellan! Line 3," shouted the sergeant from the front desk.

He picked up the wall phone. *"Oui."*

"Loïc," Marie said, her voice faint. "Guillaume's sick."

And the world stopped. All he heard was a heavy silence on the other end, then the whine of a scooter by the window.

"What is it?"

"Strep throat," she said.

Poor Marie, she must be overwhelmed to call him.

"Marie, the girls had that last year, it wasn't so serious."

"They're worried about his kidneys."

"Why?"

"For babies like him, it's serious. We're at the hospital in Vannes," she said. "He's in intensive care. As his father, I thought you should know."

The phone went dead.

He couldn't leave Marie to face this alone. Something caved inside him. And all he could think of were those little pink pearl-like toes.

He closed the files, pulled on his jacket, and hailed a taxi for Gare Montparnasse.

Wednesday Afternoon

Mathieu fingered the dried orange skin pocked with cloves, shrunken hard . . . wrinkled like a pecan. A Provençal custom, drying oranges to scent cupboards. The bittersweet remnant of the old Comte de Breuve. Mathieu's mind went back to his last visit in early September when the Comte had summoned him to the château outside Paris.

This visit was different from those on which he'd accompanied his father. The Comte, gaunt, wearing worn corduroys and an ascot tucked into his old wool Shetland vest, had aged. His nose seemed more prominent and the broken capillaries in his face more pronounced.

"Let's hurry, there's not much time," the Comte had said, his look furtive. Then he commenced complaining that he couldn't afford to heat the château, much less dwell in it. So he lived in the Orangerie, a stone and glass construction nestled among the outbuildings housing rusted farm equipment.

The catering firm that had rented out the château for parties and weddings had vacated, as evidenced by the dry fountains and overgrown gardens. Wild hyacinths peeked from between the columns. Now, only the municipality rented the ground floor and ballroom for adult evening classes.

The Comte shuffled down the musty stone cellar steps of the Orangerie, which was dug into the slope below the château. Flanked by steep staircases, it anchored the slope and remained perfectly sheltered, facing due south, its windows double glazed.

"The temperature in here remains stable, between 15° and 18° centigrade,[*]" the Comte said. "Even in winter."

Mathieu felt an even, dry warmth. Remarkable.

"These vaults once housed orange trees from Portugal, Spain, and Italy; lemon and pomegranate trees; a winter Bon-Chrétien pear tree; even a Hungarian blue pumpkin plant."

The Comte lifted a glistening dried orange from a basket and handed it to him.

"The trees produced little fruit. Most of them were decoratively pruned into topiary balls. The gardeners wheeled the boxed trees outdoors for the summer months in mid-May, returning them to the Orangerie in mid-October. They were quite sophisticated about climate control back then. They

[*] 60 to 65 degrees Fahrenheit.

114

force-ripened the oranges."

He led Mathieu to a vaulted warren of rooms filled with furniture covered by sagging old dust-laden sheets.

"This was how they hid the *Mona Lisa* from the Germans," the Comte said.

The hair rose on Mathieu's neck.

"Do you mean *here?*"

"In the Orangerie at Cheverny."

Mathieu knew the famous château on the Loire.

"I'll tell you the story," the Comte said, glancing at his watch. "Not now, another time."

But there had been no other time. The Comte had left unsaid more than he had told him. Mathieu felt it, and was sure of it when the Comte lifted the sheets and he saw the furniture. Pieces that took his breath away.

"Restore these pieces and sell them," the Comte said. "Find a buyer, auction them off *en catimini* — on the sly. Take your cut, but there must be no way to trace any piece back to me. I know I can trust you."

Mathieu bent over the mahogany piece, with its silver-framed doors, grooved and cabled, and small, rounded tapering legs. A pieta dura commode. One of three known to be in existence.

Exquisite.

Beautiful striations of wood grain. Veined white and grey marble. The interior with its seven paperboards in red morocco leather bore the *estampillé* of WEISWEILER. A piece from the period of Louis XVI.

He got to his knees, touching the wood with his fingertips like a young boy's hesitant first caress. Even if blinded, he'd know the velvety texture of the rare wood, the unique curve and supple delineation, the trademark of Weisweiler. Weisweiler had worked for Jean-Henri Riesener, furniture- and cabinetmaker to the French monarchs.

Mathieu's heart jumped. The only other eighteenth-century Weisweiler commode sold after World War II had fetched close to 70 million French francs,[*] co-bought by a millionaire and the French State, to be returned to Versailles where it had stood in the library before the French Revolution.

The next piece, stamped DELAITRE, was from 1738, *époque* Louis XV. It was a chest with two rows of drawers, in purple wood veneers with handles gilded in *faille* and bronze decorative hardware.

---

[*] At a conversion rate of seven francs to one dollar, this was a price of $10,000,000.

Would the Comte reveal their history to him?

"And the *provenance* . . . ?" Mathieu asked.

"Sell them anonymously. Don't worry, do a little work on them and they'll sell."

But Mathieu had seen the telltale red G. The characteristic mark of the Gruenthal collections. And he understood.

He might as well put the soles of his feet into the flames. Handling these would be the equivalent of waltzing with fire. All the items must be pieces the Gruenthal family had acquired from the Nazis — pieces that by rights should have been handed over to the French government for return to the original owners or their heirs. A long time ago.

And the Comte, where had he gotten these pieces . . . was he working for himself or them . . . or both? What could have reduced him to this?

The Orangerie's even climate was a perfect storeroom. He wondered how long they'd been here. And he knew he'd risk everything if he helped the Comte. But he'd be a fool if he didn't.

The Comte, he figured, couldn't risk using a *compagnard de travail* — a prestigious master craftsman apprenticed in the seven-

117

year program that dated back to the Middle Ages. A *compagnard* wouldn't touch un-provenanced pieces. Not even with a barge pole.

Envy . . . yes, Mathieu felt a *soupçon* of envy for the *compagnards*. But after years of working with his father, even though he stayed a *faubourg* artisan, he knew his craft rivaled that of a *compagnard*.

The Comte would know that someone like Mathieu, an *ébéniste* from the Bastille *quartier,* would remain discreet, too glad of the work to raise questions. And the Comte had trusted his father, knew the Cavour tradition.

So he had to play this right. Not appear anxious. The Comte needed him. And Mathieu needed the francs to buy his building in order to save it.

"Me, I repair. There's a lot of this work," he shrugged. "You expect me to sell it, too?"

"You know people who can," the Comte said. "And even you can see it's Louis XVI . . . worth, well, a lot."

"What's in it for me?" he said.

"Your father wasn't this difficult," the Comte said. "Or didn't you know?"

Mathieu hadn't.

"Listen," the Comte said, understanding in his eyes. "Once, sometime ago, your father helped me. He benefited. It's not complicated."

Mathieu remembered the Comte visiting the shop, his servant in tow, and how they'd gone out for Bertillon *crème glacée,* the best ice cream in Paris. His father had bought the truck afterward. A Renault, top of the line. Still in perfect shape.

"Don't think I won't be generous. Back the truck up, take whatever fits inside," the Comte said, as if referring to sides of beef. "I count on you."

Mathieu noticed the once-manicured, now overgrown, lime trees in planters lining the vaulted walls as he carefully wrapped and dollied several pieces of furniture to the truck. When he drove out, the Comte waved to him as if they were friends.

In the rearview mirror, the Comte, standing in the graveled court, looked solitary and sad, as if diminished by the furniture's departure. How pathetic even very rich people could look, Mathieu thought. Even a count with a château, who had only a magnificent collection of priceless antique furniture left.

Mathieu would need help to sell the pieces. And he knew where to go.

The thudding sound of a *flic* pounding on the glass-paned courtyard door brought him back to the present. He dropped the flat-edged scraper, swore, and took a step back.

Get a grip. Don't lose control, he told himself.

"Forgive me, officers," he said, opening the door of his workshop. "The older I get, the louder I play the radio."

Keep calm. They'd ask questions, nose around and they'd be gone. He gestured for the three men to come inside. One, wearing a jacket too big for him, with patches on the elbows, flashed his ID.

"Sorry for the trouble, monsieur," he said with a small smile, one hand in his pocket. He shrugged, as if to intimate these intrusions inflicted on citizens were simply a part of life. His socks were mismatched, one brown, the other gray.

Mathieu saw the *flics* surveying the cans of putty, the varnish bottles on his shelves, and the chairs hanging from the ceiling, drying.

"Any trouble, officers?" Mathieu asked, wiping his hands on his apron.

"We're investigating a homicide," he was told.

Mathieu's emotions were in turmoil. An irrational urge to babble about the past and point them downstairs welled up in him. To rid himself of his guilt, to get it over with.

Instead he reached for the turpentine-soaked rag and wiped his work table.

"Cut yourself badly?" asked the one in the ill-fitting jacket. He was older, with bags under his eyes and a bland expression. He pointed to Mathieu's bandaged finger.

"A hazard of the trade," Mathieu said. "Happens more the older I get."

"We have a search warrant, Monsieur Cavour," he said, his tone matter-of-fact. "So if you don't mind . . ."

"A search warrant?" Mathieu stiffened in fear. He tried to breathe. The impulse to confess evaporated. Had they found out about the furniture? "What do you mean?"

The *flics* pulled latex gloves from their pockets, slipped their fingers inside.

"Let's begin with your tools." It was as if Mathieu hadn't spoken. "The set of chisels. Like those." He pointed to the ones on the shelf.

Before Mathieu could summon the will to move his legs, one of the *flics* pushed over a stool, climbed up, and began taking his tools down.

What about my rights, Mathieu wanted to shout. *My rights!*

The past flowed over him. His helplessness. The unfairness. Those hired thugs had beat him up, tried to kick him out of his atelier, until he persuaded them he had money. And would keep giving them money if they just let him stay.

"Monsieur . . . monsieur?" the one with the bags under his eyes was saying, tugging his elbow. "*Ça va* . . . you're white-faced. Not going to pass out, are you?"

Mathieu shook his head.

"What are you afraid of, monsieur?" he said. "We're just doing our job. See, we have a warrant, but we prefer to have your co-operation."

"Cooperation?" Mathieu rubbed his forehead.

"A woman was killed in the next passage. We have to check everything." The man nodded. "I understand that it upsets you."

And from the look in his sad droopy eyes, Mathieu thought the *flic* did.

One of the *flics* raised his eyebrows. "Can you tell me where your chisel is, monsieur?"

"There's a whole set, they're up there," he said. "More lie in the drawer."

"What about the number 4?"

Mathieu looked up. "The number 4? It must be here somewhere, detective."

"Actually, it's *Commissaire,*" he said. "But these trademark Grifon chisels, they're expensive . . . *non?*"

"My clients, the Rothschilds, the Louvre,

want good work, Commissaire. We use the best tools," he said. "Handed down in my family."

"Like this?" The Commissaire pulled a plastic bag from his pocket. Inside lay what appeared to be Mathieu's #4 chisel.

Mathieu's eyes widened.

"We found bloodstains on this, Monsieur Cavour," he said.

"But of course, I cut myself. . . ."

"We need to test you and see if your blood is a match."

"Well, it should be." Mathieu saw the *flic* slide a pair of handcuffs from his pocket. His mouth went dry. "Where did you find my chisel?"

"Next to the victim, Monsieur Cavour," the Commissaire said, gesturing to the others. "The car's in the courtyard."

Stopped en route to the meeting called for the explosives detail, all Morbier knew was that this Mathieu Cavour was guilty. But he didn't know of what.

WEDNESDAY NIGHT

Aimée pretended she was playing hide and seek in her grandmother's garden in the Auvergne. She'd tie a mothball-scented scarf around Aimée's head, spin her around four times . . . "Count them," she'd say, then shove her forward. Her grandmother made her keep the blindfold on.

Her giggling younger cousin Sebastien often gave his location away; under the ripe plum tree or behind the trickling water fountain. Despite her impatience, she'd stand as still as she could, until she thought she could hear the high grass shift in the breeze, leaves crackle or a branch rustle. She'd smell the aroma of an Auvergnat speciality, the soft-ripening Cantal cheese, from the lunch table.

And then she'd pounce on Sebastien. Tickle him until he begged for mercy. And then it would be his turn and they'd do it all over again. All afternoon on those warm, summer days.

She remembered the grassed-in yard bordered by crumbling stone walls; on the other side lay a muddy cow enclosure. Aimée would feel her way along the pebbly stone, the outcropping of azalea bushes, over the fallen ripe plums squishing beneath her sandals, hearing the occasional crunch of snail-shells. The drone of lazy summer bees competed with the cackle of hens.

Sort of like now. Except she was hobbling over cobblestones guided by someone she'd never seen, hearing the distant roar of cars on what must be rue Charenton pulling into the courtyard of l'hôpital des Quinze-Vingts, smelling the Seine's scent rising on the wind, and feeling the sun's heat on her bare arms.

"I thought we were going to the residence. . . ."

"No room at the inn," Chantal said. "They're full. You're going to the old residence, now used by the staff and as an adjunct for old-timers like me."

"Where is it?"

"On the corner of rue Moreau and rue Charenton. I'm teaching you a shortcut past the back of the Opéra and its parking lot. Pay attention. Remember. It's important."

"Will there be a quiz?" Aimée's heel got stuck. She worked it out, awkwardly.

"Even better," said Chantal, "I can just let you do this all by yourself tomorrow."

Why hadn't she kept her smart mouth closed?

"Landmarks, learn them as we pass them, Aimée," said Chantal. "Later, we'll walk along the rue Charenton. You'll hear children at the *école primaire* on the left, that's a reminder that you've passed the hospital. If the violin maker's windows are open, you'll smell the bone marrow glue he uses; that's mid-block on the right."

125

Aimée wished Chantal would slow down. All these sensations bombarded her. Everything became jumbled in her mind and she couldn't remember.

"The traffic signal chirps at the corner of rue Moreau. A café's beyond that; keep going and you'll pass the wine bar and hit Marché d'Aligre."

Aimée felt as if she'd walked blocks, but according to Chantal, so far they'd only navigated a walkway bordering the medieval chapel and hospital courtyard. The Quinze-Vingts had functioned as the Black Musketeers' barracks in the 1770s. Later, under Cardinal Rohan, it had become the central eye hospital in Paris.

The throbbing in her head subsided in the warm, fresh air. Fresh for Paris, anyway. Didn't they say more people got sick in hospitals than got better?

Maybe it was all the concentrating, striving to hear, to understand, to remember, but something troubled her, troubled her more than she cared to admit.

The whoosh of a swinging door, stale air on her face, and the aroma of unwatered dried-out house plants greeted her.

"We're going down the hallway, then to the right." Chantal pushed open another door. "Things are chaotic. I'll help them find you a room. Take a seat," Chantal said, guiding her several steps forward. Aimée felt warmth again and found herself on a stiff plastic chair.

She didn't want to be stuck in a blind people's home. She wanted to see, she wanted them to test her until her eyes worked.

She heard a buzzing fly hit the glass window then rebound with a ping. Its wings were silent momentarily, then it buzzed, striking the glass again. And again. She felt like the fly, blinded by glass invisible to her, beating her wings in futility.

Right now, she needed to be sure the phone she'd picked up belonged to the victim of the assault. And to discover why the woman had been lured into the passage, then killed.

Aimée remembered the woman seated beside her on the banquette, murmuring into the phone. Her frightened eyes and her chain smoking.

Had the victim known the killer would be in the passage and refused to meet him? Was that why he'd called back when Aimée had answered?

But Aimée still had a sneaking suspicion that *she* had been the killer's target. She thought back to the odd sense she'd had that there was someone lurking in the hospital corridor. A foreign presence. Was it the killer, checking up to see if she'd survived?

She needed René's help. Help from a sighted person she trusted. And her vulnerability overwhelmed her again. Stuck depending on others, hating every minute of it. She'd be a sitting duck if the killer wanted to attack her again. And if the rest of her life panned out like this, she didn't know what she'd do. Lying in a hospital bed when there were things to find out . . . she had to do something concrete.

She remembered the woman's Violet Vamp nails, in contrast to her own, chipped Gigabyte Green. The dress and jacket with mahjong tiles for buttons . . . her pulse quickened. The same jacket she'd worn. She had to go to the boutique and question the owner. But how?

Aimée heard snoring, a slow wheezing grunt, from somewhere on her right.

"Time for dinner yet?" a gruff voice asked, snorting awake.

Was this a blind resident?

"We'll soon find out when Chantal returns," she said.

"New resident?" He didn't wait for her reply. "Food's awful. We regulars pay a little extra and get curry on Thursdays from Raj. He runs the South Indian hole-in-the-wall across the street. His papadams reign supreme. As good as I remember in Pondicherry."

The mention of food made her realize she hadn't eaten this morning.

"I'm Aimée Leduc, and I would shake your hand if I could see it."

"Follow my voice," he said. "Turn toward the warmth, lean, and stretch your hand."

Bingo, she thought, as a large, warm paw gripped hers. And for a moment she felt connected. Connected to others like her, for the first time since the attack.

"Lucas Passot," he said. "I lodge here courtesy of a close encounter with the #86 bus on my way back from the cleaner's last year. Ruined a good suit, too! The *salopes* tell me I'm lucky my gimpy leg wasn't re-injured. At least my left eye has some peripheral vision."

"The doctor keeps running tests on me," she said. "But a vein in my head burst. . . ."

"Don't let the jargon throw you," he interrupted. "They don't know what they're talking about. They keep our medical dossiers and tell us what they like."

Disturbing, but she knew the dossier part was true.

"I'm temporary," said Passot. "When my skills come up to snuff, so says the mobility teacher, I'm back in my apartment."

"They do that here?"

"The main residence takes independent tenants only," he said. "But here we have a small mobility program. Of course, it all depends on funding."

Aimée felt ignorant but figured she might as well ask. "What kinds of things do they teach?"

"Exhilarating stuff: dressing, calling 36 99 for the time, caring for clothes, how to shake hands, how to hear the newspaper read by a telephone service, and cane skills."

Overwhelmed, she sat back.

Would *she* have to use a white cane?

"They like those regular paychecks, these overeducated and overfed lemmings . . ."

"Running your mouth as usual, Lucas!" Chantal's voice cut through his words. "*Tiens!* Do something useful for a change, eh?"

Aimée wished she could have something to eat and then a rest. Following a conversation between people she couldn't see felt as if she were tracking the ball at a tennis match, an invisible ball.

"Why not relax, mademoiselle?" Lucas said, his voice near her ear. "Right now you're bobbing like a cork. That much I can see, and you're making me dizzy. Don't worry about following with your head. Most people think you're enthralled with their scintillating conversation if you just close your trap and listen. Relax. And wear dark glasses. That way you'll be mysterious and captivating."

Instead of blind and mistrustful?

"Trust me."

"Why would she trust a blind old fart like you, Lucas?"

And for the first time since the attack on the passage, Aimée laughed. Deep and from her gut.

"See! See Chantal . . . I'm good for something," Passot said.

"Forget yourself for a moment, Lucas, if that's possible," she said. "First, this TGV disaster, and now I hear that *flics* have taken Mathieu Cavour to the Commissariat."

"Did he forget to pay his quarterly taxes or a parking ticket?"

"It's about the woman they found murdered outside his atelier," she said.

Aimée's ears tuned in. "Tell me."

"I met poor Suzanne, his office manager, when I was buying rabbit at the Marché d'Aligre," Chantal said. "She told me that Mathieu had to close the shop. The *flics* took him in for questioning."

Aimée wondered if he had witnessed something, or if he was a suspect.

"Where's his shop, Chantal?"

"Where it's been for two hundred years, in Cour de Bel Air."

"By the Passage de la Boule Blanche?"

"You might say that," Chantal said. "They connected once."

Aimée tried to keep the excitement out of her voice. What if the man had attacked her, realized his mistake, then dodged into the next passage where the other woman had gone to escape him? Or something like that.

"But rumor says it's the Beast of Bastille," Lucas said. "So, has Mathieu been leading a double life?"

Chantal made a *phfft* sound of disgust. Then air whooshed by Aimée: Chantal had probably thrown up her arms or fanned herself.

"Mathieu Cavour and I were at the *école maternelle* together on rue Sedaine," she said. "The men of his family have been craftsmen for hundreds of years. He's no more the Beast of Bastille than I am. It's ridiculous."

"I don't know how old Mathieu Cavour is," Aimée said. "But the man who grabbed me was strong and had wine on his breath."

And the memory came back to her, his wrist . . . what was it . . . cufflinks?

From outside the window, she heard the hee-haw of sirens echoing off the stone walls.

"What do you mean?" asked Chantal, her voice incredulous. "You were attacked?"

"And it wasn't the Beast of Bastille!"

"Mon Dieu," gasped Chantal. "Mathieu doesn't drink. Never has."

"Only sadists attack the blind," said Lucas, his voice trembling. "I've met my share. I beat them off with my cane. They don't bother me twice."

A buzzer sounded several times. "Excuse me," said Chantal. "The matron of the Residence must be busy. I'll see who's at the front desk."

Chantal returned a few minutes later, other footsteps and male voices accompanying her.

Aimée felt awkward and vulnerable. She wished she could see who was there. Hot breath came close to her ear.

"A trustee tour!" Lucas whispered. "We get a lot of tours when funding deadlines loom."

So that was it.

"We hold singing practice on Thursdays," Chantal was saying. "Our choir performs in

133

the Chapel. Last year we attended the Bach choral in Prague. Snagged second place and an invitation to perform at the fall concert in Budapest."

Murmurs of approval met this statement.

"In such important ways, you board members enrich our lives," Chantal said.

"Chantal lays it on thick, but she got them to spring for new pianos," Lucas whispered. "She's working on them now to donate a minivan! If not, at least a voice coach."

"What a wonderful avenue of expression for your residents," said a low voice, smooth and warm: the cultured accent of proper and formal French.

"Monsieur Malraux, thank you for your help!"

"Big benefactor of the Opéra Guild, that Monsieur Malraux," said Lucas, pulling her closer. "He's an art appraiser affiliated with Drouot, the auctioneers. Not only that, eh, he owns a *hôtel particulier* near here, prides himself on being a *Bastoche,* you know, born and bred in Bastille," said Lucas. "But he's not like the working-class *Bastoches* I know."

Aimée's grandfather had frequented the weekly Drouot auctions where anything from Madame de Sevigné's pearls to the mundane contents of a bourgeois apartment were subject to the auctioneer's gavel. A jumble of unsorted items that could conceal a treasure or junk.

Aimée knew that prestigious art appraisers were appointed, not allowed to have commercial affiliations. "He's a *priseur?*"

"His parents were. Malraux specializes in period furniture," whispered Lucas. "He lends pieces from his collection for the Opéra stage sets."

"*Bien sûr.* We will help with voice coaches," said Monsieur Malraux. "After all, the Opéra's in your backyard, so to speak."

"*Merci,* Monsieur Malraux," Chantal said.

"Of course," another voice said. "We're all part of the Bastille community. Superb idea."

"Let me introduce a longtime resident, Lucas Passot, and our newest, Aimée Leduc," Chantal said.

"We're going to teach her the tools of the trade," said Lucas. "Important survival skills like avoiding open freight elevators in the morning at the wine bar by Marché d'Aligre."

Laughter greeted Lucas's remark.

"Mademoiselle Leduc, excuse my bluntness," said Monsieur Malraux, "Chantal's told us many residents here have been blind from birth while some have suffered an illness. What, may I ask, brought you here?"

Aimée felt she had been put on the spot, expected to perform for people she couldn't see.

"Monsieur, someone tried to strangle me. This caused trauma to my optic nerve."

"How terrible!"

Several sympathetic murmurs came from the group. She heard "Passage . . . the Beast of Bastille."

"Tell them what happened, Aimée," said Chantal.

"But it wasn't the serial killer," Aimée said, in a voice that trembled.

"I'm so sorry to have brought all this back, forgive me," he said. "Please accept my best wishes for a speedy recovery, mademoiselle."

"Please forgive us," said another voice. "Now we must move on, gentlemen. I'm sorry, mademoiselle, but we're joining the children's clinic for lunch."

The voices receded.

From the hallway came the slosh of a wet mop, the harsh acrid smell of disinfectant soap.

"Let's hope they cough up," said Chantal, rejoining them. "Tell us about the attack on you."

Aimée leaned forward and found Chantal's knee. As she spoke and they listened, smells of frying shallots and garlic wafted through the window. Her stomach growled.

"So you're a real female detective," said Lucas, sounding impressed. "And I thought they were only in the films."

"Computer forensics is my field," she said, shifting on the hard plastic chair.

"Don't tell me you have no criminal experience," Chantal said. "Private detectives are trained in all areas, aren't they?"

"Licensed ones."

"And you're not?"

"Like I said, computer forensics."

"Where's your gun?" Lucas asked.

"My Beretta's put away," she said "and I don't count on using it again. Especially now."

"You've more experience than you're letting on," Chantal said. "Certain phrases you use sound like a *flic*'s."

"Maybe because my father was one, his father too," she said. "I stopped all that after a contract surveillance for the Préfecture, when my papa was blown up by terrorists."

"I'm sorry, how awful," said Chantal. "But please, won't you consider helping Mathieu Cavour? He's innocent."

"Have you forgotten something?"

"No, what?"

"I'm . . . I'm blind," Aimée spat out.

"Quit feeling sorry for yourself," said Chantal. "So am I. But I keep going. And I know you're determined to find out who attacked you, that's obvious."

"I hear it in your voice," said Lucas.

"But that's personal," Aimée said. "I'm going to find out who did this to me, but I need help, even to find my way around the *quartier.* You'll have to assist me."

Even if they, too, were blind, they navigated in the world better than she did.

"Only if I get to shoot the Beretta," Lucas said. "I've dreamed of hitting the target at a firing range, imagining the look on their faces."

Despite her despair, she realized they could help her. Even if they were the only ones, besides René, who would.

"When my partner gets a voice-activated program for my laptop, I'll be able to get back to work."

"You're really a professional, *n'est-ce pas?*" Chantal said. "What can you do in the meantime?"

"The first thing I want to do is go shopping at *Blasphème,* the boutique on rue Charonne," she said. "You can guide me, eh Lucas?"

"Shopping?"

"And I don't want to appear too blind."

Lucas snorted. "Like being a little pregnant?"

"Give me a quick orientation course, won't you?"

"Quick . . . ?"

"Things I should know."

"When putting a drink down, place the other hand on the table first, feel around for obstacles, then place the drink next to your hand. Stairs can be difficult, especially judging the last step. Move slowly, feel ahead with your foot and keep a hand on the banister."

"Let's eat lunch." Not only was she hungry, she needed to practice.

Eating was agony. She was so hungry and the food was so hard to locate. She kept spearing the plate with her empty fork. At this rate, in order to survive she'd have to pick up her dish and lick it like a dog. She ended up lifting the dish, using her fingers, and scooping the food into her mouth.

"We all do that the first time," Chantal said. "But next meal, it's not allowed."

After lunch, Chantal took her on a tour. "Quick technique time. Let's trail the walls."

Were they going rock climbing?

"Stick your hands out a little in front," she said, pulling Aimée's arm. *"Comme ci."*

Aimée's fingers slid over metal and glass.

"That case houses a fire extinguisher," said Chantal. "You can tell by the curved handle. Feel it."

Beyond that, Aimée felt smooth plaster and grained wood beams. Her hands traveled to a thick carved banister. Hallmarks of medieval construction. Many buildings, at the core, piggybacked on medieval foundations.

"Bend down, keep your hands in front of you so objects will make contact with your forearms instead of with your face. *Bon!* Do you feel the stone . . . how cold it is?"

Aimée's fingers trailed over the chill smooth stone. Goose-bumps went up her arms.

"Remember, when you feel this you've gone too far down the corridor," said Chantal. "Turn back."

"But it seems like there's a door here," said Aimée.

She didn't know how she sensed this.

Chantal laughed. "The Black Musketeers' old escape route. They tore the rest of the building down but left this wedge. It's funny what remains."

Aimée felt Chantal grip her elbow.

"Take the Montfaucon gallows," said Chantal. "Used before the guillotine until the 1700s. They tossed the corpses into pits and charnel houses in the Bastille. In 1954, when they excavated in my uncle's boulangerie for a new oven, they found bones and remains from the Montfaucon pit. 'Scratch the Paris dirt and find a body,' my uncle used to say."

Aimée agreed. In more ways than one.

WEDNESDAY EVENING

In the bland, mustard-colored cell, Mathieu clenched and unclenched his fists. He felt naked and useless without tools in his hands. Paint had chipped off the metal bars and flaked onto the cement floor. He envisioned his clientele running in horror, his commissions withdrawn, and Suzanne quitting in disgust.

Right now, they were probably ripping up the floorboards, emptying his pots of varnish, and pulling apart priceless gilt frames. Soon they'd start on the basement. And then . . .

"Monsieur Cavour?"

Startled, he looked up and saw the *flic* . . . the Commissaire with the jowly face and bags under his eyes.

"Let's have a talk, shall we?"

The Commissaire pointed to the cell door

and the blue uniformed policeman unlocked it for him.

"I apologize for the accommodation," he said. "Come with me. Coffee, tea?"

"Water, I'm thirsty," Cavour said. "I've been here for hours, my shop can't run itself."

"Please understand, we need some questions answered."

Mathieu's jaw quivered. "I'm an artisan . . ."

"But of course, and a well-known and respected man in your craft. A member of the *faubourg* association . . . a distinguished member. Once a *compagnard de devoir,* a traveling craftsman, if memory serves."

"Not me. Only those who complete the seven-year course and finish their *chef d'oeuvre,* Commissaire, can claim that distinction." But his shoulders relaxed. This man had done his homework.

"What about your *chef d'oeuvre?*" he asked, motioning Cavour toward an opened door, the first of many in the long, linoleum-tiled hall.

"Never completed," Mathieu said. "I attended the École Boule later."

Inside, Mathieu heard the chorus to Verdi's *Requiem,* a Palais des Congrès de Paris recording, emanating from a radio. On the cluttered desk, a computer terminal screen blinked and a sheaf of papers filled the oversized printer tray.

"Not my office, I'm borrowing it," the *flic* said apologetically. "But it's tidier than mine. Sit down." He pushed a blue-tinged plastic bottle of Vittel toward Cavour and sat down.

"Tell me why the murdered woman had your chisel, Monsieur Cavour," he said simply. "Then you'll be released and I can go home after a twelve-hour shift."

Mathieu didn't want to believe this was happening. Didn't want to think of the suspicions this tired-looking man with the jowly face entertained.

"But who was she . . . this unfortunate person?"

The Commissaire sat forward in his chair, his eyes intent. "Didn't you know the woman who lived in the passage behind you?"

Was the Commissaire trying to trap him?

"I don't know people who live next to me in my own passage anymore, and I've lived there all my life," Mathieu said. He spread his arms out in exasperation. "*Bien sûr,* I know the old inhabitants, the people I grew up with. But the *quartier's* changing. Old people die and the property's sold to upstarts — architects who make apartments into lofts, developers who tear down historic buildings and ateliers to build new condos."

"Don't call me an expert but my impression is that the *quartier*'s already *mixte,* rich, gay, some craftsmen like you, young families, singles into the nightlife, couples; it's Paris today."

"All gougers and opportunists!"

"Did you classify Josiane Dolet as one of them?"

Mathieu blinked, taken aback.

He felt the Commissaire's eyes boring into him.

"Josiane? Never, she's my friend, a member of the historic preservation association . . ."

"Past tense, if you please," he said. "How did you know her?"

Sadness washed over him.

"I bury my head in my work. . . . People call me a hermit," Cavour said. "But I have so much to do, it's easy to fall behind. The apprentices from École Boule, well . . . the way they work differs from my approach. *Bon,* their technique is good but . . ."

He shook his head, lost in thought, and lapsed into silence.

Despite École Boule's prestige — the founder Charles Boule invented the chest of drawers — Mathieu knew the young ones didn't like the long hours. Or the minute attention to detail. Tedious, they'd tell him. They rejected all the things drummed into Mathieu by his father. His father never gave him a day off, yet these young ones expected holidays, sick days. Demanded it. But Mathieu was old-school and his craft would die with him.

"Tell me about Josiane Dolet," the Commissaire said.

Mathieu hesitated. Mistrust flooded him. How much should he reveal?

THURSDAY MORNING

Aimée shuddered. Sweat beaded her upper lip. She balanced herself against the smooth Formica-topped chest of drawers beside her. She'd never realized how difficult putting on her underwear could be. Forget matching or even clean. Wearing a leopard thong with the black lace bra wouldn't matter, not even if they were inside out.

First she had to find them, then get one leg in and then the other, and pull them up.

Footsteps sounded in the hall. Loud and in front of her.

Merde!

"You might want to close your door," said

a familiar voice. Aimée recognized the distinctive rolling r's of the Burgundian nurse.

"Not on duty at the hospital?"

"Time for my nap," she said. "I work a split-shift today."

Aimée heard a yawn.

"We're neighbors," the nurse said. "A perk of my job; I get lower rent, an *ascenseur* instead of winding stairs to the sixth floor, a room — not a closet like the maid's room on rue Charenton, and a real kitchen and bath."

Aimée sympathized. Living in her seventeenth-century high-ceilinged apartment with extensive foyers and a cavernous diamond-tiled hallway didn't always make up for the galleylike kitchen and postage-stamp bathrooms.

"Call me Sylvaine," the nurse said.

Aimée felt her hand grasped by a warm one.

"Aimée," she said.

"Feel free to ask for help. That's part of my rent package, too."

Aimée felt shy, but her legs were freezing. That she stood practically naked in full view from the hall hadn't occurred to her. Yet on second thought, she realized, few inhabitants would know the difference.

"I know you're tired and I don't want to impose but . . ." Aimée said. "Mind helping me get dressed? If you get me started, I think I can manage."

"Organization," Sylvaine said. "It all comes down to organizing, putting and keeping things in the same place, developing a system that works for you. Makes you independent."

Aimée liked that idea.

A half hour later Sylvaine and Aimée had arranged LeClerc's face powder, Chanel red lipstick and lip-liner, and Chanel #5 scent within reachable distance for Aimée and organized her drawer of patterned panty hose, bar of dark chocolate, and cell phone so Aimée could locate them. They'd hung her leather miniskirt over the chair back and angled her boots by the door. Aimée felt thankful René had brought her the essentials on his first visit.

"My mother was blind," Sylvaine said. "But you'd hardly have known it. At home anyway. She did everything. Even managed homemade *foie gras* for Noël. As long as someone carved the goose, she said."

"She sounds amazing," Aimée said.

A welcome breeze entered the small studio via the window.

"And bullheaded," Sylvaine said. "She

wouldn't have got far without that strong will of hers. We had our own secret way to communicate. At least, I thought it was secret until I saw some of the deaf-blind people use it too."

Interested, Aimée asked, "How's that?"

"We did it for fun. If we were somewhere and she didn't like something, she'd block print instead of whispering or being rude."

"Block print?"

"Palm printing . . . it's simple. You form the words in capitals on someone's palm or forearm. Like this."

Aimée felt Sylvaine take her arm. Then Sylvaine's finger traced lines and curlicues on it.

"It tickles."

"All the letters are composed of one to three strokes," Sylvaine said. "A U is a rounded one stroke. The V slants . . . feel the difference?"

Aimée nodded. Sylvaine's presence dispelled the cold isolation she had felt.

"What did I write?"

"The doctor was . . . no is . . . chunky?"

Sylvaine's throaty laughter filled the room.

"Do me one more big favor," Aimée said. René had left her room too soon to give her the information. "Write down on a paper the numbers from this phone's speed dial on a piece of paper. Then I promise to leave you alone."

"*Pas de problème,* but you'll owe me," Sylvaine said. "There are three numbers."

Aimée felt a paper thrust into her hand.

Then a beeping came from somewhere at mid-level where Sylvaine stood. "Oops, I'm being paged," she said. "Time for my shift."

Aimée felt guilty. "Sorry that you missed your nap."

"*Rien de tout!* Drop by my room, it's four doors down on the left. We'll have coffee and talk. I need to interview another patient for my nursing course, someone other than eighty-year-old Madame Slavinksy who falls asleep after three minutes and wakes up thinking we're in the Warsaw theatre watching a performance of *The Threepenny Opera.*"

After Sylvaine's last footsteps echoed down the hallway, it struck Aimée. For a brief time, with Sylvaine, she'd forgotten she was blind. The first time since it had happened since that night.

The phone rang.

"*Allô?*"

"I'm mad at you, Aimée," said Martine, her voice husky as usual. "Furious."

"But why? Won't Vincent cooperate . . . is he badmouthing me?"

"You didn't let on. I'm your best friend," she said. "Tell me it isn't true? You're . . . you're. . . . It's not permanent, is it?"

"I was going to tell you," Aimée said. "I didn't want to ruin your big evening."

"That doesn't matter," she said. "I feel terrible. What do you need?"

What she really needed, Martine couldn't provide.

"Don't worry," said Aimée.

"René says Lambert's *the* specialist in Paris," said Martine. "But there's always Dr. Smoillet in Lyon, who helped my father. Or the eye clinic in Genève."

Martine's father had had routine cataract surgery, and the eye clinic in Genève specialized in macular degeneration. Neither was her problem. But she knew Martine wanted to help.

"Martine, I need decent dark glasses," she said. "Miles Davis chewed on the only pair I have, not that it matters to my vision . . ."

"Say no more, they're on the way," she said. "I'll engage a nurse to help you at my cousin's apartment. Round the clock care."

"Whoa Martine, you're wonderful but I'm learning to help myself. And I need to stay here, they're still running tests."

And she wasn't really sick. Battered, blind and concussed, but that was different. She didn't need a nurse.

The phone clicked. "Sorry, I have to put you on hold," said Martine.

By the time Martine came back on the line, Aimée had gotten one of her legs into her black tights.

"This magazine will kill me yet if the typesetters don't," she said, sounding frazzled. "The typesetters were on strike, but we took care of that. Now the major account in Bordeaux has 'problems' with the concept of our article on the 'new' winemakers. *Nom de Dieu,* I have to go or they'll pull out of the coming issue. And their five pages of advertising."

"Can't Vincent go?"

"These types need the editor to hold their hand. I'll come by as soon as I get back."

Able to use the phone now, Aimée felt more confident. It had only taken her three tries to reach René.

"René, any luck finding the software I need?"

"Not too bad," he said, klaxons honking in the background. "I'm picking up cables near Montgallet Métro."

He must be on rue Montgallet, a street lined with old storefronts that housed discount computer shops, Aimée thought.

One of René's favorite haunts. Many were run by families from Bangalore, the Silicon Valley of India.

"It's a Diwali sale," René said. A diesel truck shifted, the sound of gears scraping like the ragged cry of an animal in pain.

"Diwali? The Hindu festival of lights happens in November, René," she said. "Nice try. It's still October."

"A pre-Diwali sale. Rajeev will give us a good price. He's helping me with setup."

She wondered if René, her partner, had thoughts about a future with Rajeev, who was a part-time programmer as well as a shop owner. She wouldn't blame him if he did. She realized she had to help René with Vincent's hard drive, even if it were the last job they did together. But she couldn't worry about that now. Or she would give up and fall apart.

"René, did we do a shred analysis of Populax?"

"You mean a scan to see if deleted files were really gone?" He didn't wait for her answer. *"Non."*

She detected interest in his voice.

"Exactement," she said. "Vincent's stubbornness bothers me. Let's check the operating system. That should tell us if the file system was freed."

She heard raised voices in the background. "Then we should see if the OS wrote a special one-character code to the beginning of the directory entry for any file," René said. Aimée could hear his mounting excitement over the voices in the background. "It would mark any file as deleted. But unless it's overwritten, the file info is still stored in the directory and the data still exists on the hard drive."

"Even with our low-level software tools, we could read any deleted files," she said.

She felt around for her leather backpack. Found it hanging on the hook and slipped the straps around her shoulders.

"And if we find something incriminating on Populax's system, it's better to know your enemy than be surprised, as they say," she continued. "PR and marketing firms steal from each other all the time. And since the Judiciare's not asking for anything else, just the hard drive info, suppose we found evidence of a nasty white collar crime? It would give us a bargaining chip with Vincent."

"We could even get Vincent to pay us to delete it," René said, admiration in his voice.

"But first we've got to find out what files exist," she said. "And I don't know how fast I'll be using a voice-activated program," she told him. "If you come to visit again, they moved me to the residence behind the hospital. Room 213."

"By the way, I checked the databanks," René said. "She bought her cell phone on rue Sainte Antoine."

Aimée took a deep breath.

"And she was?"

"Josiane Dolet, lived at thirty-four, rue de Cotte."

The initials J.D. . . . of course. Now that she knew her name she could find out more.

"Wonderful work, René!" On her right she heard the tap of a cane on linoleum. Closer and closer.

"I'll come to see you as soon as . . ."

"Take your time, René," she said, reaching for Chantal's elbow. "I'm going shopping."

"This is my friend, Chantal," said Aimée, making the introduction to Lulu Mondriac, the owner of Blasphème.

Chantal had accompanied her so she could navigate. Lavender oils and frangipani fragrance from the scent counter wafted across to Aimée as Lulu acknowledged the introduction.

"It's funny, Lulu," Aimée said. "You told me it was an exclusive when I bought it.

But I ran into this woman who was wearing the identical silk Tong jacket. Matter of fact, she was seated next to me in a resto."

Aimée could visualize Lulu's round blue glasses, the thick silver bracelets up her arm like armor, the red hennaed hair piled on her head and her uniform of black silk Chinese pajamas. "When I work, I stay comfortable," Lulu had told her. Aimée had bought two pairs of the same silk pajamas.

"It was the sample. I'd kept it for myself, one for you and one for me. She begged for it," said Lulu. "But the embroidery and mahjong buttons weren't as nice as yours."

If Lulu had any suspicions that Aimée couldn't see, she kept them to herself. "A John Galliano top's coming in this week," she confided. "It's brilliant. Got your name on it."

An attempt at appeasement, Aimée thought.

Lulu's racks often held surprises, an eclectic collection that might include a Christian Lacroix sweater confection with an embroidered and beaded flowered collar, a Kenzo sweater threaded with metallic Lurex, or a poem printed on an Italian microfiber scarf.

On rare occasions she'd splurge in the shop, to celebrate a new contract or when her bank balance looked healthy. When would she next have such a reason to splurge? She pushed those thoughts away.

"Was the customer who purchased the sample Josiane Dolet, a stick-thin blonde, with Violet Vamp nails?" Aimée asked.

Silence. Was Lulu nodding? Aimée visualized the small store's layout, hoping she still faced Lulu.

"It was her, wasn't it?"

"I've known Josiane for years. She's one of my best clients. So I had to let her have it," Lulu admitted. "Look, Josiane was having a midlife crisis," said Lulu, "I've had one or two of those myself."

"What did she do?"

"What's this . . . twenty questions?"

Torn between telling Lulu her reason for asking or keeping it to herself, Aimée bit her lip. Lulu might have useful information. But Aimée didn't like disclosing what had happened.

"Won't you tell me about Josiane?"

"Any special reason?"

Besides being your client and dropping big money, Aimée almost said. "Keep this between us. Josiane was the woman killed in the passage."

Aimée heard a long gasp. Then silence. What she wouldn't give to watch Lulu digesting this news.

"The serial killer . . . but how. . . . They never release the victim's names," Lulu said, almost whispering.

"The victim was wearing a silk Tong jacket with Mahjong buttons." Aimée was guessing.

"*Mon dieu*. . . . It must be her. Why hurt Josiane?" said Lulu, her voice shaking in shock.

"The *flics* will want to question you, Lulu."

The shop door opened with a gust of wind.

"Delivery!"

"*Ici*. . . ."

The rest of Lulu's words were lost in the wind, but she was moving. Disconcerted by her change in position, Aimée didn't know which way to turn. Where had Lulu gone?

"What's wrong with you?" Lulu's voice came from behind her now.

Aimée was hesitant to admit she couldn't see. That she was blind and vulnerable, dependent on another blind women to help her. She didn't feel like a detective, more like an awkward victim who asked silly questions.

"Arnica does wonders," Lulu whispered. "Reduces the swelling. Sleep sitting up. And

157

once those stitches come out . . ."

Did Lulu assume since her face was swollen and she wore dark glasses that Aimée had just had plastic surgery?

"Josiane wanted to look young, to recapture her youth." Lulu went on, apparently satisfied with her own explanation. "That's my theory. You know, some of them put on clear plastic shoes with patterned socks, carry a doughnut-shape shoulder bag, and buy a new face. You've had some work done, too, eh?"

Aimée stayed silent. Chantal cleared her throat and pinched Aimée.

"Are you a reporter, too?" Lulu asked her. Chantal must have shaken her head since Lulu went on, "Well, Josiane was blonde. Me, well my hair's red now. I should be safe."

Was it widely known that the victims were all blondes? Aimée remembered Morbier saying that, but this fact had not been mentioned the one time she'd heard about the crimes on the *téle.*

"Lulu, no one's safe."

"You're right." Lulu let out a big sigh. "We're dancing between landmines here. Complacency's dangerous. I'll get the faubourg association to do something."

Aimée doubted they could do much. If

they hadn't stopped the Beast of Bastille before, what could a neighborhood association do now?

"Lulu, he attacked me, too," Aimée said, "But Josiane was his target."

"He attacked both of you?"

"It was the jacket," said Aimée. "I think he confused us. He went for me, thinking I was Josiane."

Aimée kept her head steady and focused her eyes in what she hoped was the right direction.

"But the man who attacked me wasn't the serial killer. The *flics* won't investigate; they think it's an open-and-shut case. They're sure it was the Beast. So please, tell me about her."

"*Alors,* this goes from bad to worse," Lulu said. "Josiane freelanced as a journalist. From what she said, she mostly did pieces on human rights. A green type . . . political. But a limousine liberal, you know."

Aimée hadn't known. Did green types go in for cosmetic surgery? That seemed to strike a false note. But on the other hand, why not?

Footsteps tramped in the door, then came rustling noises, then the slinging metallic sound of clothes hangers sliding along a rack.

"Madame . . . I'll take this in medium. Here's my card."

Aimée heard clicks, a muttered curse. Lulu must have slid a credit card through the portable machine, then slammed it hard on the pink concrete counter. She'd done the same thing with Aimée's card last week. Another loud thwack and Aimée jumped. Right against something that jiggled. The beaded jewelry display?

"Piece of garbage, this thing." Lulu's voice, in a low growl, came from Aimée's right. "My clients wait, the charge doesn't go through. I end up doing this twenty times a day! Look, we'll have to talk later."

Aimée felt an arm and Lulu's frangipani-scented lip tint brushing by her cheek and realized she was being escorted out the door. "I'll do what I can."

All the way back along the slippery pavement, clinging to Chantal's arm, Aimée wanted to kick herself. She knew she must look awful. And the crowded, narrow streets and cars whizzing by terrified her. Noises jumped out from everywhere.

Something chirped and startled her. Birds . . . near the Bastille column?

"That traffic signal's for us," Chantal said. "You can let my arm loose, you know. I'll need it later and you've nearly squeezed off my blood circulation."

"Sorry," Aimée said, feeling sheepish. She was adrift in the sea of sounds.

"You need protection, now," said Chantal. "You'll feel safer once you master simple cane skills."

Chantal left her in the lobby and Aimée rode the elevator by herself. The numbers were announced automatically, and she felt proud when she got off at her floor until, once again, she sensed another presence. Someone stood in the hallway. Somewhere near her room. Her voice caught in her throat.

She took two steps. Grabbed for the railing and missed. Found it the next time and reached for her keys.

"Looking for someone?" she asked.

Silence.

Paralyzed, she waited.

Then the elevator whished open behind her. She turned, her keys pointed.

"Shopping, in your condition?" René asked behind her. "Find anything?"

"I found out more about Josiane Dolet. Now I'm certain she was the intended victim," Aimée said. "Anyone else here?"

"Just us."

"Could you look inside my room for me?"

She felt him take the door key that she held between her fingers, poised in the attack mode, and brush by her.

The door clicked as it was unlocked. "Coast seems clear," René said a moment later.

Was she paranoid? Hadn't someone been standing there when she got out of the elevator?

She told him about Sergeant Bellan's questioning and Morbier's comments about Vaduz.

The attacker had taken nothing from her. She figured he'd been in a hurry when he found out she wasn't the right woman.

"Time to get to work, partner," she said, feeling her way along the wall. After a big breath and three steps, she reached her bed and kicked her bag under it.

She located a bottle of water, twisted the top, and took a slug. Half of it went down her shirt. Cold and soaking wet.

"Here's the screen access program I promised you," said René. "Blind programmers say DOS screen readers go quicker than what we're used to. They're dealing with strings of text with no graphic interface to slow it down. I think 128 megs of RAM should be enough for you. Schematics, variable capacity and interfaces work off those.

Remember, the way we designed the Populax firewall?"

She heard the machine power up, the echoing pings as the net connection was made.

"A double password protected firewall, as usual!" she said.

"Click on Internet, then open browser," René said.

A silky robotic-tinged voice responded "Log-in completed, internet connection established."

"You're wonderful, René." Simultaneously, a surge of power ran through her. "Now I can investigate what's bothering me."

"What's that?"

"Why did Vincent tear up our contract?" she said. She nodded, her fingers finding the keys, nestling in the ridges. Enjoying the familiar little clicks, feeling at home. Her fingers racing over the keys and responding to voice commands. "What is he hiding?"

She positioned the laptop on her bed, crossed her legs, and opened an internet browser. A pleasant male voice, deep and with a slightly robotic accent, responded to her key commands.

"Sexy enough for you?" René asked.

"He's no Aznavour, but he'll do," she said.

"René, I need a favor. Please copy these numbers." She thrust the paper with Josiane's speed dial numbers at him and the phone itself.

"And then . . ." she paused. She didn't want to ask him to do this. But one of them had to comb the hard drive as soon as possible. René had provided her with the software so she could, and right now he would be better at interviewing someone.

"Up to calling on these folks and getting information from them, René?" she asked.

"It says Leduc Detective on our door," he said. "Doesn't it?"

THURSDAY MORNING

René backed his customized Citroën into a vacant sliver of space on boulevard Richard Lenoir. Never mind that it consisted of several zebra crossing stripes. A Parisian parking spot — you got in where you could.

Red-brown leaves fluttered from the trees, crackling under his feet. A weak, late-morning sun was framed by the bare plane tree branches overhead.

Opposite stood the Bataclan theatre. Once a pagoda-style folly built by Napoléon III for Empress Eugénie, then *un caf' conc'*, café concert hall, where Maurice Chevalier sang for the Germans, later a cinema. Now the marquee read "Limited run only . . . *Viva Zapata,* the musical!"

The chance to *do* something, work in the field like Aimée, excited René. Their roles were reversed, finally. But his stomach churned. The burden was on him to investigate a murder and the attack on Aimée. He'd made an appointment with Miou-Miou, the woman who answered the first number on Josiane Dolet's speed dial.

"Monsieur Friant, ça va?" said a woman with blonde ringlets who skated up to him in front of the Bataclan. She flashed a card: "Astrology readings by Miou-Miou — day or night, I rollerblade to YOU."

"Thanks for meeting me. Let's have a drink," he said, indicating the dim café.

"*Bon,* my next client's the numbers man upstairs."

René wondered if that boded well for the Bataclan's finances. He struggled to keep up with her. The curse of short legs, he thought, as he had a thousand times. Boulevard de Temple, known in the eighteenth century as the notorious "Boulevard du Crime," bordering the Marais and the Bastille, lay ahead of them.

The café, once the Bataclan lobby, looked overdue for a renovation. *At least a cleaning,*

René thought. Remnants of Chinese temple-style pillars and red lacquer beams, paint peeling off in places, arched above them. The circular zinc bar, a 50s island in the sea of café tables and rattan chairs, beckoned with a rainbow display of liquor bottles.

"Taurus . . . Scorpio rising," Miou-Miou said, with a big grin. "I'm right, aren't I?"

René nodded.

She sat down, crossed her rollerblades, and pulled her shoulder bag onto her lap. She opened it, and drew out a pile of astrological charts. "First consultation costs two hundred francs. Then I prepare your chart, which I keep with me. You can call anytime and I'll give you a reading on the spot or come to you with a detailed horoscope. For fifty francs more, I do important events or weekly forecasts."

René pulled out five hundred francs, signaling the waiter.

"I'm sorry but I didn't make myself clear. I want information about Josiane Dolet," he said. "Your number was on her speed dial."

"My client's charts are confidential." She shook her head, returning the charts to her bag as if to leave.

"Not any more," he said, forcing his eyes to move past the lime tulle ribbon around her blonde curls, the pink lips, red-and-white-striped tights, pink leggings, and green denim jacket. "Hear me out, first," René said.

A waiter old enough to be his father, bald and earringed, appeared. He wore a long white-apron and skinny black T-shirt and stood, tapping his foot.

"Un Cardinal," René said.

"What's that?" Miou-Miou asked.

"Here we call it the *Communard,*" the waiter said, writing down the order.

"Red wine, *crème de cassis,* and juice," René said. "It's the same drink, but the name lines up at the other end of the political spectrum."

The waiter shrugged.

"And you, mademoiselle?" he said, tossing a bowl of salt-encrusted *cacahuètes* on the ring-stained table.

"Une feuille morte," she said. "I like the fallen leaf autumn color of Pastis mixed with menthe and grenadine."

After the waiter moved away, René leaned forward. The table's rim hit his chest. "Josiane Dolet was murdered in a Bastille passage. Your number was on her speed dial."

"You're a detective?" Miou-Miou's eyes widened. "No wonder she didn't show for her reading. Such a shame. Josiane was a free spirit. But her chart indicated tumult. A storm brewing since August. Tempestuous relations. But I never imagined. . . ."

And I'm the Rhône ranger, René thought.

A paunchy, middle-aged man waddled into the café. He kissed the harried cashier, who paused and returned his *bisous,* then leaned over the zinc to the shaven-headed, earringed barman, a younger version of the waiter, who was polishing glasses.

"Attends," Miou-Miou said, "That's my client. I'll be right back." She glided over to the man, whose glasses glinted, reflecting the flickering neon sign advertising Picon.

Frustrated, René picked at the peanuts. Stale and oily. He looked around.

In the far corner, as if supporting the Chinese pillars, sat a pale-faced trio: a couple and a midget wearing a fedora. An aura of time suspended, surrounded them. Most cafés were lively places where people conversed or went to see or be seen.

Not here. It was like a railway waiting room.

René's radar picked up on it at once. Circus people. He hated the old fug of sad-eyed clowns and freaks away from the big top. They looked familiar, probably from the nearby *Cirque d'hiver.* Perhaps cronies of his mother. Unemployed. Or waiting for a casting call.

He felt again the trials his mother, a normal-sized juggler, had endured. The drafty circus tents, tears coursing through her makeup when money was tight, and the love she had borne him. The determination that he'd never perform as a freak.

And he hadn't.

Her amazing good fortune in becoming the old marquis's housekeeper in Amboise had helped. The marquis had attended her performances every year. He'd loved René's mother's unique juggling act and her wit.

A circus aficionado, the marquis had maintained a private museum of mechanical toys from the 1700s up to the 1930s. When she'd grown "ready for the pasture," as the circus owner termed it in his delicate way after a flaming arrow severed the tendon in her left hand, the marquis invited her to oversee his "little collection." She'd ended up running his château. And probably more, but René didn't dwell on that.

An odd but sweet man, he'd financed René's clinic bills during his stretching therapy. It hadn't worked. His hip displacement had gotten worse. The marquis helped with his education. Paid for extras at the Sorbonne. And the car.

René never told Aimée any of this. He

wasn't sure why. He liked the fact that Aimée had never asked, had never wanted explanations. She'd simply introduced herself one afternoon at the Sorbonne café, saying "Rumor says you can access a mainframe in twenty minutes."

She'd shoved a laptop across the table.

"You heard wrong," he'd told her, rolling up his sleeves and establishing a net connection. "Twelve minutes is the longest it takes me." And using the number his friend had given him he'd accessed the mainframe and done it in ten.

Her big, kohl-ringed eyes had lit up. Right there, she'd offered him a job on a project she'd undertaken. The work grew and when he ended up spending more time on computer security at Leduc Detective than at the Sorbonne, he quit classes. And she did, too.

His confused feelings about her surfaced: her terrible driving, her unconventionality, the passion she brought to things and the fierce loyalty she showed him. And glimpses of the raw inner hurt he'd seen exposed a few times. Like the hurt he'd so often felt.

He thought about her huge eyes and the funny way she hid her feelings for Morbier yet yearned for his approval.

Never mind that she didn't provide tickets

for restaurants or a Carte Orange pass for the Métro like some employers, she made sure she paid into his *seçu,* the *mutuelle* for medical insurance, and his *prévoyance.* When bills were paid and lucrative contracts signed, they celebrated with champagne and sushi. The odd thing was, his mother and the marquis had seemed pleased.

Would Aimée let him take care of her now that she was blind? Or would she push him away? Should he team up with Rajeev? Join him and form a software business, as Rajeev was urging him to?

He repressed his feelings. As always. But the thought that though she was his best friend, sometimes that wasn't enough, kept rising up. He wanted more. More of her. He pushed that away.

He drank the *Cardinal/Communard* and half of another, then stared at the old chrome coffee machine topped by a winged eagle and at the special VIEILLE PRUNE ARTISANALE 4L.-45 FRS. written in white on the beveled mirror until Miou-Miou returned. Breathless. She grabbed her drink and downed it three long gulps.

"That bad?"

She nodded.

"Another?"

He caught the waiter's eye, pointed to

their glasses.

"Does your client cook the Bataclan's books?"

"He's the comptroller," she said. "And since his sun crossed Virgo . . . very auspicious . . . he's decided to ask for the hand of his plumber's sister who lives three houses down in the same Batignolle *banlieue.*"

"At least he'll be able to fall back on his brother-in-law if the theatre business gets tight," René said. He handed the waiter several hundred-franc notes.

"*Vraiment,* I was worried about Josiane's chart," she said, reaching for her new drink. "The one I never completed. Of course not, it got stuck under . . ."

"The comptroller's?" René interrupted.

She nodded. The tulle ribbon bobbed in her curls. "Look," she said, setting down a chart. The spheres of planets were crossed by red, aqua, and orange lines. "I hadn't finished the alignment of the houses and the dominant planets . . . but Josiane called, wanting to meet. She said I could finish later, but she had an important question to ask first."

All this astral plane talk unnerved him. "And you said . . . ?"

"Clients call my hotline or hit my website

with questions all the time," she said, noting disbelief in his eyes. "I'm very good."

René grew aware of the sounds of conversation and the clink of glasses around them. Tables filling with the café clientele, the waiter rushing to fill orders and barking new ones to the younger look-alike barman.

"Sometimes I'm so good, it's scary," Miou-Miou confessed.

René avoided her eyes. He shifted on the rattan chair and wished his dangling legs could touch the floor. Just once.

"If I finish the orbit of her ruling planet . . . see how the sun line intersects . . . that shows warning. 'Tread lightly on the rungs of life's ladder.' But here," she slapped the chart, rustling the paper. "The lifeline was cut."

"When?" If she was so good she'd know.

"11:40 p.m. last Monday night," she said, glancing at her watch. She stood up, hefted her bag across her chest and snapped her green denim jacket closed.

"How do you know that?"

"She was going to call me. She didn't," said Miou-Miou. "I have to go. I've got another appointment."

Josiane's body was found Tuesday midday, René thought. But the morgue would have an estimate of the actual time of death.

Aimée sat back on her bed in the residence, frustrated.

"Searching database for requested information. Five minutes remaining," said the computer's robotic voice. René had tried for Yves Montand's silky tone. She hadn't had the heart to tell him, Not even close.

Aimée lifted her fingers from the keyboard, felt her way across the cotton duvet, and found the rumpled Nicorette gum package. She rifled inside. Each tin foil pocket punctured and empty. All gone.

Her fingers scrabbled over the duvet, found the bedside table and the plastic bottle of lemon-scented nail polish remover she'd requested that René bring her. She uncrossed her black silk Chinese pajama pant-clad legs and felt around. Where were the cotton pads? She felt something small, square, rough on one side. A box. A matchbox. Who'd been smoking . . . Morbier, *Non,* he'd quit. Bellan?

A few matchsticks rattled. She slid one out and chewed the matchhead, enjoying the gritty tang of sulphur on her tongue. Like pepper, without the kick. If only she had a cigarette to go with it.

And then she'd win the Lotto, fill every

hungry stomach with food, and discover a cure for blindness.

Dream on.

There were knocks on the door. "Delivery for Mademoiselle Leduc."

She reached for the security chain and unhooked it, then for the door knob.

"Sign please," the voice said.

But she couldn't. "Guide my hand to make an X."

He did.

"Please, what does it say?"

"Package from Samaritaine from Martine Sitbon, and four orchid plants," he said. "The card says 'When in trouble, do the frivolous.' "

How sweet!

After she opened the box she found it filled with what felt like sunglasses, in assorted shapes: round, 70s rectangular, and cat-eye shaped with bumps . . . rhinestones?

She left the orchids for Sylvaine to help her with, then tried on each pair of sunglasses. Wondered what they looked like, kept on the ones she imagined were like Audrey Hepburn's in *Breakfast at Tiffany's.* All she needed were the rope of pearls and cigarette holder.

Then her palm touched something on the bedside table . . . a crumpled cellophane packet. Too thick for Nicorette . . . dare she hope? She put it to her nose, smelled the paper . . . an acrid blond tobacco . . . Gauloise Blond? Her favorite brand?

Her fingers found them . . . two filtered cigarettes. She wanted to shout *Thank you God* except for the nagging thought: Who would have forgotten them . . . or left them for her? A sympathy gesture from Bellan? But he'd visited her in the hospital, not here. Was it a forgetful janitor's?

Would he want them back?

Never mind. And this wasn't a hospital, surely people could smoke in their rooms. She hadn't *seen* any sign forbidding it. And if some dragon complained, she'd get a kick out of saying just that.

Logistics . . . she had to plan her actions. How to smoke and not set the place on fire.

Stupid . . . such a simple thing. How could lighting and smoking a cigarette be such a big deal? But of course it was.

The matchbox fell from her hand. She heard it strike somewhere on the linoleum below her feet. Fighting a desire to burst into tears of frustration, she took a deep breath. Forced herself to look on the good side. *Nom de Dieu,* she was about to enjoy a coffin nail!

First she needed something for an ashtray.

By the time she found the espresso cup and saucer and knocked it over, spilling the dregs over her sleeve, she'd located the matchbox with her toes. With a nimbleness she didn't know she had, she clamped her toes around the matchbox, then hoisted it onto the mound of the piled duvet.

Had she closed the door to her room? If it weren't so irritating, she'd find her predicament silly. But she imagined she would appear ridiculous to a sighted person looking in her room.

Sighted . . . when had she begun referring to *others* as sighted? She'd been around Chantal too much.

With everything in position, including bottled water, just in case of fire, she stood by the window. Lifting the smooth handle, she opened the double window a crack, then pushed it all the way open. She felt vents or narrow slats. Of course, a shutter; she pushed it aside, too. Then a metal bar, with ornamental grille below, like every apartment in Paris built in the Haussman era.

A brisk autumn gust from the Seine scented with chalky soil accompanied the whirr of machinery nearby. From below came the scrape of a bulldozer. She recognized the unmistakeable grating of an earth mover in the distance.

Urban renewal in the Bastille: the thought left a bad taste in her mouth. It was worse for those displaced by it. Whole courtyards of artisan workshops were being demolished by the high-profile Mirador construction company.

Now came the hard part, lighting the match. Only three left.

The filter tip sat in her mouth. The cigarette jutted straight out. Her hands were held close to her body. She took the match from the matchbox, positioned the nubby part between her forefinger and middle finger, set the match close, and struck it. A long slow sizzle and *thupt,* it lit on the first swipe. Heat came from her fingertips.

She moved the match to where she thought the cigarette tip was and inhaled. Her fingertip burned. But had she found the tip first?

And then she felt the rush of tobacco as it caught and burned. She inhaled, the jolt from the nicotine making her head spin. The smoke rushed to her lungs. Lightheaded, she fanned the match in big arcs until sure it had gone out.

Sipping an espresso would make it perfect. Almost.

Back at the laptop, crosslegged, taking deep drags on the cigarette, she dug deeper into the Populax database. Her fingers flew over the keys, guided by the robotic voice. The impressive client dossiers revealed lucrative campaigns, especially the one for the Bastille Opéra. The Opéra's exchange with St. Petersburg, a brainchild of glasnost, now a struggle for the St. Petersburg opera house, was being promoted by the Opéra board. Layer by layer, she checked the files. She found using extra keystrokes slowed her down, but not by much.

Nothing unusual.

Just to make sure, she ran a virus scan. The semi-silky voice informed her, "Scanning time remaining ten minutes."

She sat back, grinding the cigarette out in the saucer positioned by her elbow. Trucks bleeped and the whine of the bulldozer came from below. She figured if she could see, the back of the Opéra would be on the other side of the Hospital.

The day before the assault, she'd used René's car, adjusting his customized controls to fit her height. Finding taxis on a rainy Paris night had required more good taxi karma than she'd been willing to bank on.

Running late for the impromptu meeting called by Vincent just an hour earlier, she'd dented René's Citroën in the tight first-floor

Opéra parking lot. Carrying two laptops, graphs, rolled-up flowcharts, and the thick Populax file slowed her progress. She'd asked the gaunt-faced parking attendant for help. He'd given her a big smile and showed her a shortcut. He lisped and walked with a rolling gait, favoring a shortened leg. Yet he'd gone out of his way to guide her to an unmarked blue door that led to the back of the Quinze-Vingts hôpital, with the Opéra backstage loading dock on her left, and what she recognized now was the résidence St. Louis on her right. Vincent's office on rue Charenton stood directly opposite. She'd felt about in her raincoat pocket, and come up with a damp fifty franc note.

"You're a prince!" She'd meant it, looking at the downpour. "Got any idea when they close this exit?"

"Make it back before the *guardien* locks it at eight," he said, smiling that warm smile again. "Although sometimes he forgets."

All this had happened less than a week ago. But now she couldn't see, didn't know if she ever would, and her whole world had careened out of control. Even the satisfying smoke only blunted her anxiety.

Pangs of "what if's" hit her until the semi-sexy velvet voice told her she had to make a choice between continuing the download or pausing. She snapped out of her mood of worry and self-pity. Time to work.

Loud pounding on the wall startled her. Aimée hit SAVE. Was the computer voice bothering her next door neighbor? Sharp raps at her door.

She switched off the laptop. Stood and counted her steps to the door.

"Oui?"

The knocking continued.

Aimée reached again for the security chain and unhooked it, then reached for the handle, a metal hook with padded grips and opened it.

"Who's there?"

"Don't torture me. Either close the window or give me a cigarette," said a quavering voice.

"Forgive me, but I didn't know," she said, wishing she could see who this poor woman was. "I have one more . . . share?"

"Merci."

Something furry and soft feathered her arm as the woman passed. Like her grandmother's fox collar. The same mothball musky smell. Aimée remembered the fox wrap draped around her grandmother's neck. The two beady glass eyes, the sharp claws, and how she loved to touch them. "For special occasions," her grandmother said, "baptisms, weddings, funerals, and when you graduate from the Sorbonne."

But she hadn't, and her grandmother passed away soon after.

"I'm your neighbor. Let me see you," said the demanding voice.

Aimée felt hands, wrinkled and dry, outlining her cheeks, neck, and hairline. Fingers with short nails and a clinging chocolate aroma explored her.

"Nice earrings . . . pearl studs?" she was asked.

"I'm impressed," she said. "Call me Aimée."

"Madame Toile, but you can call me Mimi. Just don't call me late to dinner."

Old joke. Something metallic jingled.

"What's that . . . your key?" Aimée asked.

It felt like a flattened serving utensil beneath Aimée's hand. "Eh? My absinthe spoon . . . I need it. Must do it properly, you know."

Aimée knew that absinthe had been outlawed for years, but figured the old biddy had her own source. Or inhabited her own world.

"Hold the sugar lump just right and sip the absinthe through it," she said, her voice misting with anticipation. "Every afternoon, Rico pours me a few drops. He's Pierre's grandson, so I know it's right."

The old woodworm liquor rotted the brain. Had it damaged Mimi's?

"Pierre supplied the *maison,*" Mimi said. "Such a well-connected man. Even when they shut us down in forty-eight." She made a snorting noise. "We moved across Marché d'Aligre. All the girls came. What else would they do?"

Was Mimi the absinthe-drinking ex-madam of a bordello?

"They called us an institution," she said. "Now where's that Gauloise?"

She felt Mimi's dry hand leading her to the bed. Using the same maneuver, Aimée lit the final cigarette and passed it to her. Mimi inhaled a long drag, then slowly exhaled. "Reminds me of the first time. He did it like a soccer player, no hands and straight for the goal."

Aimée laughed. Her first time, with her cousin's friend, had been similar.

"So why were brothels closed in nineteen forty-eight?"

"Now who cared about us, eh? Except the government! They needed the buildings. The housing shortage after the war . . . *incroyable!* So they took over the houses . . . even the Sphinx in Montparnasse, where the ministers went. Well, what went on at the Sphinx was no enigma, if you get my drift."

Aimée didn't know if she wanted to.

Madame exhaled a long smoky breath, felt for Aimée's hand, and slid it between her fingers. "Reminds me of the blackouts. We'd share fags then, too. Never light three on a match, or a sniper will get you, they said. None of *us* went to the Métro during air raids. We took our chances: after all, we were getting paid, weren't we?"

A nicotine-induced wave of dizziness came over Aimée. Was it a sign of recovery, small though it might be?

"Clothilde was the smart one. Shrewd. She still runs her bar," she said. "Right down there on the corner of rue Moreau. Banked her sous and bought the place. Clothilde knew how to judge the tide and still does. After all, the tide only goes two ways, in and out. The difference after forty-eight was that the girls stood out front on the cobblestones. That and not getting checked every week by the *médecin.* Stupid, I call it . . . with so many diseases nowadays, eh?"

"What happened to your eyes, Mimi?"

"Something I can't pronounce, but I like it when that young doctor tells me about it." Her laughter sounded more like a

184

cackle. The bed rocked. Aimée felt a sharp nudge in her ribs. "He wears good cologne and drinks Sumatra blend espresso. Know the one?"

Dr. Lambert. Mimi's sense of smell wasn't the only sharp thing about her.

"He's the department head, Mimi."

"If I wasn't so old, he'd head my department. Like him?"

"Well, he's . . ."

Another sharp nudge in her ribs. "Good salary, secure job and what a pension! A girl's got to think of these things, *non?* Looks only take you so far."

And Aimée wondered if Mimi was thinking of herself as she spoke.

"He's married, most likely."

"And when has that ever stopped anything?"

After Mimi left, Aimée ran a standard virus check on her laptop, figuring she might as well finish the tedious job before tackling the password encryption.

The slow whirr of the zip disk and then the announcement "Zip disk cleaning time remaining twelve minutes" caused her to reach for the nail polish remover bottle. She uncapped it, swished the nail polish remover onto a cotton square and rubbed away what she hoped was the chipped Gigabyte Green.

The lemony acetone smell cleared her sinuses.

More loud knocking on her door.

"Oui?"

Perhaps Mimi wanted a manicure, too? Well why not, Aimée had time. She lifted the laptop, unplugged the external Zip Drive, and set them in the drawer.

She heard a muffled voice, hard to distinguish from the increasing loud gnawing of the bulldozer and pealing church bells somewhere. Was it night . . . was it dark? No . . . the men were still working. Or were they working late on the new Métro line?

She opened the door partway and undid the chain. Her foot stuck behind the doorframe and she stumbled.

Clumsy . . . still so awkward!

A breeze sliced by her face and a splintering, cracking noise accompanied it. Her body trembled.

"Salope!" said a man with an accent she couldn't place. His sour breath hit her in the face. Then a sharp, stinging slap knocked her against the wall.

She tossed the open nail varnish remover at the man and ducked. And then she remembered the match . . . had she put it out? A fire hazard. Stupid.

From somewhere on her right came a yelp of pain.

Her arms were grabbed, then she felt a sharp shove in her back. Hard. She was airborne. Flying across the room. Good thing she'd flung her arms out to break her fall. Instead, they caught on a cold metal grille over cool fresh air.

The window was open.

She screamed. Panic overwhelmed her. A hand covered her mouth, then another big push shoved her hips over the grille. She tried to hook her legs onto the smooth metal, to cling to the bars. The next push and her legs went over. Blood rushed to her head. Good God . . . couldn't someone see her from the street?

She screamed again. And again. The air was chilly. Dank with humidity. Was it night?

The scraping of the bulldozer in the street sounded close. Too close. She was hanging halfway out the window.

Why didn't anyone see her or hear her? Was it dark? Or the bulldozer too loud?

Terror flooded her. Her fingernails scratched wood and she dug in, hugging what had to be the outside shutter. Clinging for dear life, her feet scrabbled, slipping and scraping the stone.

She *had* to hold on. Her fingers burned

from the abrading stone. Her silk pajamas flapped in the wind. She couldn't climb back into the room. She would have to take her chance with the concrete below. How far below?

"Help me!" she yelled once more.

Couldn't *anyone* hear her? Each time she scrabbled her legs for purchase, her knees hit something hard. Somehow she found a toehold with her bare feet in the metal grille guard.

She kept screaming for help. Why didn't anyone notice?

And then she became aware of gray fog, like a steamy vapor, crossing before her. And it felt so natural . . . because it was. She *saw* the fog from the Seine.

Her pulse leaped!

She blinked over and over. She could see. Furred yellow globes appeared and she realized they must be streetlamps. A foggy, grainy quality overlay what seemed a dark hulk of trees and what had to be car headlights on the street below. Dots of red and orange lights bordered the bulldozer.

And then darkness descended. It was gone.

She swung her leg on top of what felt like a stone ledge, reached out, and pulled herself up. Was this another window? Powderlike soot and crumbling concrete bits came back in her hand. What felt like a tin gutter was below her feet. She stepped onto it. It skidded and came loose. She grabbed at the nearest thing, some kind of rough weatherbeaten molding, and held on, trying to find the windowsill. Somewhere, a window slammed shut. She heard smashing and a crashing noise.

She felt a thick rock slab and then an indentation, like a little vest-pocket balcony. Nothing more. *Merde.* On her knees crawling now, and nowhere to go. Except to back up. Scarier than inching forward. Her hands, bloodied or wet from the moist railing, slipped. She smacked into a stone wall and clutched a shutter. A creaking and a ripping noise came and she clung for dear life.

Her hands slipped . . . how far were the cobblestones below? She'd never know because she wouldn't be able to see the ground rushing up at her. Her heart hammered. She didn't want to die.

Where was Mimi's room? There had to be a ledge. All buildings had ledges under the windows. Didn't they?

Wind whipped around her legs. Her fingers throbbed. If the building was as old as the Quinze-Vingts there'd be stone cornices.

Where were they?

She felt rusted pipes, grabbed them and hugged the façade. Wires snapped off in her hand and she lost her balance. Her leg slid, then her foot jammed against sharp roof tiles. Fear flared up in her. She couldn't hold on any longer.

"Somebody help!"

She heard a voice.

Raising her leg, she kicked as hard as she could. A wooden shutter banged away and glass splintered. Fine slivers beaded her calf.

"Don't move, I've got a socket wrench aimed at your head," she heard Mimi threaten.

"Mimi! Help me. Someone's trying to kill me," she screamed. "Let me in!"

"But . . ."

"Hurry up, it's cold out here and I can't hold on much longer!" Fear clutched her as her fingers loosened. Slipped. This was it. Her life was over. Then a hand pulled hers and her knees scraped over the shutters. By the time she was inside Mimi's room, she knew what she had to do.

"I must have scared him away," Mimi said.

"Call building security."

"Be my guest."

"Er, how do I do it?"

"The only security we can call is that

loafer in the front gate. Try 37 on the wall phone."

Aimée was perched on Mimi's bed, with a blanket over her feet, when footsteps sounded in the hall. Stopped. Then came a pounding on Mimi's door.

"Nom de Dieu," said a high-pitched voice. *"Quelle catastrophe!"*

Aimée opened the door. "Someone broke down my door and attacked me!"

"But property can't be destroyed like this."

Aimée choked.

"Where's security?" she asked. "Who are you?"

"The Matron, I'm responsible here," said the woman. "The hospital administration only gives us conditional use. You've had some party going on with your hall neighbor, eh? But now you've ruined it for us."

"Don't you understand? Someone attacked me in my room and could still be there, although he's probably gotten away by now."

Aimée knew there were kilometers of corridors, underground links to the hospital, the Chapel and several administration buildings. With people all dressed in scrubs and walking around wearing masks, it would have been easy for her attacker to avoid detection.

"Smashed chairs, broken windows . . ." the matron's voice trailed off. "Who gave you permission to have a room on this floor?"

"Chantal brought me here. But you don't understand . . ."

"She has no authority," said the matron. "I did not authorize you to sign in. We have strict rules. Our funding and insurance depend on upholding them."

"I heard Aimée screaming and someone thrashing around next door, breaking things," said Mimi.

"The attacker might still be here," said Aimée.

"All I see is a mess *you* created," the matron said. Aimée heard her sniffing. "What's that smell? Drugs . . . ?"

Did she mean the acetone smell of the lemon nail polish?

"Where's security?"

"*Allez-y,* you're out of here!" the matron said.

Wasn't *she* the victim here? But it was hard to argue with an irate woman she couldn't see. More footsteps came down the hall.

A shiver passed through her.

"What have you done now?" Dr. Lambert's voice asked.

Where had he come from?

"Luckily I trip a lot, since I can't see. That's what saved me or the damage to my door would have happened to my face."

"Matron, the door's obviously been forced," Dr. Lambert said. "Let's make sure security's on the way."

"Of course, Doctor," she said, her tone completely altered.

"I heard him bashing things," said Mimi, "I turned on my Books on Tape, hit the wall, then yelled. I must have scared him away."

"But I want it known this woman was in residence without my knowledge, much less my authority or consent," said the matron. "Someone's got to pay for the damages. I won't take the blame. Why should my competence be put in question?"

"Please understand, this TGV accident threw everything into chaos . . . a huge overload of cases, not enough beds," he said, trying to soothe her. "We've bent the rules a bit, but no one will point any fingers, I assure you."

Aimée couldn't believe his reaction. "I'd call this a police matter. Don't you have security cameras here?"

"At the hospital entrance, so I'm told,"

Mimi said. "Not here. Look, Aimée's been attacked. Why blame her!"

But the matron must have already bustled out of the room.

"Where are my things?" Aimée asked. *What if the attacker got her laptop and phone!* "I have to check. Please help me."

"Someone's got to clean you up," he said, "again!"

Her fingers throbbed where she had scraped them. She prayed she could still use a keyboard.

Dr. Lambert called for a nurse to medicate and bandage her hands. Then he left the room, but Aimée heard him talking with the matron in the hallway and greeting security when it arrived.

As soon as the nurse arrived, Aimée had her search the room. "Tell me what you find."

"Well, the mattress is turned over, sheets and pillows everywhere, chairs upside down."

"Please look in the closet."

"Leather jacket, shoes all tumbled about. A mess."

"Can you look in the drawer?"

"There's a laptop computer," said the nurse.

Thank God.

"Tubes of Ultralash mascara, a Chanel red lipstick, lipliner, powder, and perfume bottle on the floor. A black silk teddy mixed up with what looks like red and white wires."

Her phone-line splicer cables. "What about my cell phone?"

"No sign," the nurse said. "Not even under the bed."

Great. Now they could get to her another way. Nothing remained private anymore. France Télécom held a wealth of information, if one knew how to crack the database. She'd done it often enough herself.

Still, she'd had Josiane's phone in her pajama pocket. That at least was safe. And she guessed that the assailant had wanted it. That's what this was about. And he'd find out soon enough he'd taken the wrong one.

She called the Commissariat and asked for Sergeant Bellan.

"Not here. What's this about?"

By the time she recounted the circumstances and been transferred to the correct department, her lip trembled nonstop. She was afraid her words were no longer clear enough to be understood.

"We'll send someone over," a policewoman said, "but it could take a while. A big rig overturned on the Périphérique and it's a mess."

She asked the nurse to help her cancel her cell phone service.

"I'm sorry this happened, but you can't stay here," Dr. Lambert was saying. "Normally it wouldn't matter. But with the property damage and matron upset . . ."

"I don't care if she is. I've called the *flics*."

She felt a finger on her lips. Nice and warm. His?

"I understand. Our reaction may seem callous but I'll try and explain. The Ministry of Health's threatened to close some hospitals. Our funding's under review, so we all feel stretched right now. Services are tight, and the proposal to expand the day clinic's outreach for the *quartier's* underserved residents is crucial. We'd rather not make waves right now." She felt Dr. Lambert's arm around her shoulder.

"I think the attacker came back looking for . . ."

"Accommodating you here was my idea," Dr. Lambert interrupted. "A bad one. But from now on, we'll keep you safe. Forgive me, but you need to be checked often. The timing's critical . . . we must monitor you closely until we know the extent of your vision loss."

Despite his irritating stupidity, she liked how his warm hand felt on her shoulder, his lingering Vetiver scent, even his starched cardboardlike lab coat. How smart would it be to jeopardize any chance of regaining her vision?

And then she remembered. "But Doctor, I forgot. For an instant I *could* see. I saw gray fog, streetlights shining, and cars. It was so wonderful."

Silence. "Just don't hope for too much. Be thankful for what little you get."

"But I saw again! Even if just for a few seconds . . . so it means I'm getting better . . . *non?*"

"Often that happens . . . a gray cottony film or fog?"

She nodded.

"That could be *flottes,* random detached tissue. Or it could be due to the easing of the pressure. Whether full vision will return permanently . . . that's a hard call."

Crushed, she turned away. She didn't want him to see her in tears. Or shaking from fear. She had to find her phone, get out of here, find a place to stay.

"We'll locate a bed for you in the hospital. It might be in the hallway but . . ."

"In case you forgot, if the attacker found me here, he'd find me there. No thanks, I'll stay with friends."

But who? René's tiny studio brimmed

with computers. Too small. Especially for her *and* Miles Davis. And too far away, as well. Martine's boyfriend's place, in the ultra bourgeois 16th arrondissement, wouldn't be comfortable, now that all his children were living with them.

Live in her office? She'd done it before, but it wouldn't be safe to stay there.

Martine's cousin's Bastille apartment was nearby, but having only been there once, she'd have to become better at navigating before she could get there, much less live in a strange place.

Outside she heard the bleating siren of a police van. She imagined the white police car, the flashing blue lights and red arrows striping the side. Was she nostalgic for the *flics* now? Pathetic.

"It's imperative that you stay nearby," Dr. Lambert said. "The way things look right now, it's difficult to schedule another MRI, which you need. I'll have to try to fit you in when there's an opening. Can you pay rent?"

"If need be. Why?"

She heard him tapping on a cell phone. Then his voice.

"Madame Danoux, *ça va?* Still need a boarder? *Bon* . . . one of my patients. . . . You are a lifesaver, *merci!*"

■ ■ ■ ■

Aimée, her laptop and bag hanging heavily from her shoulder, walked with Chantal to the rear entrance of the résidence. They caught a taxi which dropped them off on rue Charenton, just a block away. But she'd had the taxi circle the area several times until she felt safe. Chantal helped her count out the francs for the fare. Each bill was folded differently, so she could distinguish its denomination.

"You've got more to learn, Aimée," Chantal said. "We've got to get your orientation scheduled. But luckily you didn't end up on the cobblestones. Things could have been a lot worse, eh?"

True. But her lip hadn't stopped trembling. Thank God Chantal couldn't see that.

"Chin up." And with that Chantal left her on the second floor landing of a building that smelt of old cooking oil and musty corners.

"Crap!" seethed a soprano voice.

"But Madame Danoux, you mustn't sell the lace panels," said a middle-aged woman's voice. "Such intricate work, remnants of a past time. Nostalgia passes over me when I think . . ."

"Nostalgia for what?" Madame Danoux's voice interrupted. "Nostalgia is when you want things to stay as they were. I know so many people who stay in the same place. And I think, my God, look at them! They're dead before they die. Living is risking."

A complete contrast to Mimi, Aimée thought. She had lifted her bandaged hand to knock when the half-ajar door swung open.

"Who's there?"

The woman must be looking Aimée over, deciding whether to let her in . . . despite Dr. Lambert's introduction.

Aimée took a deep breath, wishing she could see who and where she was. "Aimée Leduc, Dr. Lambert's patient."

Aimée wondered if her hair stuck out, if her black boots were scuffed, if the seam of her leather miniskirt was misaligned, or if the bag of salvaged belongings on her arm bulged open. "May I come in?"

"We'll talk later, Madame Danoux," said the middle-aged woman. A chair scraped over wood. Footsteps clicked away.

"Of course, I need a tenant," Madame Danoux said, her words measured and careful. "Such a saint, that man, Doctor Lambert. I help him whenever he asks. You know, he saved my husband's eyesight after that amateur botched a simple cataract operation."

Unsure, Aimée remained in the doorway. Where was that chair . . . was there a rug to trip on . . . tables to run into?

"Thank you, if you could tell me . . ."

"Come inside, make yourself comfortable," Madame Danoux said, her voice edging away. "I'll just see to some tea. You take tea, of course . . . I require it for my throat, must have it."

And then she'd gone. For a moment, Aimée wondered if the woman knew she couldn't see. . . . Wouldn't she have guessed from the doctor's call?

She reached behind her, closed the heavy door, then played back in her mind the conversation she'd overheard, the chair scraping and the direction in which Madame Danoux's voice disappeared.

Cautiously Aimée edged forward, her arm outstretched. Dr. Lambert had given her a cane but she refused to use it. A lingering scent of roses wafted from her right; dribbling hot air warmed her wrist. She figured the purring cat signaled a chair by a window with a southern exposure, still containing the heat of the day.

Hammering came from below, the whine of a saw and then a soaring contralto voice.

"No, no, *no!* The emphasis falls on the half-note!" A piano key was pounded repeatedly. "*Zut!* Go home and practice. That's all for today."

Then she heard the flipping of a radio channel, quick and impatient, then what sounded like a grainy radio interview. The tinny sound came from the AM radio:

"Joining us this evening on *Talk to the People* is Michel Albin, sociologist and author of *The New Violence: France in the 90's.*"

Just what she wanted to hear, a paperback sociologist spouting his theory and hawking his book!

ìMonsieur Albin, since the early nineties the crime rate has soared. Whatís happened?î

ìLetís give it a historical perspective,î Albin said.

ìThe fties and sixties were a time of social reform and recovery from the war. The seventies were political, going into the eighties brought drugs and drug traf cking. Digicode security replaced front doorbells and concierges and Parisiens pushed minorities into the suburbs. Weíre living with the results today.î

ìBut monsieur, violence isnít a new phenomenon."

"Violence constantly evolves, mirroring Society and depending on the period."

The windows slammed shut. "Blah, blah, blah, talk is cheap. That and six francs gets you an espresso," said Madame Danoux. "We need him to tell us the country's going to the dogs? Have some tea and I'll show you to your room."

"*Merci,* madame," Aimée said. "Picture the face of a clock. Can you tell me at what time the tea cup is?"

"Three o'clock," she said. "Sad, to lose your sight so young. Need treatment, do you?"

Aimée nodded. Sad wasn't the half of it. She'd been attacked now for the second time. What would the radio sociologist theorize about that?

Somehow, she'd fathom a way out of her predicament. But right now, she didn't know how.

"Do you sing in the Opéra, Madame?"

"Nodules grew on my vocal cords," said Madame. "Otherwise . . ." she trailed off. All the *what ifs* in life were encompassed in that long pause. "This Bastille Opéra house was an architectural disaster. Can you believe it? The building tiles fall off. They're keeping them in place with cargo nets in the back! The dressing rooms are notorious for being filthy. Mulitiple shows go on, so someone else has used it the night before you go in. At least, the costumes are put in place every night by staff, the makeup person comes to your room. And the acoustics are marvelous. I preferred Châtelet — more beautiful, great backstage crew and the sets: huge. But at least I've got my health."

Despite Madame Danoux's words, Aimée felt she did miss her former profession.

"Mademoiselle, did you know Cyrano de Bergerac lived nearby?"

What a shift! Aimée's brows creased in surprise. Madame Danoux was giving her an overview of the neighborhood.

Meanwhile, where were the *flics?* Chantal had promised to send them over.

Several shrill rings came from the front of the apartment.

Aimée heard a rustling and footsteps on parquet. "So much coming and going, busier than the Galeries Lafayette!" said Madame Danoux. "Excuse me."

"Mademoiselle Leduc?" asked a deep voice. "I'm Officer Nord from the Commissariat. You reported an attack."

"Bon!" she said, turning in the direction of

the voice. She wished she could see him. He sounded young. "Madame Danoux, may I impose, some tea for the officer and use of this . . ." she stumbled . . . and gestured with her arm . . . what kind of room was this?

"Parlor," Nord finished for her.

"Bien sûr," Madame Danoux said.

Officer Nord showed her to a seat. The low hard divan cut into her back. Aimée fidgeted. She tried to concentrate. The better she explained and painted a picture for him, the more clues he'd have. What he did with them depended on how well he'd been trained.

Aimée heard the hissing of hot water being poured as Madame Danoux served him tea, then left.

"Why don't you tell me what happened," he said.

She started with the attack in the passage. Then she described the assault in the residence.

"You know the *flics* treated the first attack on me as the work of the Beast of Bastille," she said.

"Now we're treating it as an isolated assault," he said.

Good. She realized something new must have taken place.

"Why?"

"I'm not at liberty to discuss that," said the young *flic,* clearing his throat.

"You've found the Beast of Bastille, haven't you?"

No answer. Had her message reached Morbier? And she thought about that night. She remembered who'd been brought into custody.

"You're charging Mathieu Cavour, the *ébéniste?*"

Silence.

"But why . . . what evidence did you find?" she asked.

She figured he must be searching for a way to answer this. He couldn't have been out of the police academy for long.

"Look, my father was a *flic.* I know the score," she said. "Give me the truth."

"They said you were a troublemaker."

"I am. But tell me anyway."

"Sergeant Bellan's my superior," he said.

Merde! Bellan had it in for her. No wonder he'd sent a trained lackey. A nice way to show how low she rated on the totem pole.

". . . and Sergant Bellan's a good one," she said, gritting her teeth.

It stung to say that. Especially after the way he'd badmouthed her father. But it was best for her to compliment Bellan if she wanted to learn more. When Bellan stayed off the liquor, kept his rage under control, and didn't take things personally as he did with her, he scored high marks in the Commissariat. Word had gotten around he was up for promotion. "Of course Bellan's good, my father trained him."

She hoped that sank in.

"Would you say," he asked, "robbery was the motive for the first attack?"

Robbery?

"Does it make sense for Mathieu to attack and rob someone in front of his atelier?"

Had Bellan been saddled with a new recruit he had no time to work with? Silence.

"I'm the one asking questions here," he said. "Let's move on. Could robbery be the motive for this incident?"

"Not in the way you think," she said. "My laptop and things were left. Only my phone was taken."

"Mathieu Cavour was released. This morning."

So they'd let him go? At least she'd learned that. She wanted to stand up, get the kinks out of her neck, feel the warmth from the heater. Her thoughts flowed better that way.

If only she could see his face, read his

movements. But she couldn't. All she had were intuition, some sensory antennae and whatever she could glean from his words. She had to get him on her side. Get him to cough up more of the latest info.

"Let's assume, after luring out Josiane Dolet, the attacker got me by mistake," she said. "I'd picked up her phone. We were wearing the same jacket. He realizes his mistake too late, after he's bashed in my head. People come down the passage, frightening him away. But he finds Josiane in the next passage. He kills her, the most important part, but we don't know why, then wraps her in an old carpet which isn't discovered until later the next day. Meanwhile I'm blind, out of commission, but Josiane's phone is nowhere to be found and eventually he realizes I must have it. He figures his number's on the speed dial or it incriminates him some way, so he discovers where I am and breaks into the room . . . but he gets my phone . . . not hers. Thwarted again."

"So Mademoiselle Leduc, why not give me the phone," said Officer Nord.

He'd learned something from Bellan after all, how to listen. Josiane's phone was her face card . . . the only one. The murderer wanted it. So did the *flics*.

208

"Tell me how you're investigating the attack on me," she said. "If you've found any suspects, and what's happened to Vaduz, the Beast of Bastille."

"If you're trying to negotiate by withholding evidence needed in a homicide case, mademoiselle. . . ."

"Negotiate? Someone attacked me. So viciously, Officer Nord, that it blinded me. The doctor doubts I'll ever see again."

Silence.

She wouldn't give in unless he met her halfway. "I want to discuss this with Bellan."

"That's impossible."

No warmth in his voice. Was he writing this down? He sounded far away . . . had he moved?

"No more until I talk to him."

"Sergeant Bellan's away."

"Away? A workaholic like him?"

"Family problems. The baby's sick," he said.

For the first time, the *flic* sounded human.

"Aaah, sorry to hear that." Her back felt stiff from sitting on the hard divan. "Then to Commissaire Morbier."

"He's assigned to another case. The Beast of Bastille won't strike again. That's the official story, anyway," he said, his voice faltering. "I didn't know you'd lost your sight. Sorry."

He grew more human every minute.

"Has Vaduz confessed?"

"As far as the Prefet's concerned, as good as."

"So where is he?"

"After a rampage outside Porte de la Chapelle, he crashed the car he stole. We're not supposed to reveal this yet, especially to the media, but whatever they found was sent to the morgue."

"You mean . . . Vaduz is dead. . . . When?" Why hadn't Morbier told her?

"No announcements. No details released to our unit, anyway. So please keep it to yourself."

"I want to, but if Vaduz died before I was attacked in the residence, that's important."

"How?"

"It could mean that someone else attacked me in the passage and killed Josiane, the same one who later came to the residence. That's why I have to talk to Morbier."

"Sergeant Bellan's handling the case. Everything goes through him. Of course, you'll mention Josiane Dolet's phone and reveal its whereabouts when I pass on the message to call you, won't you?"

She nodded. "So they said I was trouble?"

"I made that up," he said, "but looks like I got it right."

Thursday Late Afternoon

René pressed the second number he'd copied from the list on Josiane Dolet's speed dial.

"Architecture Brault," said a middle-aged male voice.

"I'm calling concerning Josiane Dolet," he said.

A pause. "Who's this?"

"I'm with Leduc Detective," he said, glancing up from the courtyard at the gleaming limestone buildings on the steam-washed cobblestoned alley. One could eat off the pristine stonework façades. A decade earlier, many would have avoided the area. It had been a district of weed-filled *cours* and small dilapidated porcelain and bronze fixture factories. These stood next to former seventeenth century nunneries that had once held an army of nuns in cloistered convents, seats of wealth and power that had rivaled the king's. "Please spare me a few moments," said René. "I'm downstairs."

A head appeared at a window. All René could see was a halo of copper hair.

"I've got a backlog of clients . . ."

"We should talk in person," René said. "Your number was on Mademoiselle Dolet's speed dial."

"My firm deals with many people."

"This concerns Josiane Dolet's murder. I just thought we should have a chat before I talk with the *flics*." René let the silence hang.

"Ten minutes. Between clients," he said. "The code's 43A6, second floor, first door on the right."

René took off his jacket, undid his right cufflink, rolled up the sleeve of his pink tinged custom-made shirt, got on his tiptoes, and just managed to hit the digicode.

The door buzzed. He pushed it open and reassembled himself in the glassed-in foyer, which melded two old factories. An ingenious arched portico opened up to an azure glass-roofed courtyard. Ochre-stained pots of bamboo bordered a minimalist bleached-wood desk. The reception area lay empty.

René took the lift. The wet weather kicked his arthritis into an aching winter mode early. He'd cut back his martial arts practices at the dojo. Not details he would share with Aimée in her condition. Or ever.

A man with thinning copper hair, small black-framed glasses, and a pale complexion stood as René entered. Surprise painted his face for a moment. René was used to that, and to the customary downward glance at his long torso and short legs.

"René Friant, of Leduc Detective."

"Brault, of Brault Architecture," the man said, extending his hand. René saw no welcome in the pale, guarded face.

René approached the side of the desk and shook hands. His arms wouldn't have reached across the desk.

"You understand, I have a few minutes only," Brault said, his thin mouth working in his long face. Expensive mechanical pencil tops showed in the pocket of his shirt. He wore tailored black denim jeans, a charcoal gray shirt and jacket, blue socks, and black hiking boots. All Gaultier by their look.

"Please sit down," Brault said. "I'm concerned, but I don't know how it involves me."

After one glance at the tall, olive Philippe Starck-designed chair, René preferred to stand. *"Non, merci,"* René said. "I'll get to the point."

Instead, René headed to the window, shaking his head. He stood silently, figuring his next move, hoping to throw Brault off guard. The office window opened onto the coppered roof connected to the glass skylight. Vestiges of a bas-relief on the wall and verdigris-patinaed rain spouts stood out against the gable walls. Beyond, he saw a niche with a worn stone figure where the building roof overhung the street. Probably St. Anne, the patron saint of carpenters, René figured.

"What's this about?" Brault said, breaking the silence.

"Josiane was protecting you, wasn't she?" René asked, taking a stab in the dark.

A pencil lead cracked.

"Go ahead, talk to me. I'm not a *flic*," René said. "What you tell me . . ."

"Goes to your boss, right?" Brault interrupted. "That *salope* of an editor who wants corroboration from two sources before he prints a fanny-licking article that makes it to *France-Soir* by nightfall."

René struggled to keep the surprise from his face. "We don't have to play it like that," René said.

"Josiane was a good journalist. I don't know why she associated with the likes of you."

"Me?" René wielded his short arms in mock defense. What the hell was going on here? Brault had jumped from coolness to white-heat without a warm-up. He wished Aimée were here. He needed clues on how to proceed. And his hip ached.

"She had to pay rent like the rest of us," he said.

"Josiane?"

Merde . . . had she been wealthy . . . had he blown it?

"There's a lot you didn't know about her," René said, hoping he could bluff this out. He regretted it immediately. How lame it sounded! Why couldn't he have a script or a computer program to guide him?

"Look, I won't involve the *flics*," said René, "if you tell me what you and Josiane were working on."

Brault's stainless steel intercom buzzed. "Planning commission's assembled and waiting in the conference room, Monsieur Brault."

"Tell me or I turn over my info," René said. "I'm waiting."

"What guarantee do I have you'll conceal the fact that my number was on Josiane's speed dial?"

Behind the small designer glasses, Brault's eyes glared.

"We're not the Brigade Criminelle," René said, and winked. "One source works for me." If that didn't confuse Brault even more, he didn't know what would. "There's no benefit for me in involving the *flics*. I'll erase your number."

"Your boss knows, doesn't he?" Brault glared.

Knows what? But René returned the glare in silence. And waited.

Brault snapped the mechanical pencil lead in and out, but it didn't break. Just shot a little rain of pencil lead onto the Berber carpet.

"They hire flunkies to clear the tenants out," Brault said. His tone was harsh and he spat the words out.

"Who does?"

"Mirador."

"The big construction developer Mirador?"

Brault nodded.

"The Bastille Historic Preservation Society can't compete with the palms greased by developers like Mirador. The Romanian spilled the beans one night after some 80 proof vodka. He plastered ceilings, did occasional jobs for us. There's no reason to doubt him. The rue des Taillandiers project seems to be just the tip of the iceberg. That's what I told Josiane. And that's all."

"What happened on rue des Taillandiers?"

"Forget the November to March ban on tenant evictions. Mirador evicts anytime."

Brault's words sounded like code to René. But not the kind of code he could decrypt.

"The Romanian?"

"Dragos."

"Then Dragos can verify . . ."

"Don't bother to check," Brault interrupted. "He's disappeared with the wind. That's how they work. They hire transient Romanians, Serbs, or Russians."

René nodded, hoping he didn't look as clueless as he felt.

"Josiane wrote the article to put a spoke in Mirador's wheel," said Brault.

René's ears perked up.

"Would it be big enough to stop Mirador from evicting illegally?"

Brault's office door swung open. Two men in suits beckoned him. "The representative of the *Bureau de la Construction*'s here. We can't hold up the meeting any longer."

Brault strode out of his office, leaving René to see himself out, laboriously, with short steps. René's mind spun. Whirled. He'd promised Aimée he'd call after interviewing Brault. But he couldn't stop now; he had to find out about Mirador.

René labored several blocks to rue Basfroi, in the northern part of the Bastille. He headed to his friend Gaetan Larzan's prop rental, where he knew he'd get information. Maybe even a decent glass of wine.

"Business good?" René asked.

"Terrible!" said Gaetan, brushing off his stained overalls, then slicking back his hair.

Always the same reply. Like his old uncle.

Gaetan, who stood near a tarnished knight in armor, returned to consulting a checklist, marking things off.

"These television crews, they're more careless than monkeys," he said. Beside him stood a garish green plastic palm tree, bent as though weeping on his shoulder. Ahead lay a hall full of coat racks: wood ones, bamboo, mahogany, metal, lucite, every size and shape imaginable. In a cavernous room strewn with clawfooted bathtubs, old screens, and mirrors propped against the wall, René saw a massive stuffed polar bear towering between low-slung chandeliers.

"Time for a glass?" Gaetan asked.

"Twist my arm and I might," René said. Gaetan's uncle and René's mother had become friends when she'd foraged through the shop for props for her act.

"How's your uncle?"

"Spry, as usual. He escaped from the home last week," Gaetan nodded. "But his leg gave out. He didn't get far."

His uncle's wooden leg, a souvenir from the Austerlitz battlefield hospital, intrigued René. After the war he'd refused a prosthetic, saying so many had died, he'd been lucky to get the stump, and he wouldn't let anyone forget that. René felt empathy for him. "Makes a nice pair of salt and pepper shakers," he'd heard some workers laugh behind their backs, "a tall cripple and a short one."

At the secretary's desk, littered with piles of yellow invoices under a stuffed hedgehog, Gaetan cleared a place for René. He reached back and pulled out a dusty, unlabeled bottle. In the pencil holder he found a corkscrew, then rinsed two long-stemmed wine glasses with bottled Evian, flicked the water into the waste bin, and poured.

"Château Margaux nineteen seventy-six?" René swirled the rich rust-red liquid, sniffing the cork.

"Close. You're quite the connoisseur. Nineteen seventy-five was a vintage year."

René wondered how Gaetan managed to get hold of such excellent wine. He wouldn't mind a bottle.

Gaetan shrugged. "Fell off a truck in Marseilles," he said.

Comme d'habitude — as usual — René thought. Business must be booming, or else he was paid in wine.

"Didn't I miss your party this year? . . . Here's a late present. Don't drink it all at once. Happy birthday." Gaetan pushed another bottle toward René.

"*Salut.*" They clinked glasses. The wine poured down his throat like raw silk, full-bodied yet light.

"*Merci,* Gaetan."

Gaetan's prop shop overlooked a narrow passage. Beyond lay a dirt lot, fenced in by jagged aluminum siding and stone building walls pockmarked by old, peeling wallpaper.

"Wasn't there a ceramic factory here?" He remembered his mother buying a piece of *faience,* a flowered vase from the flawed seconds batch. It had sat in the kitchen hutch for years. He still had it.

"The *patron* died. No one to run it. Soon to be a parking lot," Gaetan said, making a *moue* of disgust. "Developers!"

A pity, René thought. He went to the window. But he couldn't read the construction sign which had been defaced by silver and green graffiti.

Gaetan would know about Mirador. He'd grown up in the *quartier.* "I hear Mirador's hiring Romanians to kick people out of old buildings."

"Wouldn't surprise me, but I know nothing firsthand," Gaetan said. He broke into a wide grin as he announced, "I'm getting married. Remember Giselle?"

The long-legged dancer who taught at the dance studio. "Of course, lucky man!"

"We're moving to Tours."

"*Félicitations!* But your business?"

"Pierre, my cousin, is the manager now, he's more involved."

"Where's Pierre?"

"Hiking in the Pyrenées. He deserved a vacation."

René's brow furrowed. "I need information about the evictions."

"Not your style . . . *Aaaah,* it's one of your friends, *non?*"

So he told Gaetan what had happened; about Aimée and the story Josiane supposedly was working on. By the time he'd finished, darkness had descended over the tiled rooftops.

"René, I'd like to help, but I'm hardly here these days," Gaetan said, looking away. "Not everything in life checks out."

But René could tell Gaetan was withholding something.

"There's a load of returns in the yard," he said, standing up. He flicked on the switch, flooding the office with light. "You know your way around; stay as long as you like."

Was he afraid?

"Look, I'm worried about Aimée. You must know someone who can help me."

"Don't take this detective stuff so seriously," Gaetan said. "Look, genius, your *métier*'s computers."

"She's blind, Gaetan," he said, "and my job might go down the toilet with this picky Judiciare."

Gaetan picked up a folder of invoices, tucked them under his arm. He avoided René's eyes. "*Desolé.* Don't forget your wine. I'll send you a wedding invitation."

"Here's my cell phone number," René said. "Pierre might know, or be able to give me someone who does."

Dejected, René didn't know which way to turn. Calling Mirador and asking them about evictions probably wouldn't garner information. On his way back, René passed the fenced-in lot, but he still couldn't read the graffiti-covered sign.

After some blocks, rounding a corner, he just missed running into an old woman. She wore a faded scarf knotted at her neck, and a sealskin coat that had flaked off in patches. She stood in front of the dark Gymnase Japy. Yellow pools of light from the just-lit streetlamps glistened on the wet brick walls. She was knocking on the tall wood door.

"I promised Maman to do better. Every time the teacher says *fois* in the *dictée* I will write it correctly," she said, then repeated in a falsetto voice, slow and measured:

"Il était une *fois* une marchande de *foie* qui vendait du *foie* dans la ville de *Foix*. Elle se dit ma *foi* c'est pour la première *fois* que je vends du *foie* dans la ville de *Foix*."

She uttered the passage again and again, faster and faster. René watched her, unsure of what to do. How could he help?

A blue uniform turned the corner. A young *flic* on his beat. "*Bonsoir,* Madame," he said, taking in the situation. "The gym's closed now."

"But the tutor's supposed to meet me. He's waiting . . ."

"Not tonight, eh, it's late. Let me accompany you."

The old woman gave him a toothless smile. "Maman would like that."

"*Bon,*" said the *flic,* taking her arm gently, "let's take you home, it's time for your supper, *non?*"

"But they won't let me back in," she said. "I tried." She pointed her ragged glove at a bricked-up, soot-coated, eighteenth century *hôtel particulier* facing the square. A jewel in its heydey, René thought. Fronted by doric columns, with arabesques of rusted iron balcony railings and nymph-bordered plaster detail. A crane with a dirty black wrecking ball stood suspended over the building. Large placards across the door said "Villa Voltaire — Luxury Apartments Ready Soon."

"*Alors,*" said the *flic,* "they've moved you someplace, *non?*"

The old woman shook her head. "I want to go home."

"We'll just go find out now."

The *flic* noticed René. "Do you know Madame?"

Before René could shake his head, a second floor window opened and an old man leaned out, a pipe in the side of his mouth. "Madame Sarnac's lived in the *quartier* all her life," he said. "Right there." He took the pipe from his mouth and pointed at the *hôtel particulier.*

"Can you help, monsieur?" the *flic* asked, his tone polite. "She's confused."

"That was where she lived. She worked in the *magasin* below," he said. "She went to school here. So did I."

"But where does she stay now? I don't want to bring her to the Commissariat."

"It's sick, throwing old people out. *Armée du Salut* sheltered some and the Maison des

Femmes, too. But just the ones who had no families to take them," he said. "She's here everyday, doesn't know what else to do. Me, I took action. It was I who got them to put up that plaque."

He pointed to the plaque on Gymnase Japy that was just visible in the fading daylight. René could only read the last part. It was signed the ASEJD: *Association en souvenir des enfants juifs déportés du XI.*

The *flic* walked away, escorting the old woman, and the man shut his window. But now René knew who to ask about Mirador.

Looking around, René observed BANQUE HERVET lettered in silver, a small beauty salon and dimly lit brasserie. Beyond was a fire-gutted building — scorched black stone and broken windows — overlooking the gym opposite the center of the square.

He turned and stood under the rippled glass awning held by curlicues and spokes of wrought iron. A chipped and faded hotel sign was wedged inside an iron circle. The bubbled glass of the door was covered by a metal grillework pattern of flower bouquets and palmettes. He pushed the buzzer.

The door opened to display a diamond-patterned black-and-white tile foyer. The tiles were cracked and worn but the period staircase of white marble and swirls of

225

scrolled ironwork retained its grandeur.

René climbed. His short legs pumped up the wide stairs. The ache in his hip increased. Tired, he'd resolved to make it the last interview of the day. On the second floor landing, he knocked on the door.

"Oui?"

René's eyes lifted to the old man's face, wreaths of smoke coming from his lit pipe. His white hair curled around his ears and down over the collar of a gray wool cardigan. He wore Moroccan leather slippers with turned-up toes and kept one hand in his pocket.

"I'm with Leduc Detective," René said, flashing Aimée's detective badge quickly.

"I don't talk to strangers," the man said, peering down at René.

"Neither do I," René said, "but you saw me with Madame Sarnac, didn't you? I want to help her."

"A detective, eh? I didn't know they made them so small."

René flinched. He'd sat behind the keyboard too long. He'd forgotten it was always like this.

"You seemed the helpful type," René said. "Guess not. I won't stay up nights worrying when it happens to you. Being evicted, I mean."

The old man leaned over and peered closer at René. "Who did you say you work for?"

"Leduc Detective. I'm investigating the reporter's murder."

"The landing's drafty, come in," he said, tugging at René's shoulder. *"Vite."*

Surprised at his change in attitude and the swift tug at his shoulder, René followed him inside. The scent of sweetish cherry-laced pipe tobacco filled the air.

The old man's apartment, high-ceilinged and surprisingly tidy, faced the square on two sides.

"Let me introduce myself: Yann Rémouze," he said, gesturing to a chair. "I didn't want to talk out there . . . the walls have ears. Please sit down."

René used a low ottoman to heave himself up onto a comfortable chintz armchair. He'd promised to call Aimée but it would be better to have some information to give her when he did.

"Bet you see a lot from your windows," said René.

"I hear a lot, too." Yann remained standing, surveying René.

René noticed a collection of flutes and woodwinds on a shelf ringing the wall. "You're a musician?"

"Once I had an instrument shop; I made flutes," he said. "Now I do repairs for a few old clients."

An antique silver flute gleamed on the shelf.

Yann followed René's gaze. "That belonged to a man who created color. That's what a virtuoso flutist does. Plays with a simplicity that's vivid."

This old man lived in his memories, but René didn't share them.

"Monsieur Rémouze, what happened to Madame Sarnac and those in her building?"

"Should I trust you?"

"Why not? You've already let me into your apartment."

"Good point." Rémouze sank into the chair beside René. His eyelids were heavy, tired. "Last week, the *démolition* signs went up and the trucks came. But the place had been emptied the week before that. I heard them in the middle of the night."

"What did you hear?"

"Nothing that hasn't happened time and again. Only this time instead of *flics* rounding up the *juifs* for the Gymnase and deportation or Apaches collecting interest on an overdue loan, it was Romanians hustling them out at three in the morning."

228

"Mirador hired them?" René kept his tone even.

The old man nodded. "Let's put it this way. Not long ago, a man on the fifth floor was offered a cheque to vacate the apartment he's lived in for forty years. He refused, his neighbors got similar offers and refused too. Everyone was incensed. Suddenly, returning from Marché d'Aligre where he shops every day, he was attacked. Broken bones and bruises, then his heart gave out in L'hôpital Saint Antoine. Now lots of old people are awakened in the middle of the night, told they're lucky not to get their hips broken. Now they don't even get an offer of a cheque. They fold like a deck of cards. Intimidated."

That agreed with what Brault, the architect, had told him.

"But why hasn't someone gone to the authorities?"

Yann rolled his eyes. He lit a match, stuck the burning tip in the pipe bowl, and puffed in a steady rhythm.

"Think about the complaint system, the forms one has to fill out . . . no one's stupid enough to identify himself. And for the rest, pockets are lined to look the other way."

"Give me names," said René. "Then I can do something."

"No one will point a finger," he said, "so it's all hearsay. One of the *flics* said the old people are haunted by phantoms from the past. Poetic, probably true, but a nice excuse for inaction."

"What do you mean, phantoms?" Was the old man going to ramble now? René wished Aimée was listening, instead of him. She had a better take on criminals than he did. She heard old men and women talk and put their stories together. She could find the thread. For such a restless person, she had a fund of intuition.

"Past indiscretions, like informing the *Milice*," he said. "Ignoring black shirt thugs looting apartments of the deportees."

"That's long ago," René interrupted. "What does it have to do with now?"

The old man puffed several times then looked up. His eyes were wide and full of an almost palpable sadness.

"What *doesn't* it have to do with now? The past informs the present. Memory makes the map we carry, no matter how hard we try to erase it."

True. René still didn't see how it related. Paris had legions of the old, sitting on park benches or at kitchen tables telling stories of the war to grandchildren or others hostage to politeness.

"Some talk about it," Yann said. "Many remain silent."

René had enough problems without going back to what happened during the war. Leave that to those whose memories stretched that far.

"Can you read it, the plaque?" Yann beckoned René to the window.

To the memory of the more than 600 children, women and men of the 11ième arrondissement, assembled here and then interned in Loiret camp before being deported to Auschwitz. . . .

"Do you know how long it took our association to erect the plaque for our classmates?"

René shook his head.

"Simon was my friend; he lived down the hall," Yann said. "Big family. Poor, but Simon had a beautiful steelie marble, topaz cat's eye. Superb. He let me borrow it one day, his treasure, but he was like that. Generous. And I didn't give it back. He asked me again and I stalled. Kept saying I'd forgotten it. And then one night we heard noises down the hall."

Yann looked at René, his eyes clouded. But René felt he wasn't seeing him. Just the past.

"Those noises. The ones making you hide

your head under the covers, the frantic whispers of Maman telling me not to look out the window. And they were gone. Never came back. The apartment taken over by someone else, their belongings too."

"So this is how you return the marble to Simon?"

A bittersweet smile crossed the man's face. "Fifty years too late."

True, there was no escaping the past, but René wanted to pull the focus back to the evictions and Josiane Dolet.

"Look, I can't find out about the thugs unless I know where to look."

"After they do their job, they don't stick around for coffee," he said. "Big *mecs,* bodybuilders, East European by the look of their clothes."

"How's that?"

"Hard to say, but a lot of them wear those track suits, the cheap designer copies with words misspelled."

René knew the knockoffs sold at street markets. A Tommy Hilfiger with an F missing. Romanian chic.

"One wore a ponytail," he said, "stringy hair. You know the type."

"What else?"

"One night I heard this runt below my window calling out. 'Draz,' " he said.

"Draz?"

"That's all I understood. Then this gorilla, this Draz with the ponytail, beat him into pulp against the wall."

René said, "Here's my card." He knew Aimée handed hers out all the time. It looked professional. And ran up a high printing bill. "Please call if you remember anything else."

By the time René reached his car, the line for the outdoor soup kitchen, part of a network organized by Coluche the comedian, snaked up boulevard Beaumarchais. He knew authorities left a Métro station open when severe cold hit. A well-kept secret among the *clochards* and junkies. He hoped Madame Sarnac wouldn't end up there.

THURSDAY EVENING

In the hôpital Quinze-Vingts waiting room, Aimée heard the evening sounds from Bastille and inhaled the Seine's scent from the open window. She remembered seeing a teddy bear floating in the swollen Seine in the spring. After so much rain, the river had overflowed the quais. The image haunted her all day . . . had a child dropped it from a bridge, a spiteful older brother tossed it?

Did wet tears soak a pillow and an anxious parent rush off to the Samaritaine Department store to replace it . . . as her father had tried?

When she was ten, her *doudou,* a ragged mouse named Émil, dropped from her bookbag into the Seine. Émil was the one thing left from her mother. The only thing her father hadn't had the heart to throw away. Stained and threadbare, with missing whiskers, Émil had been the subject of her mother's drawings and stories. The day he fell from Île St-Louis ranked as the second worst day in her life. The first was when her mother left and never came back.

Émil had fallen at twilight; the dusk, a rose-violet slash under the fingernail crescent of a moon. Her papa had told her the moon's lit face always turns toward the sun. And to imagine Émil in the turquoise-green Mediterranean enjoying the sun-baked sand. She'd shaken her head stubbornly.

She'd begged her papa to call Captain Morvan, an old colleague and police diver, who'd checked with the Seine dredgers. After he'd reported no luck, she insisted they search the water-treatment plant beyond Bercy. But Émil must have floated away.

Then one day a package had arrived,

covered with British stamps, official customs forms, and coarse brown twine. It was addressed to her. In it, she found a toffee-furred bear wearing rainboots, blue slicker, and luggage tag from Paddington station, London, on it, saying "Please take good care of this lost bear."

After her father's death, in his drawer, she'd found a yellowed receipt from an English department store for a stuffed bear for a Mademoiselle Leduc. And after all these years, her Paddington Bear still stayed on her bed.

Her dog Miles Davis and the stuffed Paddington Bear were the only men in her life. But wasn't that how it turned out . . . a successful career and money, but a sour love life, or conversely, madly in love, business falling apart and broke?

Was it just her? Or the fact that bad boys were her downfall?

The last time she'd been happy had been with Yves, now a news bureau chief in Cairo. A problematic relationship at best. Then a few flings, all disasters.

Her tastes were simple. Someone who could make her laugh, had nice eyes, and had the same taste in champagne. Veuve Clicquot. And a bad boy side that made up for any other deficiency.

A nurse's voice interrupted her thoughts. "Dr. Lambert's ready. I'll help you to the MRI."

Why was she thinking about men? It wasn't as if she'd had a future with anyone before, and now the prospect seemed even more remote. Zero. She couldn't see and didn't know if she ever would.

"Nervous?"

"Me?" she said, hoping her voice didn't crack with tension.

Chantal had taught her to endow someone with a face or a feature, to "give looks to voices." She turned to the voice and nodded. The movement felt more natural, less odd than before.

"Ba wey," said the young nurse for *bien oui,* with that hesitant Parisien drawl. Aimée felt her slowly expelled breath. "Can't stand enclosed spaces myself, but Dr. Lambert will be staying with you. That's quite unusual, you know."

An eye surgeon and head of the department at the MRI? Didn't they have technicians for that? But she was reassured. She wouldn't mind having him explain what he saw or giving her the chance to ask questions.

A buzz of voices met them in the imaging department.

"Dr. Lambert, the cranial sac shows distension . . ."

"Here's the case we're going to study: female suffering severe blunt trauma to the head, partial asphyxiation, and subsequent vision blurring and loss."

Great. She was to be his guinea pig for students. And he hadn't even told her.

"You forgot the resulting concussion, Dr. Lambert," she said.

Silence.

"So I did, Mademoiselle Leduc," he said. "Anything else slip my mind, or does that about cover it?"

A snicker came from somewhere in the shuffling group she felt standing ahead of her.

"You're the doctor," she said. "I hope you explain everything. And the real prognosis."

"This is the type of patient, doctors, that will be your rare curse and luck to treat," he said, his voice serious. "Strong-willed and a fighter."

What about smart?

And despite the fear gnawing at her insides, she focused on his voice explaining the neurons, ganglia, arteries, veins, and whatnot causing the trouble. Or what seemed to.

"Notice the nice embolizing technique of

Robards, the neurologist at hôpital Saint Antoine," Dr. Lambert said. "He redirected the bloodflow and supported the blood vessel at the weakened site. Not in a textbook, but it makes good sense. Remember that."

Aimée concentrated on Dr. Lambert's words, but even with a few years of premed, she felt lost. Nevertheless, she could appreciate Lambert's observations, his way of injecting guidance, of teaching them to think. Maybe if she'd had a professor like that in the *école des médicins* she'd have stayed. But then the dissection of corpses had gotten to her.

She took a deep breath as the gurney wheeled ahead. They wrapped sheets over her and slipped her into something that echoed. Drafts of air shot across her. And from all around the noise of the giant machine, as it powered up, enveloped her. As if she'd been shoved inside a wind tunnel.

From outside came the muted clacking of equipment, moving of knobs and other adjustments.

"Try these earplugs; it gets noisy," said a loud voice. "Small space bother you?"

"A little." She was terrified.

"Try to remain still."

The nurse had given her small sponges,

telling her to let out her tension by squeezing them. At least they kept her fingernails from digging into her palms.

The students had gone and Dr. Lambert stood near her. Elevator bells pinged down the hallway. The smell of the hospital laundry soap clung to his lab coat. She managed to sit up, then to stand.

"Got a clearer idea of the problem, Doctor?"

"Right now I've got a clearer picture of what's *not* the problem," he said. "The brain stem's a complicated highway. But, to tell you the truth, the doctor who reads the MRIs won't analyze the films and report until tomorrow."

Great. Her knowledge had increased by zero.

"Let me reexamine your eyes. I want to check something," he said. "Tell me if anything changes."

She felt his hand on her chin, lifting it up. He must be tall. His fingers lifted the edge of her eyelid. Gently. A metallic clicking sounded by her nose.

Desperately she wanted to see. Anything. A blur, something. She tried.

Only darkness.

He pushed her hair off her forehead. His

hands were warm.

"You want it straight?"

"Will I need a drink to hear this?"

"Are you always so . . . ?"

"Feisty?" she interrupted. "Only when I'm scared, only when my life's collapsing. Otherwise I'm easy."

"Your life will change, it has to," he said. Something moved on the linoleum, as if his feet shuffled. "But it doesn't have to fall apart. Shall we have that drink?"

Now she was really scared.

"Fine, let's hit an Orangina machine in the lobby," she said. "My treat."

She thought back to books she'd read about Helen Keller, all unkempt and wild with rage before she learned Braille, and that movie, *Wait Until Dark,* with Audrey Hepburn, blind and gorgeous in Givenchy, defeating killers. But she wasn't like either of them.

It hit her like a load of bricks. Her vision loss was permanent. She didn't need him to spell it out. She needed to find somewhere to fall apart, but not in front of him. Then somehow she'd manage to call René.

She realized how nice Dr. Lambert was. He'd cared enough to find her a place to stay. He'd tried. Above and beyond his duty. The poor guy must have a heavy schedule, case overload, and a wife and kids dying to see him after a long workday.

"Look, let's make it some other time. You've got a life, probably a big day of surgery and appointments tomorrow," she said, giving him a way out. "We can talk when the detailed MRI report comes in. Unless, of course, I wake up to a halo of miraculous light and can finally do my nails. Then I'm out of here."

"You know that's the first time I've seen you smile," he said.

Had she smiled? She felt warmth spreading over her hand. From his.

"Let's go," he said. He placed her hand on his bended arm. "Amaze me with all the tricks Chantal's taught you."

Perform like a circus animal?

"What do you mean?" Dumbfounded, she stood paralyzed.

"Relax. You're pretty uptight. Show me how you walk on rue Charenton to the *bar-tabac* on the corner of rue Moreau, for a start," he said. "Or do you have stage fright?"

She didn't want to go to a lighted, noisy bar full of people. Or to pass by the passage where she had been attacked. She wanted to crawl into a hole, curl up, and cry.

"Scared?"

"Me? Where's that bar?" She strode ahead, pulling him along with her and prayed to God she didn't run into a pillar or stone wall.

By some odd quirk of fate, she'd been to the *bar-tabac* on the corner of rue Moreau. It was on the rainy night she'd parked in the Opéra parking lot and the attendant had showed her the shortcut through hôpital Quinze-Vingts. She'd stopped for a quick espresso, knowing she was late for the impromptu Populax meeting but figuring she'd need to key up with caffeine to match Vincent's nervous energy.

She remembered the fifties-style bar, but not its name. Comfortable and utterly Parisian, like the one around the corner from her apartment. They still existed. Timeworn, with a stumpy, rounded counter. The soccer calendars with team schedules on the nicotine-burnished walls. The smudged, beveled mirror with the specials written in white over the Lavazza coffee machine, crowned by rows of cups. Upside-down liquor bottles anchored to the wall with silver stop-cocks that gave metered doses. The brown mosaic tile floor littered with sugar cube wrapping and cigarette butts, where one bumped elbows with neighbors. Not chic but centime-conscious.

"Later on they sing," Dr. Lambert said, taking her elbow and guiding her onto a leather banquette. "Clothilde shuts the place at midnight, the accordion player hands out sheet music, and people stay until dawn."

Clothilde. Where had she heard that name?

"The new generation craves a whiff of the past. To sing their grandparents' songs, to dance the *bourrée* from the countryside in three quarter time."

She knew the past could reassure. Or frighten.

"You know most people in Paris come from somewhere else," he said. "What about you?"

"A Paris rat," she said, leaving out the fact her mother was American. "And you?" she asked.

"Born in Chambery. The snowy Savoy."

What did he look like? she wondered.

"But my grandparents . . ." she went on.

"Let me guess," he said. "Auvergne?"

She nodded. "That's easy."

Paris was filled with Auvergnats. Between the wars and during the Depression, Auvergnats, nicknamed *bougnats,* had fled the mines and their bleak farms in the Massif

Central, migrating in droves to Paris. The well-known tale: coal merchants, hoping to make their fortune in Paris, often ending up carrying coal on their backs. The more affluent opened bistros, accounting for the large number of Auvergnat-based menus one still saw. She remembered her grandmother telling her how in Cantal, the calcium carbonate-rich springs coated any object put under them with a shiny translucent layer. Like the pervasive *bougnat* influence in Paris.

Her senses had been pared to the essence. People, slapping eath other's backs, and smoking, involved in discussions, as they were all over Paris tonight. Their energy hit her. And she felt curiously part of it.

"Pastis?"

She needed something strong.

"Double, please." She shoved a fistful of francs at him.

While Dr. Lambert got drinks, she pulled out Josiane's cell phone, found the number pad, and called René.

"Allô?"

Aimée heard klaxons and the revving of engines in the background.

"*Ça va*, René?"

"I'm stuck in the motorcycle rally in Bastille," he said.

"But that's on Friday nights."

"Maybe you should let *them* know. *Alors,* traffic's jammed," he said. "Where are you?"

"Not far, buying my doctor a drink," she said.

Pause.

"Aren't there ethical considerations . . . doctor and patient, eh?"

"It's after my MRI. He's trying to break it gently to me," she said.

"MRI?"

"Standard procedure. He'll know more tomorrow." She didn't want to tell René she'd be blind forever. "Look, he feels sorry for me." She felt the edge of the table, worn and sticky. "What did you find out?"

The revving of engines increased. She wished he'd shut his window.

"Aimée, get this. Romanians intimidate residents and old people, using strong-arm tactics to force them out. They don't even try and evict them legally," René said, his voice rising with excitement. "Seems a construction company moves in then and restores or demolishes the building. Josiane was working on a story about this."

"Would that have got her murdered?"

"Makes more sense than that she was a victim of the Beast of Bastille," said René.

René was good. A natural.

"Quite the detective, aren't you? Tell me more."

And he did. The architect Brault's allegations, the roller blading astrologer's predictions, his friend Gaetan's evasions, and the old woodwind maker's information.

"Draz?" she asked. "This old man heard the name?"

"Seems Draz was a *bon mec.* The old flutemaker heard him beating someone to a pulp below his window," René said. "I don't imagine that's something you forget."

"Good job, partner. Listen, someone stole my phone," she said, wanting to downplay the attack. "Try my number, see who answers."

She clicked off. René called right back.

"Your voice mail answers," he said. "Your phone's probably in the Seine with the fishes."

She wasn't so sure of that.

"I'm staying somewhere else tonight," she said.

Another pause.

"With your doctor?"

How did René make that jump? Was her flicker of attraction to the doctor so obvious?

"An opera singer rents rooms . . ."

"What about the residence? You need care!"

She appreciated his concern. He was the only family she had besides Morbier, who was keeping to the margins of her life.

"It's complicated," she said. "Look, my door got carved up and I had a close encounter hanging from my window railing."

"Someone attacked you in your room?"

So she told him.

Right now, she was so worried that she might not see again, that everything else faded in importance.

"Stay at my place."

"René, the doctor wants me near the hospital, available for tests. He can't schedule in advance, he calls me in when a space opens. But thanks for the offer."

The air brakes of a late evening lumbering bus hissed in the background.

"Of course," he said, his tone resigned. "You need to be close to the hospital. Lucky the attacker didn't take your laptop."

"He came for something else: Josiane's phone. If he saw the laptop in the drawer he ignored it. My phone must have sat in full view on the bed but I'd put Josiane's in my pajama jacket pocket after the nurse copied the numbers for me. I'd forgotten it was in there."

She heard René's intake of breath. "By now he will have discovered he's got the wrong phone. You are in danger."

"That's why I moved. Only you, Dr. Lambert, my landlady, and Chantal know where I'm staying."

"Good."

"Listen, why don't you make an appointment with Josiane's editor?" she said. "Find out what she worked on, see if the editor will share her notes."

"Tomorrow. I'm beat."

He sounded more than tired.

"We know she lived near Marché d'Aligre."

She pictured the streets leading to it, one of the few covered markets left in Paris. Her grandfather had bought pheasant there. She'd accompanied him, transfixed by the beady-eyed stuffed guinea fowl and the bright-plumed pheasants. Rabbits hung by their feet upside down. Under the glass and wire-framed roof, he'd buy Meaux mustard sealed in its crock with red wax, and containers with olive oil from Provence they decanted into small bottles.

The *marché* hosted a thriving outdoor produce trade and secondhand dealers, too. On the outer fringes, under the arcade of a 70s "monstrosity" (according to her grandfather), stood the curve of flats replacing Haussman era buildings, where street people spread blankets, hawking odds and ends. A marketplace since medieval times, the Marché d'Aligre was the only spot in Paris to continue the tradition unbroken.

Aimée tried to view the map in her mind. Had it made sense for Josiane to go through that passage where she was killed on her way home to rue de Cotte?

No, the passage lay several blocks in the opposite direction.

Then why would Josiane go there? But she knew why . . . the phone caller, the man had begged her to meet him.

She knew because she'd heard him.

Again she wondered if they had been having a lover's quarrel.

"René, what if this involves jealousy?" she said. "Love problems. Plain and simple."

"Since when is love plain and simple?"

He had a point.

She smelled Dr. Lambert's Vetiver scent before his thigh brushed against hers in the booth.

"René, I'll get back to you later," she said and clicked off.

She felt her hands laced around a frosted cold glass.

"The new bartender recommended Fire

and Ice. A speciality of the Antilles, where he's from, too. He swears this will get anyone through a rough night."

"So, doctor, what gets you through?"

"Call me Guy. If you keep calling me doctor, customers will descend on us to describe their illnesses."

Laughter. Low and melodic. Nice.

"So what gets you through the night?" she asked again.

"Sunrise."

What a cop out! She might as well head back to the opera singer's and try banging her head on the wall. Maybe that would jiggle those neurons into action. It might even restore her sight.

She chugged the Fire and Ice, a mixture tasting of tomato and strawberry zinging with tabasco. Curiously wonderful.

"Look, I appreciate the drink . . ." she said, making as if to stand up. Hard in the cramped booth when she didn't know which way to turn.

She felt a tug on her elbow and decided to stay put. She wouldn't have known what direction to go anyway.

"Blame it on a school trip to England," said Guy. "We saw dawn rise through the pillars at Stonehenge. And it changed my life."

He sounded serious.

"I was fifteen," he said. "Since then I've photographed hundreds of sunrises all over the world. After an eclipse comes the best sunrise. Incredible."

And she knew what he meant. She loved sunrises herself. Watched them from her window lighting up the Seine with a luminous glow. The quiet time before the city burst alive. Like a still breath before a large exhalation, feeling as if she were the only person on the planet.

Yet, she'd imagined him otherwise; a life filled with surgery, consultations and patients. "How do you find the time?"

"The baker loves me. We share a coffee. He's the only other one awake at dawn on my street except for the newspaper truck. Or once in a while, kids coming home from rave parties."

"What was sunrise like this morning? Describe the colors."

Pause.

He attempted to change the subject. "I live behind an old hardware store, famous for doorknobs. It's been there since 1862, has more than 130 kinds. They specialize in Louis XIII style."

Why was he avoiding her question?

"Did you miss the sunrise this morning?"

"I don't think it's healthy," he said, his voice hesitant, "talking to you about this . . ."

"Please, tell me about the colors," she asked again. If she couldn't see the sunrise, she'd like to hear about it. Visualize it.

"As I said . . ."

"But I want you to," she said. "Then I can see it in my mind. I miss seeing the sunrise."

"So you like them, too."

A pause.

Had she made points with her doctor? He grew more human all the time.

"A band of pewter fog covered the Pont Neuf," he said. "Peach lightened up the horizon, spreading and reaching for the blue."

"What kind of blue?" she asked.

"Innocent. Baby blue. The stars and streetlights twinkled until the bands of color became one brightness."

She wished she could see him; the shape of his eyes, how his mouth moved, if his cheekbones slanted, and how light glinted in his hair.

"It's not something I broadcast," he told her. "Some might say I seem obsessed."

"Having a passion isn't necessarily obsession. I'm just wondering what you look like."

That must be the Fire and Ice talking.

"Chantal's a bad teacher if she hasn't . . ."

"But she has," she said, interrupting him as she passed her fingers over his face. Tentatively, she traced his chinline, felt the stubble and the soft border of his lips. His mouth. It would be rosy and he'd have straight white teeth. Her fingers traveled his earlobes, then his long fringed eyelashes that never seemed to end. Black or dark brown hair? Maybe tobacco red? She felt his forehead, smooth and . . . she stopped. *Down girl . . . try and control yourself.*

"Like this," he said, taking her other hand, sliding it, with his, along her eyebrows and framing her eyes.

"I'll leave it to the professional," she said, enjoying this. Now if he could only give a massage.

The next table had gone quiet.

"Encore?" asked a voice near them.

"Feel like that pastis?"

"You buying?"

"Two double pastis, *merci,*" he ordered.

After the drinks landed on the table, she felt proud as she hooked her pinky over the glass's edge to gauge just the right amount of water to pour into the milky pastis. The anise aroma hit her along with the buzzing conversation, the hiss of the espresso ma-

chine, and the smoky atmosphere. Comfortable and familiar, even though she couldn't
see. The feeling that things could be worse
crept into her mind. After all, there was a
man at the table.

Not her man. Not her table. But it was a
start.

Arm-in-arm they walked to Madame
Danoux's. She heard the hushed sound of
the cars passing over the cobbled street. It
must have rained while they were in the
café. The car tires sounded different.

"Not many people appreciate sunrise," he
said, his tone low in the damp street.
"They'd rather sleep."

"My father pulled the all-night shift. When
I was little, the only time we'd have to talk
was before I left for school," she said.
"Sunrise was the best time of the day for
me." She remembered his worn bathrobe,
tired face, and grin as he poured her
steamed milk and chocolate. His thick,
unread work files on the table by her bookbag. She shook off the memory.

"What's on this street, Guy?"

"Café, fabric store for decorators, the of-
fices of the La Rochelle Film Festival, and
of *Médecins san frontières*," he said, pausing.

Was there something else he wanted to say?

"There's a uniform manufacturer, a public relations agency . . . it's written in Chinese but it looks like a wholesale accessory shop. In the courtyard there's an organ grinder's supplier. He's the only one who still makes the music rolls."

She recalled something: the sheets of music from Clothilde's café . . . and the sheet of music René found in the garbage at Mathieu's. Did they connect? But she'd think about that later. At the door, she reached for his hand, not knowing where to plant the customary *bisous* on his cheeks.

"I didn't learn much about the MRI," she said. "But I enjoyed myself. *Merci.*"

"That's the point," he said. "Chantal and the others frequent the bar we went to. The owner was a madame way back when, a 'character,' as people say."

"A colleague of Mimi's?"

He laughed. "That's the rumor. People watch out for each other here. The *quartier* takes care of the non-sighted."

Her heart chilled. "Not well enough. I was attacked in the passage and Josiane was killed."

"But the serial killer's . . ."

"It wasn't him. It was someone who knew

Josiane."

"Let's concentrate on the present," he said.

And then she felt his fingers on her lips. Then his lips on hers. Warm and searching.

And she was 16 again . . . late kisses in a hallway at night, stolen and wonderful. Something mysterious revealed for the first time.

"I've wanted to do that for a while," he said.

What did he see in her?

The door opened. "Dr. Lambert . . . is that you?" Madame Danoux's distinctive contralto filled the hall.

By the time Aimée got to bed, her tiredness had evaporated, leaving a brittle restlessness. Didn't patients fall for their doctors all the time? What a cliché.

Again, she wondered what had appealed to him? She was blind. Had it been pity . . . a mercy gesture?

Yet, he hadn't said he was married or involved. She hadn't felt a ring on any of his fingers.

And what good would she be to a man? How could it go anywhere? Did she want it to go anywhere?

Stop.

But he knew how to kiss. If she didn't quit

this, she'd be fantasizing about him all night. Forget counting sheep. She had to switch gears, distract herself, but she couldn't call René, it was too late.

She felt for the laptop, trying to ignore the mustiness and mothball scent emanating from the corner armoire, wishing Miles Davis, her puppy, was curled at her feet. As usual.

But thank God, he was with René's neighbor in Les Halles. He needed care and she couldn't provide it. Maybe they could enroll in the guide dog course together.

After booting up the laptop, she created a file, titled it *Chanson* and typed in what bothered her. A big list in no particular order. And as she typed, the voice repeated the words. After five minutes she played the list back.

Over and over.

Then she arranged them in order of importance. Blindness, Vincent's obstinate refusal to furnish the hard drive, and Mirador with Draz, the scum, rated as the top three.

And René. She worried about his health, what he'd found out, and what he might miss. She often missed things, only to notice them later. Or details might hit her as she walked away or in the middle of the night.

Like now.

This was the kind of thought process she'd learned from her father and grandfather, growing up in a household of policemen. Not to mention the smoky Pelote nights with half the Commissariat playing cards around the kitchen table. The talk. The nuances, the glances, the tipoffs. The way they treated their *indicateurs*. Every *flic* nourished informers. Had to. By osmosis, she'd absorbed what to be aware of, what to suspect, and how to tell when something was being withheld.

Fat lot of good that did her now. She wasn't in the field. She had to depend on René. And part of her worried about people's cruelty to him because of his stature.

She wanted to tear her short, spiky hair out, but not seeing the result would ruin the pleasure. All she could do, besides stew, would be to put her fingers to work. She felt around, made sure the modem wires hooked into the phone line.

She couldn't do much about her blindness. But she could find out if Mirador had a website and garner info from it. René would get the scoop from Josiane's editor, but in case it might help . . . she'd call in the morning and butter up whoever hired the casual labor . . . assuming she got that far.

"*Bienvenue à* Mirador," came a slick media-trained voice at the website. She found the fiscal and corporate structure, how they complied with building codes governing construction.

She hoped René had reached everyone on Josiane's speed dial. . . . Had the killer's number been listed? Was that why he wanted the phone? Or did he think the last call could be traced? That thought jarred her.

Of course, if *she* planned to murder someone she wouldn't be that stupid. And she didn't think he was. But the attack on her, the similarity to the Beast of the Bastille's method bothered her. In its very similarity, it seemed too planned to resemble the serial killer.

Disturbing. This was someone with access to inside knowledge. Fear danced up her spine.

Draz, the Romanian, might have prior convictions. A long shot. She didn't even know his last name. Or if he was in the country legally. But checking on the off chance that he had a prior record would save a lot of time if he did. Her father always said "follow your nose."

What he left out, but adhered to faithfully,

was procedure. She'd grown up intimately acquainted with investigative procedure, having done her homework, and lost several baby teeth, on the Commissariat marble floor. Following procedure, if nothing else, eliminated unnecessary legwork — now at a premium, since there was only so much René could do on his own.

She found the cell phone, hit the number of Le Drugstore . . . once the sole all night pharmacy and café in Paris. The worn 70s decor, pricey service, and the location on the Champs-Elysées deterred her visiting. Not to mention the suburban backwash attracted by the seedy glitter.

"Martin, please."

"You are . . . ?

"Aimée Leduc, Jean-Claude's daughter."

Pause. He must be checking.

"Call back in three minutes."

"D'accord, merci."

Standard operating procedure for contacting Martin, her father's old informant. At least he was still alive and he seemed to be in operation.

After one a.m., despite rain, sickness, or citywide strikes, Martin held court at a back table. He sat near the rear exit, where he could easily slip away.

The phone cabinet, down the tiled stairs

branching left from the restrooms, functioned as his communication center. No cell phone, but he brokered information, traded it like a commodities broker. If he didn't know, he'd find out. Not always a lot, but quality. And worth every franc.

He owed Aimée's father for saving his skin at least twice. And being of the old school, that counted. Certain ethics prevailed and debts transferred, like a legacy, to offspring. Aimée knew she could count on Martin for something.

She counted to 180 then called the number for the phone cabinet.

"*Bonsoir,* Martin."

"*Aaah, ma petite mademoiselle!*" his voice boomed, gritty like gravel on an unpaved road. "Such a long time. *Ça va?*"

She imagined his oversized tortoiseshell glasses, his gray wavy hair combed back, prominent nose, and dancing eyes. A charmer in his own roguish way. Her father always said Martin could have been a first class ship's cruise director if he'd only trod the straight and narrow.

The last time she'd seen Martin was the day before the bombing in Place Vendôme that had killed her father. He'd furnished information about a gang in the eighth arrondissement. Unrelated. But countless nights, when she'd woken up, she'd wondered if it really was.

The department hadn't sent flowers when her father died, but Martin had. A bouquet of yellow jonquils. And a donation to the war widows, her father's favorite charity. Crime created strange partnerships.

"And your dog, smarter than ever?"

The pang of missing Miles Davis hit her.

"Smarter than me, Martin," she said.

"You need an appointment?"

That was his term.

"Not the usual way, Martin," she said. "It's urgent. Thugs evicting tenants in the Eleventh, a Romanian named Draz."

"You know how I operate."

He required a personal visit to impart information. He used the phone as a tool, brief and to the point.

"The murdered reporter, Josiane Dolet, what's the word on her?" she said.

"I want to help you but . . ."

"No disrespect Martin, but I *can't* come to meet you," she said. "Logistics problems." She didn't want to admit her blindness. Never show a vulnerable side to a thief; it came back to haunt you.

"These days I've cut back," he said.

She doubted that.

"It's not like before," Martin said. "The

new gangs, new ways of operating . . ."

Paris had plenty of crime to go around.

"You're the best, Martin," she said. "Who else knew the Hsieh Tong sliced the bookie in the Thirteenth but you?"

Few penetrated the Asian underworld around Place d'Italie, but Martin had his sources. Even the *flics* used him there. Stroke his feathers enough and he should fly.

A low throat-clearing came over the phone. He slept all day but must smoke two packs a night. She'd never seen him without a lit cigarette between his fingers or burning in a nearby ashtray.

The thought made her wish for that Gauloise she'd shared with Mimi.

"Quality's important, Martin, that's why I've come to you."

She heard a low chuckle. "Not that I owe you?"

"Life's a flowing river, currents combine," she said.

"You're so like your father, bless him," Martin said.

"It's been five years, Martin," she said.

She remembered the explosion, searing heat, and crawling on the bloody cobblestones. The charred limbs of her father, his shattered reading glasses somehow forgotten in her pocket. And the emptiness that followed.

"We were set up, Martin." As always she wondered why. "You know that, don't you?"

Pause.

"Don't you work on computers now?" he said. "Gangs in the Eleventh seem too low-rent for you."

"Evictions, they're rent-a-thug style," she said. "East European bodybuilder types. But they must stick their thumbs in other tartes. See what you can dig up. I'll call you later."

"Tomorrow or the next day," he said. "It takes time. I'm an old man, remember?"

She hoped Martin could deliver. Time passed, and she knew, to solve a homicide, new information couldn't come soon enough.

She punched in several numbers and finally connected with the central office at the Quai des Orfèvres.

"I'm Commisaire Vrai's adjutant," she said, "requesting a search on an East European, goes by the name Draz. No surname known. I'll wait."

She knew they'd find Vrai was on leave if they checked. They did. Good.

"No luck with your computer?" the voice asked.

"We want to cast the net wide."

"Searching Draz." Whirring came from the background. "Nothing."

"Try entries with D."

Aimée heard a yawn.

"Twenty-three entries. But there might be more; not all the files have been made available online."

"Meaning they're sitting in the Commissariat files?"

"Or moldering away in the Frigo."

"Any 'D's' in the Eleventh?"

"Right now the only person detained in the past six months with a D is a Dicelle . . . transvestite trafficking in amyl nitrate. Sentenced."

"Thanks for checking."

She sat back. The clock ticked. Too bad she couldn't see what time it was. Why hadn't she asked Chantal for one of those talking clocks?

The lack of police interest in the attack on her bothered her. But as Morbier implied, if the Préfet wanted things nice and tidy to close the Beast of Bastille case, there stood little chance they'd exert themselves.

Would Morbier help? He was edging toward the finish line of retirement, too. These days he seemed more withdrawn than ever. And Loïc Bellan detested her.

If only she could interface with Europol.

She needed a last name. Had to have it. Tomorrow, she'd get René to lean on the architect . . . he might know more.

Meanwhile, she checked in with the answering machine at Leduc Detective. It felt like not just a few days but forever since she'd been there. She accessed and listened to the voice mail. A query for security work referred by a current satisfied client. Nice.

Then another message. No voice. The machine clicked off.

She felt uneasy. Even though she'd canceled her phone service right after her cell phone had been stolen, the attacker had time to find her addresses, home and business.

The third message, her connection from *la Proc*'s office, bothered her in a different way.

"The Incandescent hearing's scheduled for Monday afternoon at sixteen hundred hours at the Palais de Justice. If your client's not there, his firm goes on the docket for issuance of a subpoena."

Merde!

And then she fell asleep. She dreamt in color. Blood-red and tamarind-hued leaves spiraled down from the autumn trees in Place Trousseau. Children kicked the leaves, scattering them in a red-orange whirl, then ran to the quivering gloss-green see-saw. The crooked fingernail of a moon, its outline burnished in blue, swayed to accordion strains. The "piano of the poor," her grandmother had called it, as she slipped the worn straps around her shoulders.

The colors pulsed and throbbed; she'd never witnessed anything as beautiful. It grew larger than life, surreal and wonderful. And she didn't want it to end.

But it did. The colors faded. Disappeared. Waves of sadness hit her as she woke up.

Then she'd dozed off again, curled around the laptop, with the cursor flashing on Populax's logo. Better get back to work, she thought, rubbing her eyes and wondering what the bright thing was on her toe. A patch of sunlight surrounded by gray fog.

Her heart leapt. She could see!

She squinted, tried to focus. And the image slowly evaporated into more fog. A fog that shifted and moved.

She wanted to shout and dance. Her sight had returned. A little, a very tiny bit, but she'd seen her toe! It was only when she struggled into her T-strap high-heels that she realized the fog, now a dense charcoal color, remained.

Depression descended over her. Would her eyesight ever come back?

Friday Morning

"Which editor do you want?" said the man in the T-shirt to René.

René, wiping his damp forehead with a handkerchief, noticed the man's stringy hair and the ASK ME ABOUT THE BERLIOZ OPERA button on his sleeve.

Hard sunlight beamed down from the soot-laced skylight. Men hammered and saws whined in the background of the newspaper building.

"Someone in charge of investigative reporting, please," René said, wishing he knew how to word it better. And wishing, too, that he'd foregone his early workout at the dojo.

"All reporting's investigating for truth . . . so you could say, they all would do," said the man, looking down at the clutter on his reception desk.

"How about the city desk?"

"If we had one, it wouldn't be on this floor," he said.

Great. Forty minutes of wading through construction workers and over cables . . . for this René had tramped all over this tank of a building and had ended up in Accounting?

"What about the eleventh arrondissement?"

"It's not cheap anymore, eh, especially around the Bastille, but my former girlfriend lives there and still has a great rent."

Frustrated, René threw up his short arms in supplication. "I mean articles, an exposé about illegal evictions in the Bastille area, the eleventh . . . who'd edit that?"

The man's eyebrows arched. "Check with Dossiers. Behind the Archives section, second floor. That's if they haven't moved."

"Moved? Don't you know where they are?"

"They're installing new fiber optic lines," he said. "My phone's dead. I've tried all morning."

By the time René reached the right desk, his hip ached more than it had yesterday. Was pain cumulative? He gave a small smile to the young woman with black cornrow braids, wearing blue lipstick and a tight, bright blue jacket.

"I need to speak with a reporter about an exposé on evictions . . ."

"I'm sorry," she interrupted, "those articles come from stringers. Freelancers who've established a relationship with us. They turn in the finished work, someone copyedits it, and it's printed."

"No internal control?"

"Our stringers know the rules. Of course

everything's run by the head editor."

"May I speak with him?"

"Give me your name and number. He returns the day after tomorrow."

Frustrated, René handed her his business card and went to sit on the island on boulevard du Temple. He wedged himself up on the green slatted bench, wondering what to do next as he watched the old men play *pétanque* in the dust. A crowd of bystanders looked on in the dappled sunlight under the plane trees. Still leafy, but changing color to signal autumn's approach.

His phone rang.

"René?" asked Aimée.

"No luck with Josiane's editor, Aimée," René said. "But I left a message, maybe he'll get back to me the day after tomorrow."

Pause.

"I tried the last number on her speed dial," he said. "But I don't know what it means."

"Tell me."

"It's in Taverny, outside Paris," he said. "A Dr. Alfort's office at the Nuclear Commission. The receptionist says he's out until Monday. But I left both our numbers."

"*Bon* . . . good job. When you talk with the editor, René," she said, "don't forget to ask what else Josiane worked on. Maybe she was also writing an article about the Nuclear Commission . . . seems she was active in the Green party."

"A real socialist-with-a-trust-fund type!"

"Or a woman with a conscience, René," she said. "I found out that Vaduz died in a car crash near République."

"Vaduz, the Beast of Bastille?"

"The very same."

"When?"

"That's what you've got to find out from Serge."

"But he's a forensic pathologist."

"Exactement," Aimée said. "The *flics* are keeping their cards close to their chests. Letting no word out. So, on the quiet, you're going to ask Serge. And find out the cause of Josiane Dolet's death, too. You know, what he thinks. Ask him if it differs from the serial killer's MO."

"Whoa . . . after my last visit to the morgue, when we came through the sewers, I decided to skip any future ones. Except maybe my last."

"Please, René, I tried, but it's too risky for him to give information over the phone."

"How can I just walk into the morgue and get him to talk?"

"But you won't have to," she said. "He's willing, I've already arranged it. He's lectur-

271

ing at the musée des Moulages."

René drew a breath. "The Plaster Museum?"

"Part of l'hôpital Saint-Louis; it's in the Dermatology research wing," she said. "Where are you?"

"Boulevard du Temple.

"*Bon,* you're two Métro stops away."

"I like to drive."

"Even closer. Park by the northeast entrance," she said, concern in her voice. "Your legs bothering you?"

"Me? *Pas de tout,* not at all, doing great, I need this exercise, it's keeping me in shape," he said rubbing his aching hip. He lifted his swollen ankle to rest on the green wood-slatted bench, wishing he could ice it. "Don't worry about me. Take care of yourself."

By the time René found the musée des Moulages in hôpital Saint-Louis, he realized this was the third hospital he'd been in this week. And a temple of dermatology, René noted, renowned for the treatment of plague victims, syphilis, psoriasis, ringworm, and leprosy.

Built by Henri IV, in rose-colored brick and stone, the walled hospital resembled a medieval internment camp. Distinctive, but less beautiful than the Place des Vosges, his other seventeenth century construction, the hospital had been built to combat epidemics. And isolate the Black Death, the plague raging at the time.

And getting around in it was hard on René's short legs.

The Musée des Moulages, reminiscent of a nineteenth century natural history museum, would have made Jules Verne feel at home. One hundred and sixty-two glass showcases containing plaster samples illustrating various skin diseases lined the four sides of the huge rectangular room. More lighted showcases were reached by spiral staircases leading to long balconies running the length of the room. Glass-enclosed wooden cabinets held all manner of leprous fingers, limbs, ears and even faces pocked with bumps and lesions. Faded numbers in old script were tacked above each.

René cringed at the life-like portrayal of these diseased body parts. The wood floors creaked and a stale smell emanated from the showcases.

A sign informed the visitor that Baretta, a shop owner in the Passage Jouffrey, who made casts of fruit to display his produce, had been discovered by a dermatology doctor who used Baretta's skills to document skin diseases. So helpful was Baretta that the museum still displayed more than 2000 of his casts documenting every form of skin disease on every body part imaginable.

Finally, René located Dr. Serge Leaud, full black beard over a rosy complexion, standing on a podium before a screen, pointing at slides. An audience of a hundred or so men and women sat on folding chairs surrounded by the glass showcases. Many wore white labcoats and some, René figured, were medical students.

Léaud indicated a slide on the screen, showing a purplish and yellow lesion. "Here's an excellent example of the small ulcer, less than a centimeter, another manifestation of the various infectious complications of intravenous drug usage. In this case, an ulcer has developed as a consequence of a thromboembolic event associated with bacterial endocarditis. Of course, I'm sure you remember the cutaneous ulceration and destruction of the underlying tissue so reminiscent of the profound heart valve damage due to the antibiotic-resistant organisms we observed this morning."

René suppressed a groan. He pulled the laptop from his bag, averted his eyes from the screen, and did some work.

Finally, Léaud finished and the group of students surrounding him dispersed. René stood and smiled at him. Serge returned the smile, motioning toward a side chamber with a lowered ceiling and even more lighted displays. More intimate and quiet.

"Riveting stuff, Serge."

Serge nodded. "It's a little-known killer. In the morgue, we've seen only three incidents of this in the past thirty-five years. But last month, an ulcer reached a woman's varicose vein." He snapped his fingers. "Bled out like that."

"Fascinating, Serge, but I'm short on time. Did Aimée tell you . . ."

"You didn't hear this from me," Serge interrupted, looking around and lowering his voice. "If you repeat it, I'll deny every word."

"Deny what?"

"The Dolet autopsy findings," he said. "I assisted. Saw most of the preliminary examination. But the final pathology reports take time. All the other Beast of Bastille victims' autopsy findings, according to the attached police report, were consistent. Only Dolet's evidenced nothing of a sexual nature. But then, maybe he was interrupted."

Serge moved toward a window facing a display of syphilitic noses and leprous, misshapen ears. René winced but followed, as Serge tamped the end of a nonfiltered Gauloise and lit up.

"That can kill you," said René.

"So my wife tells me," Serge said. He glanced at his wrist, a red Mickey Mouse watch with a EuroDisney strap on it. "A birthday present from my twins," he said, in explanation.

"We know the victims ranged from twentysomething to fortysomething blondes living in the Bastille. Party types," said René. "Vaduz waited in the passages they lived in or walked through, slipped in the door behind them, and attacked."

Serge nodded. "Not the most innovative or original serial killer. Boring but consistent. He did it every time. The DNA was monumental."

"So what distinguished Josiane Dolet from the Beast of Bastille's victims? That's what I need to know," said René. "What made her different from the others, the serial victims."

Serge buttoned his pea-coat, lifted his briefcase. "According to the Préfet, we don't have serial killers in France. That's an American phenomenon."

"What do you call Polin and his predilection for slicing up old ladies in Montmartre?" asked René.

Serge grinned. "We called him an old lady killer."

"So how did Vaduz get released?"

"Technicality. Verges, his lawyer, knows the game. And how to play it after a *flic* makes a procedural error. This Verges, known as a big civil liberties crusader, moves in the lofty Lefty circles."

René remembered what Aimée had asked. "Were the autopsy details released to the public?"

Serge shook his head, puffing away. "Never. That's why it was so hard to nail him. The *flics* didn't enlist the public's help until the last murder. The one before Dolet's, that is. It was only then the newspapers put it together, labeling him the Beast of Bastille, saying he killed women in the passages. The next day they found him. But no thanks to whoever routed the file to the wrong arrondissement."

"Like Aimée says, Napoleon's centralization of the military, police, and administration decentralized their power. But it bolstered his. They couldn't overthrow him," said René. "And still couldn't today."

"We let Waterloo and the Russian winter do that," Serge said.

"When did Vaduz die in the car crash?" René asked, as Serge edged toward the door.

"He's dead, what does it matter?"

"That's just it," René said, wishing Serge would slow down. His hip hurt again. "If Vaduz stole the car and died before Aimée and Dolet were attacked, it's proof he couldn't have attacked them. Even if he died later, but before Aimée was attacked in the residence, we'd know there was another culprit."

René had followed Serge out under the colonnades, glad to escape the musty *musée* and its contents.

"She didn't tell me about that." He shrugged. "I asked around. The dossier's been moved. Seems they found Vaduz like steak tartare, mostly raw and scattered, his edges burnt when the engine caught fire. They cremated whatever bits were left."

René winced.

"Serge, you have to find out," he said.

How did they do it on those TV shows? They always had some clever way to obtain information. All he could think of was mundane.

"Can't you find out what time they delivered Vaduz to the morgue? Someone must have logged it."

He was guessing but in a bureaucratic system one needed a signed, stamped certificate for everything, and even more so in the police.

A breeze laced with damp leaves from nearby Canal Saint Martin wafted under the stone arches to them.

"I want to help, René, but I'm late for the lab," Serge said. "*Alors,* tonight's our wedding anniversary, my mother-in-law's coming to babysit. If I'm late they'll both shoot me."

René racked his brain. What could he do?

"Look, Serge, when you leave the morgue can't you go out the back?" René said. "Through the gate used by the vans and ambulances. On your way, have a brief chat with the drivers, the men who unload bodies. Say you're just wondering about something and check their log. It will only take a minute, then you're on your way home. I'll meet you outside."

"How bad is Aimée?"

She must not have told him.

"She's blind, Serge."

René saw anger in Serge's eyes.

"See you at five."

René stopped at Leduc Detective to check the mail and messages. He needed to get some work done, rack up some billable hours, and honor their security contracts.

Someone had to keep their income coming in. And he worried, as he had since Aimée's attack, about how they could make things work now. Or if they could.

As he hung up his jacket, the phone rang.

"Monsieur René Friant?"

"Speaking."

"I saw him again," said a hesitant man's voice.

René took a breath. "Who did you see?"

"Draz, only he's not called Draz. These Eastern European names confuse me. He's called Dragos."

Now René recognized the voice of Yann Rémouze, the flutemaker who lived in the square overlooking Gymnase Japy. And Dragos was the name the architect Brault had mentioned, too.

"So tell me more, Yann."

"You gave me your business card but I didn't want to call you too early. They had one of those loud techno parties in the abandoned building."

"Who's they, Yann?"

"Those East Europeans."

René stopped unbuttoning his coat.

"At dawn they milled around in the square," said Yann. "This Dragos, they were calling him. He was surrounded by his comrades. Some fight broke out around the block, the *flics* car pulled up, then they all disappeared."

So Yann had called to tell him of a missed opportunity. Late again. René figured getting any information about Josiane from the Romanian *mecs* who evicted people had to be a long shot anyway. "Next time call me when you see him, Yann. Anytime."

"But his friend's still here, sniffing around."

René froze.

"Which friend?"

"One of the gang who evicted old people. Tracksuit, big shoulders."

"I'm on my way. Try and keep him there," René said, grabbing his keys.

"How can I do that?"

René heard the panic in Yann's voice. But if he'd got up the courage to call him, there was hope.

"You'll think of something Yann. Call me on my cell phone if he leaves. 06 78 54 39 09."

René gunned his Citroën down rue du Louvre. He thanked God he'd filled the tank earlier as he crossed three arrondissements. He'd passed through the Marais and lower Bastille in record time when his cell phone rang.

"He's getting on his bicycle, this *mec,*" said Yann.

The cell phone reception buzzed and wavered.

"Can you speak up, Yann. What's he wearing?"

"Navy blue tracksuit with those stripes down the side; he's on an old battered bike," said Yann, his voice brimming with excitement.

Not so different from many of the cyclists René passed. At least two people wore that type of gymsuit.

"Can you tell in which direction he's headed?"

"Turned onto rue Gobert," said Yann. "He's either headed down Boulevard Voltaire or . . ."

"I'm on Boulevard Voltaire," interrupted René. "Does he have a ponytail like Dragos?"

"*Non,* short black hair," he said. "There's a funny straw basket on the front with plastic flowers."

And there he was, in the bike lane. Leafy trees canopied the wide boulevard, casting dappled shadows on cars and pedestrians.

"Got him," René said. "He's ahead of me, Yann. Call me if you see Dragos again. *Merci.*"

René slipped the phone in his pocket and edged the Citroën closer. The man, pedaling hard, wiped a brow glistening with sweat. He appeared intent on the busy traffic, turned right on rue Charenton and weaved his bicycle through the crowded one way street to Avenue Ledru Rollin.

René kept pace, glad he was behind the wheel. The only other time he'd followed anyone had been with Aimée in Belleville. At least he didn't have to run this time.

After crossing Avenue Daumesnil, right behind l'hôpital Quinze-Vingts, the bicyclist turned into a small street leading to the pedestrian bridge crossing the Bastille's canal. Moored on both sides of the canal were upscale boats and several *péniches,* remodeled barges.

René pulled over, stuck on a one-way street. He jumped out of his car, ready to pursue. But he saw the man pedal the bike across the bridge, then coast down to the long dock lining the basin of the canal that fed into the Seine.

The man propped the bike against the pitted stone wall, Henri II's fortifications surrounding the former fourteenth century moat. The bike was below a niche in the old, worn wall. Weeds wormed their way in its crevices. He hopped onto the narrow gangplank and disappeared.

René pulled out the cell phone and called Aimée, determined to keep his tone light.

"Aimée, I followed one of Dragos's friends to a *péniche* moored here in the Bastille basin."

"Dragos?"

"Yann got the name wrong," René said.

The churning water lapped the quai below René, as a *péniche* with bright red geraniums, lace curtains, and a child playing with a dog on deck, chugged by.

"What's he doing?"

René told her. "It's a waiting game now. Until he comes out. But I have to meet Serge at the morgue when he gets off work."

"So tell me René, if this Romanian, Dragos, thought I was Josiane . . . why did he want to kill her?"

"How about this?" he said. "She wrote an exposé of Mirador's illegal evictions. He tried to stop her."

"That fits. But why make it look like an attack by the Beast of Bastille?"

"A good cover." He wished for the thousandth time Aimée had never picked up Josiane's phone and answered it.

"Somehow, I doubt it," she said. "It's not the immigrant thugs' style. Bold as they are, they'd have to know a lot more about the serial killer to plan it. Who knows how much French they understand? Besides, they'd speak with an accent."

She made sense.

"Whoever called on that phone knew Josiane, and was trying to lure her into the passage. He got me instead. The Romanians' trademark isn't subtlety."

"So that leaves us . . . ?"

"With more questions."

Below on the quai, the man René had followed emerged.

"He's come out," said René. "I've got to go."

"*Alors,* be careful."

The man strode at a rapid pace, mounted his bike, and was down the quai before René reached his car. By the time René arrived at the Place de la Bastille roundabout, circling the Bastille column surmounted by the gold-winged figure of the genius of Liberty, the bike had disappeared. He could have gone in any of the 11 different directions radiating from the column.

What to do now?

Only one thing. He drove on and parked along the Boulevard de la Bastille.

Fear flickered over him as he crossed the bridge on foot. The man had seemed to be in good shape and Dragos, or others like him, might be on the boat. His confidence ebbed despite his martial art practices and black belt from the taekwondo dojo.

René took a deep breath and walked up the gangplank.

FRIDAY

A hundred things weighed on Loïc Bellan's mind, which was webbed by a dull receding hangover, the least of which was the *mec* from a derelict building rave party allegedly selling Ecstasy. Bellan also had several cases on his desk. On top of it all, the little doubt about Aimée's attacker being the Beast of Bastille still nagged him.

But the duty detective leaving his double shift had dumped everything on Bellan's desk and rubbing his tired eyes, said, "Welcome back, we're short staffed. Your date's in lockup four."

Bellan considered himself lucky to have grabbed a bed in a building used for out of town *flics* on temporary assignment. At least by working late he'd avoid facing the dormitory-style bunkhouse with its bare walls that would drive him to finish the flask of scotch malt whiskey in his pocket.

And he'd avoid Marie's silent accusing face that woke him up at night, slicing through his dreams. And the small bundle in the Vannes hôpital, his son Guillaume, who'd lapsed into renal failure and was fighting for his life.

Bellan opened the thick metal door and stood in front of the wire cages in the Commissariat where they kept the prisoners. Like animal pens, he'd always thought. He stared at a sullen young man sitting on the narrow bench, a sheen of perspiration on his face.

"Iliescu, D." said Bellan, consulting the file. "Come with me."

Iliescu wore a skinny T-shirt and baggy sweatpants. He lurched toward the grille. He kept rubbing his nose and looked flushed and feverish. *Shakes like a junkie,* Bellan thought. *But more buff than the usual twitching skin-and-bone types.*

They went back to an office.

"Looks like you had some bad shit, eh?"

"I don't do drugs," Iliescu said, with a thick Romanian accent. He heaved, then covered his mouth with his hand as if about to throw up. "Never, I work out."

All through the short interrogation, Bellan noticed Iliescu fighting waves of nausea.

"Where do you come from?"

"Budapest."

One of his palms had numbers written in

ink on it. Numbers with odd curlicues on them.

"What's that?"

"I write notes to myself," Iliescu said, breathing faster. "If I don't write down the time, I'm late for work. Listen, I've got a job."

"We'll have to search your domicile," Bellan said, cutting it short. "I've applied for a search warrant."

Iliescu's eyes rolled up in his head. He gagged and fell back in his chair. Alarmed, Bellan pulled on some latex gloves, from a box kept handy on the desk. He grabbed the wastebasket almost in time for Iliescu to spew inside it.

And then Bellan saw the blackened skin under the man's arms. Big charred places, some cracked and bleeding. Cigarette burns? He looked closer. Bigger. He'd never seen anything like this.

"Get the on-call medico here. Right away," he shouted into the hallway.

The sounds of scuffling and the banging of metal drawers came from the hallway.

"Nobody answers," said a duty sergeant. "Will a paramedic do?"

"Anybody, quick!"

A short man with a graying beard wearing a lab coat rushed in.

"What's up?"

"Look at his arm."

"Spanish Inquisition time eh, Bellan?" said the paramedic. "Burning your victims these days?"

"They're not new burns," Bellan said.

"But recent. Notice the blackened skin." He pointed.

Iliescu's eyes fluttered. His skin appeared clammy and moist, but he was still coherent. "They'll fire me if I don't show up at work," he said, his voice hoarse.

"You mean you'll lose your drug connections," Bellan said.

Iliescu tried to sit up as the paramedic brought in another man to help him.

"No drugs," said Iliescue. "Never."

"Take him to Hôtel Dieu," Bellan said. Hôtel Dieu, on Île de la Cité, one of the oldest charity hospitals in Paris, treated prisoners and the indigent.

"*No!* I'll lose my job!"

"Where do you work?"

"The loading bay at the Opéra," said Iliescu.

Something clicked. Vaduz, the serial killer, had worked there, too. "Do you know Patrick Vaduz?"

Bellan saw recognition in Iliescu's fevered eyes.

"That pervert!" said Iliescu. "He made everyone's skin crawl. We avoided him."

After wheeling Iliescu out, the paramedic looked back at Bellan from the door,

"It's odd, but it's as if he has a major case of sunburn. A megadose."

Bellan stared at him.

"What do you mean?"

"But no one gets sunburned in just one spot, do they?" said the paramedic, tugging his beard.

FRIDAY

René clutched the rope railing as the gangplank swayed. He wished he could suppress the churning of his stomach. A porthole snapped shut on a boat down the quai.

The bright glare from the water and greasy oilslick danced in front of him. *Seasick* had been one of his middle names growing up. *Le petit* was the other.

The slim dark blue *péniche,* moored in the Port de Plaisance, swayed in the wake of a tugboat. The barge's hold had been converted to a covered living space. STARLA was lettered in white across the hull.

"*Allô?* Anyone there?" called René. His words caught in his throat. He didn't know what he'd say if the door opened.

290

No answer.

He knocked on the door. Again and again.

The lapping of water against the wooden hull was the only response.

He looked around then turned the door-knob.

Locked.

Weathered wrought-iron chairs and a glass table took up the deck space. On the other side, by some piled deck chairs, he saw a round porthole. And another larger one, circled by rusted bronze. Unlocked. If he opened it wide enough, he just might squeeze through.

Should he?

He saw no sign of life on the next boat.

Breaking and entering was more Aimée's *métier*. Yet, if he continued to stand here, he'd learn nothing.

Alors, he might as well try. He pulled the deck chairs over as a shield, opened the porthole wider, and shimmied inside, landing on a slick pine floor. Newspapers were strewn across the counter. René looked. The mastheads read *Romania-Libera.*

He pulled on the latex gloves that he'd taken from his pocket, as he'd seen Aimée do countless times. Then rolled up his jacket sleeves and got to work, hoping to find something that dealt with Mirador. He'd have to find it soon and get out.

In a drawer, he saw names, hours, and what looked like break-times, listed on a sheet. A work roster for different shifts? He glanced down . . . Iliescu, Dragos.

His excitement mounted. He'd found Dragos. At least where he'd been known. And he'd found it all by himself.

Footsteps pounded on the wooden gangplank.

Merde . . . he was coming back!

René looked for somewhere to hide.

Where?

The doorknob turned. Locked.

René dodged under the table that was bolted to the floor. Against the bulkhead were the built-in knee-high cabinets. He heard footsteps circling the boat like he had, someone trying the windows. Out of options, René opened a latched cabinet and backed himself inside a musty damp space big enough for a trunk. A man with longer legs would never have fit inside.

He prayed that he wouldn't sneeze. His hand fell on a dirty beige canvas bag. Slants of custard-hued light came through the space where the cushioned seat missed meeting the wall.

In the cramped, hot space, René's hip throbbed. On his right were glass cylinders.

Long, fat, test tube-like, poking out from a bag.

But his gaze caught on the bag's dirty canvas flap that bore the initials DI . . . Dragos Iliescu! He wished whoever was tramping about outside would leave so he could exit with Iliescu's bag.

In his dreams.

He tried concentrating on the rays of light, not the swaying of the boat. Or his claustrophobia. He heard the barge ropes strain against the hull.

And then his cell phone trilled in his pocket. *Merde* . . . why hadn't he put it on vibrate? How dumb!

A shadow blocked the light. He couldn't answer it. After three rings, he shut the phone off. And prayed.

He heard the windows jiggled from outside. He held his breath. Finally, the footsteps clomped back up the gangplank.

René used his elbows and scooted out. But not before he'd slipped the sling of the canvas bag around his shoulders.

FRIDAY AFTERNOON

Bellan crossed the hotel courtyard, whose dark stone walls were covered by ivy and climbing roses, to find the room listed as

Iliescu's residence. He followed the hotel clerk, a short squat woman who walked with a cane. If Iliescu sold bad Ecstasy, Bellan wanted to find the drug before anyone else did. And confiscate it.

Lemon trees in old washtubs tilted on the cobbles. Bellan's interest grew as the woman, who leaned heavily on her cane, climbed the winding metal back staircase. There was a certain rundown charm about the place. Reaching the third floor, the woman turned the room key and a door creaked open.

"Iliescu's room," she said, stepping inside. She looked around, then beckoned Bellan to enter.

Bellan's nose crinkled at the room's stale smell. It had been closed up for a long time. The only personal touch was the pile of dirty sweatsuits on the floor.

"My uncle rented rooms by the month on this floor until the sixties, the rest were . . ." she cleared her throat, "on a more temporary basis."

A brothel before they'd been outlawed in 1948? Now a rent-by-the-hour prostitute's hotel? No questions asked, Bellan figured. So it would feel safe and convenient for a dope dealer like Iliescu.

The tall, half-shuttered windows faced

south to the narrow street. A maze of alleys really. Shafts of sunlight slanted across the wooden floor, dust motes dancing in their light.

In the afternoon sun, it was apparent that the march of time had dulled the glint of period wall sconces. The pre-war floral wallpaper was smudged and worn; the heavy-legged writing desk and the metal runged bed hadn't been changed since the forties, Bellan figured. He felt as if he'd stepped into a time warp.

The hotel clerk's eyes narrowed. "My *tante* Cecile lived here until last spring," she said. She buttoned her mohair sweater vest, worn despite the heat, and wiped her nose with a tissue. "*Tante* slipped on the icy street during an early thaw. God took her in her eighty-third year. She managed the hotel until the day she died."

No wonder it had an old lady smell. Hard to get rid of after all those years.

"Sorry to hear that, but I need to look around," he said, flashing his badge.

The woman shook her head. "What's the *quartier* coming to these days? Full of crime and overpriced boutiques! My grandfather moved here because it was cheap; he carted his own charcoal and drew water from the well. They've cemented it over now."

"When did Iliescu rent the room, madame?"

"Yesterday, but he left almost at once."

She seemed awfully knowledgeable. Most non-star hotels made a point of not knowing their tenants' movements or whereabouts.

"How do you know that, madame?"

She stood back, her hands on her ample hips. "I was cleaning the filth out, wasn't I?" she jerked her cane toward the room across the hall. Halfway ajar, the door showed a scene of upside-down chairs and general upheaval. "A pigsty. Must be what they're used to where they come from, some Slavic way of living. Not in Paris, I told them, and kicked them out."

"Did Iliescu have any visitors?"

She nodded. "Nobody I saw."

Loud buzzing came from the courtyard.

"That's the Reception buzzer. If you'll excuse me, I've got a hotel to run," she said, heading out the door. "Lowlifes, all of them."

Disappointed, Bellan searched the room.

All he found were several bodybuilder-type magazines. He searched the desk, cracks in the wall, the floors for any loose floorboards. In the back of the armoire, he found a yellowed and tattered old programme from the Balajo, the club on rue du Lappe. It bore a photo of Edith Piaf and Jo Privat, the well-known accordionist.

But no drugs.

He raised the window sash. From across the way, a piano *étude* trilled, the notes rising and falling over the passage.

What was he missing?

And then he saw it.

"21, Port de Plaisance, 16:00" written in pen on the window's wooden frame. He recognized the odd curlicues of the numbers. Like Iliescu's writing on his palm.

The same funny curlicues.

Bellan copied the address. Wasn't that the dock where pleasure boats moored in the Bastille?

Friday Afternoon

René headed toward Place Mazas to meet Serge at the morgue. A gray metal Métro bridge spanned the Seine, looping just behind the morgue's back gate. René wondered if Métro passengers on high realized what they viewed, in close proximity, for a brief few seconds.

The nineteenth century redbrick building, bordered by the expressway to Metz, looked more like a school than the Institut médico-légal, the central morgue. Built on the Seine to receive bodies sent downriver, it proved a macabre curiosity stop for *fin-de-siècle* Parisians eager to view cadavers. In 1909, a handcuffed Houdini had jumped off the morgue gates into the Seine, emerging long minutes later with freed hands, waving.

René parked his car by the wide, massive gate. He saw a van drive through. Within, men in white labcoats hosed down the courtyard and two men sprayed their short white boots.

René cringed. He didn't much like contemplating what they were cleaning up.

At the gate Serge, his pea-coat buttoned and a navy cap low over his eyes, slapped a man's back. They laughed. And in a few seconds, Serge leaned through René's passenger door window. René took the rolled up racing newspaper, Paris Turf, that Serge thrust at him.

"A hundred francs says Josiane in the eleven p.m. race and the Beast by a long shot in the five a.m.," said Serge, poking his head in, "but that's if I was a betting man."

"Merci," said René.

Serge turned toward a man in a trench coat. "*À demain,* Inspecteur."

"Tomorrow's your turn to buy coffee," said the man. "Don't weasel out of it this time, saying you've got an autopsy."

Serge laughed and waved as the man went by. But his eyes weren't smiling.

"I did some homework," said Serge, turning back to René, lowering his tone. "Lambert's the best optic trauma specialist, at least in Paris. I just spoke with him. Asked about Aimée's prognosis. There's not a lot to do besides monitor the optic nerve, run tests, and work on reducing the inflammation. If and when that subsides, then they'll assess the damage. Let's pray it's not extensive."

"Tell me what that really means, Serge," said René.

Serge sighed. "I'm sorry, René. We put men on the moon and orbit satellites, but we don't know the idiosyncrasies of brain stems. Or their reactions. Don't count on things getting better, René. *Alors,* it's so hard to say this," Serge stumbled. "Better plan for the worst."

René's head felt heavy from the weight of his words.

"But I can't tell that to Aimée," said René. "She needs hope."

Serge smacked the car's hood.

"That's why I work with those who don't need explanations any more." Serge looked away, shaking his head. "This shouldn't have happened. But I'm being honest, René."

"Me, too," he said lifting the parking brake and shifting into first.

René drove back to the quai and opened the racing pages. Serge had been busy. Inside lay photocopies of the daily intake and outtake log of the morgue since Monday. And it made his head spin.

"Allô?" said Aimée, sitting up in bed.

"Serge photocopied the morgue log," said René. "I'm trying to figure it out. But the handwriting's terrible."

"Good job. Look at Tuesday, under white female, late thirties or early forties found in . . ."

"*Voilà.* Estimated time of death: eleven p.m.," he said. "Of course Serge said as much. Don't you remember . . . the astrologer Miou-Miou predicted Josiane's time of death?"

"René, hurry up. Read the rest."

"Further on, at five a.m., body parts of white male, early twenties deposited from a charred automobile. Vaduz!"

"Does it give any time for the accident?"

"Non."

"René, look for an attached police report. Sometimes they submit it with the body. A blue sheet. The writing on the photocopy will be fainter."

She heard René inhale, the rustle of paper as he thumbed the attached sheets.

"Most of these seem like copies of lab requisitions . . . wait a minute," he said. "In the middle of the sheaf one's labelled Commissariat de 11ième arrondissement. It's just legible.

"*Tiens,* Serge's a genius," said René. "This report states that a black 1989 Peugeot was reported stolen at ten-thirty p.m. Monday night. A couple attending a film near the République Métro saw a man breaking into their car. He fit Vaduz's description. They couldn't catch him and he drove away. The same car was involved in an accident later."

"Voilà," she said. "Vaduz didn't attack me."

"But he could have driven from République . . ."

"I left the resto at ten-thirty," she interrupted. "Somewhere, I have my receipt with the time; I needed it, to bill Vincent. So Vaduz couldn't have attacked me if he was stealing the car. It's doubtful that he could have killed Josiane in the next courtyard."

Aimée paused.

"I'm trying to add all this up. Make a timeline."

"Go on," said René.

"If we can make the connections, I'll call Bellan and demand that he reopen the case."

"And Vaduz certainly couldn't have attacked you in the Residence," said René, his voice mounting in excitement. "He died early on Tuesday!"

"*Bon.* So according to the police log," she said, "Monday night Vaduz stole a car at the same time I was attacked in Passage de la Boule Blanche."

"But Serge attached another police report," said René. "It's not blue either."

"Which states . . . ?"

"A man resembling Vaduz, identifiable by those horrible teeth, driving the stolen Peugeot, hung out at a café near Porte la Chapelle. Then he took off with one of the local drug dealers named Barzac."

"That's not so good," she said, worried. Dope dealers were notorious for bending their stories. Especially if the dealer was caught with dope. "The drug dealer probably cut a deal."

"Meaning?" asked René.

"If the dealer's mentioned in the report, the *flics* interviewed him. So his testimony can go either way," she said, "depending on what he's up for. And how the *flics* prefer he testify."

"Then what does it matter?" said René. His voice sagged.

"Are you all right, René?" Was she being insensitive, pushing him too hard? She'd heard fatigue before in his voice.

She was obsessed, but she didn't want to use him at the cost of his health.

"I'm fine," he said. "What about the MRI . . . what did the doctor say, the one you went out with for a drink?"

Pause. Should she tell René the way he'd kissed . . . the little, growing fantasy of regaining her sight and cooking the doctor dinner after a long day in the hospital? Dinner? . . . She didn't know how to cook.

"He likes watching sunrises."

She heard the rustling of paper.

"Look, we're banging up against a brick wall, Aimée. That's what I mean. The *flics* want to pin the blame on Vaduz; satisfy the victims' families' thirst for justice, and ensure the Préfet's smooth retirement. They'll ignore this, *non?* It's easier for them to place the blame on Vaduz and pretend you're crazy."

"We need to talk with the café owner, René," she said. "Feel like a drive?"

Aimée felt the car shudder as René downshifted and parked. According to Morbier,

Porte la Chapelle's reputation as a cesspool had grown worse in the two years since she'd been there; it had high dope traffic and East European prostitutes had set up shop under the concrete Périphérique and along the rail lines shooting up from Gare du Nord.

"It's called Café des Roses?" asked René.

Aimée nodded. Then she wished she hadn't, as resulting fireworks flashed in her head.

"Nice name for a fixer-upper," he said. "Broken shutters, cracked pavement, peeling paint. And that's just the outside."

"So, no stars in the Michelin guide," she said. "Tell me what you see."

"The café's across from a *serrurie,* with a big green key for the locksmith sign. That's the only other functioning business."

"Handy," she said. "All the times I've locked myself out, I wish a *serrurie* had been nearby."

"Several young men wearing dark windbreakers are standing out front of the café," he said, "and on the pavement. The rest of the buildings are old, Haussman-era, with windows bricked-up."

Rundown and anonymous. Like much of the area had become.

She heard him turn the ignition off.

"Cars stop," René reported. "These men go to the windows, hold brief conversations."

"Then what, René?"

"One just drove off."

"Drug dealers," she said. "Let's have an espresso."

"Me, I worked the counter that night," said the café owner, who had a northern, Lille accent.

A former truck driver, Aimée figured. Many bought cafés upon retirement or when their backs gave out from crisscrossing France in 18-hour shifts, 52 weeks a year.

"My wife came down with *la grippe*. White-faced and weak. I sent her upstairs. Busy. That's all I remember. Worked my feet off all night. My corns still ache."

Aimée's hand circled the espresso cup. She knew her hesitant entrance, gripping René's shoulder, had brought them immediate attention. She heard the skipped beat of conversations, felt the weight of eyes on them. Heard a few guffaws from the corner.

The stale smell of beer, the sticky counter, and grit from the unswept floor bothered her. But not as much as being the center of attention.

"Monsieur, has Barzac been here to-night?" she asked.

No reply. Only the gush of water in the sink and gurgle of beer from the tap.

"Are you shaking your head no?"

"Look, the *flics* were here already," he said. "Barzac talked with them. Haven't seen him since."

"Did the *flics* speak with anyone else?"

"Not that I saw."

She pulled out the 20 francs arranged the way Chantal had taught her; one edge folded for 20, half-folded bill for 50. A length of the rectangle fold for 100, and a double folded rectangle for 500 franc notes.

"That's only 10 francs," said a slurred voice to her right. Garlic breath wafted over her.

"Take it easy, Franck," said a voice in the rear.

"I always do," said the garlic-breath.

She felt him lean into her elbow.

"It's twenty," she said. "More than enough for two espresso." She almost added *in a dump like this.*

"You challenging *me?*"

Snickers of laughter came from the corner.

"Don't pay attention, Aimée. Let's go," René said.

"What's your hurry, *petit?*" said Franck.

"The circus leaving?"

The laughter got louder.

"He doesn't like the clientele," she said. "Neither do I."

"Ouch," said Franck, his voice slurring more. It sounded like he was about to be sick.

"Franck, leave it," said the café owner. "It's on the house. I don't take money from the handicapped."

Her hand shot out in the direction of the owner's voice and she felt an Adam's apple. She hoped it was his and squeezed. Chairs scraped across the floor, voices quieted, and whoever's throat she gripped choked.

"Like that?" she challenged.

"Let's go, Aimée!" She felt René tugging at her bag.

She pulled the Beretta from her bag, clicked off the safety. The only sounds were the hiss of the dripping steam in the espresso machine and the rumble of trucks outside on the boulevard.

"Somebody did this to me. But harder. Now I can't see," she said, and let go. "But I pay my way. Got it?"

"Sure."

"My partner's a black belt," she said. "If you want some action, get in line."

No one said anything. No one laughed.

"So where's Barzac?"

Silence.

"I start shooting in ten seconds. And my aim isn't too good these days. But it's effective. I can hit the espresso machine and cost you several thousand francs damage. That's for starters. I'll bet there's a gray smoky mirror in front of us. I don't like those; maybe I'll start with that."

Behind her she heard an *ouff* as something connected with breaking glass. "You okay, René?"

Then the sounds of someone being sick.

"I am. But Franck's looking poorly. I showed him a new jujitsu move."

". . . seven seconds, eight seconds . . ." she said.

"Barzac lives above the *serrurie,*" said the café owner. "Second floor."

Aimée threw down a fifty franc note. "Keep the change."

They were standing at the door of the apartment building.

"Some new pills making you feel better, Aimée?" asked René.

"I'll feel better when I talk to Barzac," she said.

Her instinct had made her reach for the Beretta. Thank God she hadn't used it.

"I thought you left the gun behind," he said.

"It makes me feel safe."

She wondered if he understood. Maybe no one could unless they were blind.

She heard René ring the buzzers. None of the apartments answered. Wind gusted around her legs. Cold and damp.

"No lights in the upstairs windows."

"Let's try the *serurrie*," she said.

"Looks like he's about to close," said René.

She heard knocking, the door creaked open, then René pulled her hand. Aimée heard a man coughing, the low drone of a television soap opera with a crescendo of music. A dog growled somewhere from the right. Deep and powerful.

"Be careful. Two steps," René said. "Sorry, monsieur, are you about to close?"

She lifted her foot, felt her way.

"I'm open twenty-four seven," said a man, interrupted by coughing. "*Arrête,* Brutus."

The dog ceased growling.

"He's a sweetheart, take no notice."

Sounded like a Doberman to Aimée.

"We're detectives, like to ask you a few questions," she said. "I'm Aimée Leduc; my partner is René Friant."

"Mind closing the door tight?" he said.

"My heater's on the fritz."

"Bien sûr," said René, shutting the door hard.

"We'd like to talk with Barzac, a tenant in the building," she said. "Any idea where we could find him? No answer upstairs."

"There wouldn't be, would there," said the man. "Skipped to Marseilles, the concierge told me. Owing two months rent."

Great. A dead end.

"Were you here on Monday night, monsieur . . . ?

"Piot. Alex Piot. Been a locksmith here since 1974," he said. "Let me check the daily work log. I have to write every transaction down, or I forget."

Aimée heard the television sound lowered, footsteps shuffle over the floor.

"People love me here," Piot said, his voice closer. "I get everyone out of a jam. Keep my stock current. Why, you lock yourself out of your car or your flat and I've got your key: Fichet, Picard, Bricard, Muel, Keso, Pollux, Vak, Réel, even the Medeco line. Not many keep that on hand. But I get truck drivers, businessmen, doctors, nuns, philosophers; you name it, since I'm near the Périphérique."

He liked to talk. Maybe he'd seen something.

"What about Vaduz, the serial killer? We heard he picked Barzac up in front of the café."

Only the rustle of pages.

"Monsieur Piot?"

"I rented *Dr. Zhivago* that night," said Piot. "They don't make movies like that anymore, eh. That Russian winter scene, Julie Christie's cheekbones . . . a classic!"

Disappointment sat heavy on her.

"But monsieur," said René, "your shop window overlooks the café."

"I don't watch those types. I avoid them and the trouble they bring."

"So you didn't see Barzac, the drug dealer?"

"Like I said, I watched the video. Only a one-night rental, you know."

"Let's go, Aimée," said René.

But she didn't want to let it go without one more try.

"Are you sure, Monsieur Piot, you didn't see Vaduz?"

"Well, I've had an archbishop, but never a serial killer. I thought they only had those in *Amérique.*"

"He's called the Beast of Bastille."

"Aaaah," he said. "The only transaction that night was for a black Peugeot," said

Piot. "Man with bad teeth. He sat in here a while."

Stopping in her tracks, Aimée pulled René back. "Tell us about him, monsieur."

"He used my bathroom. Acted funny after that."

"Did he buy drugs from Barzac?"

"I wouldn't know," he said. "But it wouldn't surprise me. He said he didn't like the types in the café, so he wanted to wait here while I worked. I don't mind company when I'm grinding the key. Makes the time go faster. And Brutus, well, no one tries anything funny with him here."

"Did you write the man's license plate number down?"

"Certainly. It's required," the man said. A bout of coughing overtook him. "74 89 56 04."

She felt René nudge her.

"Can you repeat that Monsieur, please?"

He did.

"It matches the report of the stolen black Peugeot," said René.

"So you made this man," said Aimée, "a key for a stolen car?"

Why would Vaduz get a key made? If he was planning on a long trip it would be easier with keys!

"Did I know that?" Irritation sounded in

Piot's voice. "People lose keys all the time. Most of the time they run into the *tabac* for Gauloise and leave them on the counter or drop 'em down the sewer, five minutes from their house. They end up spending a couple hours trying to get back in."

"Please tell me how long he was in here," she said.

"Let's see, the first fit didn't work," he said. "Then I had to refit the shank, since those older Peugeots have a different ignition system . . ."

Aimée tried to keep her booted feet from tapping . . . why couldn't he hurry up?

"Looks like, aaah, now I remember," he said. "After I tried that I watched the rest of *Dr. Zhivago,* you know the scene years later when Zhivago sees Lara. But he falls down with a heart attack . . . and he was right there and she didn't see him?"

"What time, Monsieur Piot?" asked René.

"Until midnight, I'd say. Then he drove off."

All the way back in René's car, she sat hunched over, trying to imagine the streets and people. Flashes of light blinked every so often in the gray haze before her eyes, and she realized it must be the globes from the streetlights.

Was this progress? Shades of light and dark? Hope sputtered in her. What if her sight returned? She pushed that aside. No time to think about that now.

At least they had proof Vaduz was in Porte la Chapelle at midnight. Even if he U-turned and went to Bastille, it would have taken him a while to cross the eastern part of Paris. No matter what Barzac might say, the *flics* would take a bonded locksmith's word over a drug dealer's.

But she knew that something stared her in the face and she couldn't see it. Literally or figuratively.

"We're missing something, René," she said. "Like Piot said, it's right there but we don't see it."

SATURDAY

Aimée sat in the clinic in l'hôpital Quinze-Vingts hugging her bag. The rustle of magazine pages amid frequent calling of patient names from the reception indicated efficiency. To her it also said impersonality.

She fingered the hem of her leather miniskirt, tugged it down, and felt for the zipper. Good, it was on the side, where it should be. She couldn't stand the waiting, the doing nothing. And the darkness.

After last night, everything made her edgy. She figured the attacker would strike again to get Josiane's phone and finish the job. He'd be stupid not to.

The *flics* continued to do nothing. And she wondered again why Bellan hadn't called.

"Leduc, Aimée," said a loud voice over the scratchy speaker. She was gripped by the elbow.

"Come this way," said a young woman.

Blasts of dry heat hit her legs as they walked down a corridor echoing with footsteps, conversations, and doors whooshing open and closing.

"I'm Dr. Reyaud, the retinologist," a man said.

"But I thought Dr. Lambert . . ."

"Let's see what we have here," said Dr Reyaud, guiding her to what felt like a smooth plastic chair. "He referred you to me."

Without telling her?

"But he hasn't . . ."

"Have a seat," he said.

She felt a glowing heat on her eyelid.

"What's that?"

"Don't worry, mademoiselle, this won't hurt."

His patronizing tone bothered her.

"Did you see the MRI results, Doctor?" she asked.

"Machines show us some details, but not everything," he said. "Deciphering the brain's architecture takes time."

"Does that mean my retina's involved?"

"Like I said, we see the damage but not necessarily the immune defenses and healing process battling it."

No, he hadn't said. But he wasn't saying much.

"Dr. Lambert wants to run more tests . . ."

"I've taken over your case," said Dr. Reyaud. "He has transferred your file to me."

A sinking feeling came over her.

She'd made a fool of herself the other night with Dr. Lambert. Guy, as he'd wanted her to call him. Must have drank more than she'd realized. But he'd seemed amenable. More than amenable when he'd kissed her.

Dumb. She'd scared him off. Or had he scared himself off, wary of obligation?

He'd tried to be nice, that's it. Got carried away and realized on his way home. Doctors didn't get involved with patients. Who cared? Not she.

"Doctor, my vision came back," she said. "Not very clearly or for long. Last night I saw light and dark. But I did recognize things."

"That's quite common with trauma to the optic nerve," he said. "Does your vision flicker in and out?"

She nodded. All the blinking sparks and pepper-like fog must mean bad news. "Doctor, will things get worse . . . can the inflammation affect other parts of my brain?"

She heard metal scratch. His stethoscope against his name badge. She felt him take her hand in his. They were large and warm.

"Mademoiselle, you're young, healthy and strong-willed, according to your chart and from what I hear from Dr. Lambert," he said. "There's so much going for you. No one can predict the future. But let's try a new anti-inflammatory medication, see if it reduces the swelling more effectively. Schedule your next appointment for Monday."

By Monday she could be dead. And that wasn't her depression speaking.

An older nurse guided her to pick up her prescription. By the time she'd made it back to Madame Danoux's, she felt so tired and dispirited that she fell asleep.

She woke up to a chill in the room. It must be evening. Blind people must save a lot on their energy bill since they used so little electricity for light, she reflected.

Then, from outside the window, she heard a church bell strike twelve. Only noon.

What if the Romanian had an arrest record, but it was sitting on someone's desk? Or had been filed with the morning reports, like so many of the backlog cases. Over-worked *flics* got to them when they had desk time. She knew they always aimed to clear their desks by noon.

She had to do something until she could check with Martin. That wouldn't be for hours. She called the Commissariat again, asked for the records department.

"Lieutenant Égérie? I'm Aimée Leduc. My father worked with you."

Pause. She heard raised voices in the background, like an argument.

"So you're Jean-Claude's daughter!"

Égérie, whose name meant *muse,* suffered teasing because of it. He'd been the dispatcher on her father's shift. A tall man, thin as a rail, he lived with his mother. He had a prominent Adam's apple that bobbed when he talked, which had fascinated her as a little girl. Sometimes, in the Commissariat, after school when the others were busy he'd bend his double-jointed fingers and do amazing tricks.

"I remember when you got those roller-skates, not like the ones they have today," said Lieutenant Égérie. "The wheels came off . . ."

"And you were the only one who could fix them," she said, "everyone else was helpless. Just like now."

He laughed. "Still the same. But you're not asking me for help now, are you?"

She told him about Dragos.

"Let me see," he said, his voice tired, "we're down four investigating officers due to flu. They've pulled staff for the explosives case. Everyone here's doing double shifts."

Funny, Morbier hadn't told her that.

"Of course, just thought I'd ask," she said. "What explosives?"

"Very hush-hush," he said. "I haven't heard much."

And he usually did.

"I'll sniff around for you on Dragos. No promises."

She hung up. And for a moment, thoughts of Dr. Guy Lambert crossed her mind. She wondered if he'd watched the sunrise this morning. For half a franc, she'd call and ask him what colors had painted the dawn.

But he'd referred her to another doctor. And hadn't even told her. Forget him.

A minute later she dialed his office.

"Dr. Lambert's in a meeting," the receptionist told her.

"Please have him call me . . ." she paused. This was about her health, not about some silly kiss after several drinks that he regretted. A delicious kiss. Of course, he'd done the classic French naval manuever . . . made for the target, then veered off and run. "This concerns my MRI results."

And it struck her again . . . did his opinion matter? She feared the worst. The retinologist hadn't even responded to her queries.

Chantal and Lucas led full, active lives, adapting and managing without sight. She could learn to live with the darkness. Even if she didn't want to. Even if it wasn't fair. Even if the man who caused it was still out there somewhere.

And she would.

She had to keep telling herself that.

She'd never saddle René with a whining, awkward burden. That's if he would still want to work with her. She'd have to organize her life, adapt her apartment and the office, learn Braille, train Miles Davis to cope. And pay her bills.

But first she had to find out who was after her, before they came calling again. And deal with Vincent's predicament, as she'd promised René.

She booted up her laptop and opened the Populax file one more time. Checked each entry pertaining to Incandescent, the gun-running firm Vincent had unwittingly represented. After two tiring hours of examining data via the robotic screen reader, she felt convinced Vincent had honored the marketing duties outlined in his standard short contract.

Why would he fear showing his clean laundry in public? Why had he torn up their contract?

Curious, she delved further, checking his e-mail. Then his deleted e-mail. Common thinking was if you deleted e-mail it was erased from the hard drive. But that was true only if you didn't know where to find it. Once written or received, nothing left the hard drive.

After reading Vincent's e-mails, she concluded that he was having an affair. A very hot one, almost worshipful in tone, with someone called Inca.

If it was exposure of these e-mails that bothered him, she'd ask René, see if he thought they could have a word with *la Proc.* Try and work out a deal citing the intimacy factor. They'd done it before and saved face for a few of their clients.

When she was about to end her search, the robotic voice said "Unable to read encrypted e-mail file."

Startled, she sat back, alarms sounding in her brain.

Vincent had encrypted part of his e-mail! That bothered her. Why just some of it, not all?

She checked the date. A Friday. René picked up all client backup tapes on Friday mornings. A routine. And then it occurred to her that Inca . . . might be short for Incandescent . . . or someone who worked there.

Was Vincent having an affair with someone at Incandescent? Had he wanted to withhold the hard drive because of an affair with an employee . . . an employee in a company being investigated?

She wondered if René's standard backup files would display the e-mail before it had been encrypted. A long shot, she figured, but worthy of scrutiny. Otherwise she'd ask René for software to crack the encryption. But depending on the code, and with her handicap, it would take time. Longer than they had.

She rummaged in the laptop carrying case, feeling for the velcro tabs holding the tapes, assuming they were where she hoped René kept them.

Sun beat down on her leg, warm and lush for October. A nice break from the rain.

From somewhere in the apartment, a parakeet's song trilled.

Below, a Frexpresse delivery man announced his arrival with a shout from the courtyard. "Delivery!"

What she wouldn't do right now for an espresso and a cigarette! Yet she wasn't up to navigating Madame Danoux's kitchen, redolent of bay leaf, without any help. It would be as daunting as negotiating the Métro platform without a white cane.

Twenty minutes later, after much experimentation, she found the right Populax backup files. They had an extensive batch, since Vincent had been a client for several months. After another two tries, she found the tape.

The robotic voice enunciating the contents of Inca's hot e-mails was almost funny. But something nagged her. Why hadn't Vincent told her? Or had he been embarrassed because she would know the recipient?

She put that thought aside to follow up later.

After Inca's torrid e-mail correspondence came a series of innocuous messages from Popstar. The subject read *Marmalade tea.* Then she deciphered:

Call 92 23 80 29 for a good time.

Why encrypt this sort of thing? Something

smelled off. Way off.

She decided to check each detail; she reprogrammed the software. Now the robotic voice read each word of the e-mail header. Her system had trace route capability, so she converted the e-mails' IP address by using a DOS command line and pinging the name which came back as a number: 217.73.192.109.

This pinging, as it hopped on the IP's traceroute, indicated how many servers the e-mail had gone through. She figured if she listened long enough, she'd hear a pinging symphony.

Excited, she kept going. After twenty hops, it landed.

243ms 246ms 239ms head.rambler.ru

ru . . . the origin of the message was Russia.

She sat back, surprised. And tried several more. Every time it went back to the same server in Moscow. That made sense. Even though the Wall had fallen and the Soviet Union disintegrated, she knew Big Brother in Moscow still looked at all e-mail. They probably hadn't enough money to change their system.

Yet.

Now she had to figure out why Vincent was getting spam-like e-mail from Russia that he kept encrypted. Was he the intended recipient? Was it going first to someone else?

The phone rang. Josiane's phone.

She hesitated then answered.

"Allô?"

"I've just got a minute," Lieutenant Egérie said. "This came across my desk."

She picked up an unusual, tense note in his voice.

"I appreciate it."

"In the process of being charged, a man became ill," Lieutenant Égérie said. "A Dragos Iliescu."

That was the name Yann Rémouze had given to René. She held back her excitement.

"Where's he now?"

"Hôtel Dieu, but he's due to be charged with drug trafficking in the 11ième."

"Merci."

The Hôtel-Dieu, on Île de la Cité between Notre Dame and quai des Orfèvres, supposedly dated from Druid times. However, Aimée's lycée teacher had insisted it was only from Emperor Julien II's era. And her parish priest had cited Saint-Landry, the bishop of Paris in A.D. 600, as the builder of this hospital for the needy.

Any of them were good enough for her.

She knew how to circumvent the Hôtel

Dieu switchboard, archaic, but still functioning.

"Bonjour," she said. "I'm calling on Commissaire Morbier's behalf about prisoner Iliescu."

The woman at the other end of the line coughed; papers rustled. "Let me transfer you to the ward nurse."

Clicks and buzzing accompanied her call.

"Ward 13C," said a brisk voice.

"Checking on prisoner Dragos Iliescu. The Commissaire's interested in his health status."

"So he's a doctor now, your Commissaire?"

"Not in this life," said Aimée, trying to inject a world-weary tone in her voice as if she did this every day, "but he wants to know if this Iliescu's healthy enough for arraignment."

"Let me check," she said. "Aaah, that one. Transferred from CUSCO to intensive care."

CUSCO was the prison section of Hôtel Dieu.

"Can you elaborate? Why?"

"He needs twenty-four hour care and supervision," she said.

What was wrong with him?

"Sounds serious. Want to share it with me

so I can give my boss a time-frame here? Two days, a week, or . . ."

"Third degree burns, high fever, nausea," the sister said. "Hard to say."

"Burns?" she asked, perplexed.

"Like he'd been on vacation, but only his arm got sunburned. Bizarre, eh?" she said. "Time for rounds, excuse me."

Bizarre.

From the window, Aimée felt the Seine-scented breeze waft inside. If only she could take Miles Davis for a walk right now along the quai.

If only.

But food and rent weren't paid with *if onlys.* She had to move on.

And then she thought about what René had recounted to her after his conversation with Mathieu, the *ébéniste,* in the passage. She had some questions; it was time for her to visit him.

"I appreciate your taking me, Chantal," Aimée said.

"No problem," said Chantal, "It's on my way to the Braille library on Avenue Parmentier. I work there this afternoon."

"Work?"

"What people do to earn money, yes," she said. "I supervise the reading room."

Aimée felt Chantal's dry hand on her elbow, guiding her. And the uneven cobbles beneath her feet. She didn't want to admit how afraid she felt. How vulnerable to attack.

But talking with Cavour could give her information about Josiane.

Or not.

But she had no one else to ask.

"You know, there's a Braille beginning class starting next week. Two nights a week, an accelerated class."

Aimée thought about all the CDs she wanted to hear. And how if she put off learning Braille, it would just get harder.

"Sign me up, Chantal," she said, anxious to arrive.

"Fine. We're almost there," said Chantal. "Feel the wall, how it curves; it's the way medieval entrances were built."

Aimée's hands, guided by Chantal's, felt the pocked, cold stones, the crumbling pebblelike mortar in between. Grayish film swam in front of her eyes, coarse and grainy. Like ground pepper. Her heart skidded. Was she seeing what she was feeling?

"Dr. Lambert's referred me to a retinologist," she said. "Why couldn't the geek have done it in the first place?"

"Geek . . . are you kidding?" she said.

"Everyone says he's . . ."

"*Pardon,* madame et mademoiselle," said a quavering voice near them.

Aimée slid the sunglasses up on her head. And for a moment, a glint of silver hair flashed in front of her, superimposed on the pepperlike film. But there was no depth. No distinction between close or far.

The world tilted. Dizziness overwhelmed her. She grabbed at the wall, pressed her forehead against the cold stone, gray and furred with lichen. Ecstatic to see, and yet so dizzy.

"*Alors,* Aimée, I must hurry," said Chantal. "I have to open the reading room."

"But Chantal . . ."

"Mathieu, Mathieu!" said Chantal, interrupting her, pulling Aimée along.

She felt as though she'd stepped into a Dalí painting. No depth of field, everything pasted together. Colors colliding. Weaving and wonderful and surreal and sickening.

She picked a point and tried to focus, but every stone, each bar of woven grille work, disoriented her. Her nose brushed the wall, yet she'd had no idea how close she was.

Her head ached. She wanted so much to see and so much to close her eyes.

And then it began fading. Fading. Images of a hammer, and a man in a wavy, blue workcoat, coming in and fading out . . . a gauze-like haze hovered, never quite lifting.

The man's mouth was moving in the haze, he was saying "Chantal . . ." The granular film descended, succeeded by gray mist.

"No, no," she said, rubbing her eyes, trying to rub the film away.

But Chantal didn't answer. Nor did the man. Silence, except for the birds singing in the distance. She realized they'd entered Mathieu's atelier. And there had been large chairs hooked on the walls and gilt frames stacked against tables. She'd seen it. Work-worn, real. Good God, she'd seen it!

She felt a tentative hand on her shoulder.

"Mademoiselle, *ça va?*"

And she realized her face was wet. Tears streamed down her cheek.

"I'm sorry," she said, rubbing them away. The vision had been so brief. So beautiful. Her body quivered. "Forgive me. Your atelier's wonderful."

"But it's a mess!" he said, his voice edged with amusement. "The only other person it's brought to tears was myself when I was twelve and forbidden to go to the cinema until I cleaned all the solvents my dog spilled. A long, tearful process."

A cloth was pressed in her hand.

"Please, take the handkerchief."

She wiped her face, rubbed her nose. "I forgot about . . . rocks, tools, the hue of fabrics, how things glint and catch the light."

She shook her head, put her fist over her streaming eyes. "Forgive me. I saw an old woman's silvery hair, your mouth moving, your face . . ." She turned away, trying to get hold of herself.

"You shame me," he said, his voice saddened.

"I'm sorry," she said.

"*Non.* How I think nothing of my sight and my hands, mademoiselle," he said. "Hearing you humbles me. You're too young. It's not right."

The finches sang in his courtyard. Water gurgled from what sounded like a fountain, and the scent of honeysuckle wafted inside.

She could never forget seeing sunrise over the Seine, how the first peach violet light stained the roofs, skylights, and the pepperpot chimneys, or the Seine's green mossy quai, the brass doorknockers shaped like hands that invaded her dreams. Just one more time she wanted to trace the dewed veins of a glossy camellia leaf, see the tip of Miles Davis's wet black nose and his button eyes. The memories passed before her; her father's smile, the signature carmine red lipstick her mother had used, her grandmother's worn accordion strap.

Get a grip, she told herself. She turned to where she thought Cavour stood. Again, she wished her emotions hadn't gotten the upper hand. She had to salvage this visit, find out if the *ébéniste* knew anything. Better to deal with her emotions in private.

She ran her fingers along the rough wood counter permeated with smells of turpentine, wood stain, and sawdust. Her hands touched a handle. Then what felt like a rectangular plane with wood shavings curling on it.

"Attention!" said Mathieu.

Too late. She'd knocked it to the floor. Things clanged and clattered by her feet.

"I'm so sorry. What did I spill?" she said stooping down and feeling with her hands to locate whatever she'd knocked down. She had visions of having ruined a priceless piece. "I'm so clumsy!"

She felt a cold slick sheet of . . . alumininum? No. Too dense and stiff for that.

"Forgive me." Guiltily she tried to pick up whatever her hands touched. They slid beside what felt like a long, round-edged salt shaker. But something was attached to it, like a panel.

"Let me help," he said, taking things from her hands.

"You work in metal, too?"

She heard him grunt, then his hands taking things from hers. "Once in a while."

She marshaled what grace she could and climbed her hands up the worktable leg. Helpless and awkward again.

"If I broke something, let me replace . . ."

"No harm done," he said. "Don't worry."

She felt even more awkward, but had to find out if he knew anything.

"My partner René spoke with you about the attack on me."

"So it's you," he said. "The one hurt in the Passage, *non?*"

"Oui."

"I didn't help you," he said. "I am sorry . . ."

But could he have helped? Suspicion crossed her mind. The police had questioned him. But would he have attacked her in front of his own workshop?

It was Josiane who had been the target . . . everything pointed that way. And the police had let him go.

What if he had witnessed something he was unaware of?

"Tell me what you remember, Mathieu," she said.

"The old lady you passed, the one whose hair you saw," he said, his tone wistful. "I caused her to be hurt, too."

Why did he sound so guilty?

She sensed he'd gone down another track. Again, in her mind she saw his blue work coat, the way his mouth moved, and his hands caressing the wood chair.

That's what she'd forgotten. The more she thought, the more briefly glimpsed images came back to her. The way he'd touched the wood, the atmosphere in the atelier, his obvious love of his craft.

How did it come together? The attack on her in the passage, Josiane's murder, the Romanian thugs, Vincent, and Mathieu's atelier? How could it? Yet somehow, in her gut, she knew it did.

Her brief moment of vision illumined her sense of Mathieu, and she was thankful. Intuitively, she knew he was a good man. But good men make mistakes, like bad men, like everyone.

"Look Mathieu, try to remember where you were when you heard. . . . Had you seen Josiane?"

"Josiane loved the Bastille," he said. "She spearheaded our association to save this historic *quartier.*"

That piece fit in the puzzle.

"So could you say Mirador was alarmed by her investigative reporting?"

"I don't know."

"Would Mirador encourage her to reconsider her article on the evictions? Or hire thugs to threaten her?"

Only the finches chirped in response.

"We can keep it between us, Mathieu," she said. "Mathieu?"

"Since when do you have such pretty visitors, Mathieu?" said a man's voice behind her.

Aimée stiffened. She knew that voice.

"Monsieur Malraux," said Mathieu.

"No wonder the piece isn't ready, eh. A nice distraction to occupy you."

Was there an edge in the man's tone?

But she heard a warm, slow laugh.

"I like to tease him, mademoiselle," he said. "He hardly ever gets out, shuts himself up with his work."

"Let me check for you," said Mathieu. His voice receded along with the clop of wooden clogs — *sabots* her grandmother had called them — over the floor.

"What brings you here, Mademoiselle Leduc?" asked Malraux.

Now she remembered. She thought fast. "Trying to solicit a donation for the Résidence, Monsieur Malraux, just as we are from you trustees."

Again that nice laugh.

"*Bon,* but you could have asked me to intercede with Mathieu. I'd be more than happy to help you. Don't tell Chantal, let's keep it between ourselves for now, eh, but I've got her a van."

"That's wonderful!" Aimée turned to his voice. But he was moving. She tried tracking him and then gave up. Too much work. She pulled her dark glasses on. "Chantal will be thrilled."

"I really feel I should be doing more," he said. "Especially after Chantal explained how vital these programs are. She's a wonder, that woman: working, volunteering. Never stops."

Aimée felt a pang of guilt. What a caring man. . . . So what if he was an Opéra patron, well-connected and wealthy? Unlike most of those social climbers, he shared, helping those less fortunate. A rarity.

"Chantal's wonderful," said Aimée. "She teaches me a lot."

"Matter of fact, just between us, I'm getting two vans donated," he said. "My cousin's father-in-law's a Renault dealer in Porte de Champerret."

That's how it worked. Through connections. Her friend Martine would no more consult the Yellow Pages in the phone book than eat food off the floor. It wasn't done.

One went through a friend or a work colleague or a great-aunt's cousin, in the time-honored tradition. Probably unchanged since feudal times.

Malraux rose higher in her estimation. Favors begat favors. Now he'd owe the donor.

Where was Mathieu?

A gust of damp, subterranean air encompassed her. Accompanied by a strong scent of paint.

"Have you commissioned a work from Mathieu?" she asked, turning her head and hoping she faced him. Sun from an overhead skylight warmed her. Was it her imagination or did pale haze creep from the corners of her vision?

"Indirectly. My client needs a special *vernissage* on a piece."

She liked the smooth cadence of Malraux's voice. Imagined what he might look like. Tall, well-built. She figured he paid attention to detail.

And then her mind went back to Vincent. He obsessed over detail. But Vincent was short and bursting with nervous energy. While Malraux projected an aura of effortless charm in dealing with people and projects . . . like an *aristo,* someone to the manor born. Or maybe that mode of operating was *de rigueur* in the art world.

Vincent . . . could he have . . . ?

"So, of course, I come here," Malraux was saying. "Mathieu's one of the few left who know this *vernissage* technique."

Malraux seemed very sure of his status, something she sensed Vincent craved. A hunger coloring all his efforts.

She heard the clop of wooden sabots up the stairs.

"I'm sorry, but the last layer of lacquer won't be dry until tomorrow," said Mathieu. "Not today."

"But they must pack . . . well, the back-stage prop manager told me he's loading the container this evening."

So Malraux was having a piece fixed for the Opéra? But he'd said for a client. If the client was the Opéra, she wondered, did Malraux know Vincent?

Mathieu's voice cut in on her thoughts.

"Linseed oil takes time," said Mathieu. "You know it's not always possible to predict the drying rates in changeable weather. Especially these past few days."

"But this needs . . ."

"The work will be ruined," Mathieu asserted. "It's still wet."

Something in Mathieu's voice was strained. Was it because he had to refuse

Malraux's demand? But it wasn't only that. She heard an underlying tension. Was Mathieu stressed about Josiane?

"Excuse me," said Malraux. "I'm late for the Opéra board meeting. Mademoiselle Leduc, I've enjoyed talking to you. Hope to see you again."

She heard footsteps, then the door shut. Aimée was wondering at Mathieu's silence when the phone in her pocket rang. Josiane's phone. The one she'd been attacked for.

"Allô?"

"Where are you?" said René, his voice raised. In the background she heard klaxons blaring.

"In Mathieu's shop in the passage."

"I found Dragos's bag," he said, his voice vibrating with excitement.

"Dragos's bag?"

"No, I stole it," said René. "I've never stolen anything in my life!"

Aimée realized Mathieu was beside her, silent.

"Go on, René."

"You have to see this," he said. "I can't describe it over the phone."

"Slight problem, René," she said. "I can't see."

"Get your white cane, come out to rue

Charenton in three minutes."

Her heart thumped. She didn't want to walk there. Again.

"I don't have a cane."

"Why not?"

"A dog's better."

She didn't want to admit she'd refused the white cane. Pride had prevented her from learning how to use one. Stupid. Face it. She needed one now.

"The Citroën's too wide to get by the construction. My God, Aimée, it's a medieval passage. Come out in two minutes, you've got less than fifty meters to walk."

Her head hurt. Her brief period of sight with no depth perception, the resulting lack of balance had disoriented her. But she gathered her bag, thinking back to the layout she'd seen. Unease lingered in her mind. She didn't want to ask Mathieu for help.

All she could think of was that awful choking. No air. Having to walk there alone, again. Her hands went to the dressing still on her neck, covered by a scarf.

"Excuse me, Mathieu," she said. "My partner's waiting."

Mathieu guided her to the door. She refused his offer of further help. She stretched her hands out, felt the cold stone, and took small steps, guiding herself along the wall.

The passage felt much warmer than on the night she'd been here. Noises of trucks, the chirp of someone's cell phone, and the smell of espresso came from somewhere on her left.

Something gnawed at her. Stuck in the back of her mind. But what was it? Immersed in the fear and frustration of blindness, had she missed details . . . important ones?

Now it all came back: the dankness from the lichen-encrusted pipes, the dark sky pocked with stars, the cell phone call's background noise, the tarlike smell of the attacker.

She felt sick . . . had it been Mathieu? Had he thought she was Josiane?

"René?" she said, hearing the familiar Citroen engine.

"Door's open."

She smelled the leather upholstery he'd oiled and polished. And what smelled like fresh rubber latex.

"Put these gloves on and feel this." She felt René thrust latex gloves in her lap, then what felt like a glass tube.

The car shuddered as he took off down the street.

"Wait . . ." She wanted a cigarette. And for the fireworks to subside in her head. Her pills. She'd forgotten to take them. She found the pill bottle inside her pocket, uncapped it, and popped two pills. Dry.

"Let's stop. I need water and a pharmacy." As the Citroën sped down cobbled streets, Aimée was glad for the smooth suspension.

René pulled up at the curb. "Here's a pharmacy. Let me . . ."

"I'll manage," she said, feeling her way on the sidewalk. "How many steps to the door?"

But the doors opened automatically. Pharmacy smells and warm air enveloped her. Now if only she could find the tar shampoo. The one the attacker smelled of. She took small steps and listened for voices.

"May I help you, mademoiselle?" said an older woman.

"Water, please," she said. She smelled floral bouquet soap. "Am I near the shampoo?"

"Keep going, end of the aisle, on your right."

Aimée felt slick plastic bottles, smooth boxes, and more perfumed smells. Not what she looked for.

"Madame, what about the medicinal shampoos?"

"Here's your water," the woman said, grasping Aimée's hand, putting a cold bottle in it. "Right here. Which one would you like?"

She craned her neck forward, sniffing the boxes. Both rows. And then she smelled it. "This one. What's it called?"

"Aaah, super-*antipelliculaire* shampoo. This one really fights dandruff. Tar-based. It's the most effective."

"*Merci,* madame." She paid for the water and shampoo and edged her way back to René's car.

"What was all that about?" asked René.

"Whoever attacked me has dandruff," she said. "And uses this shampoo."

"Him and thousands of others," said René.

"It's a start," she said. "How often does it say to shampoo?"

"Once a week, but for increased effectiveness, every three days," said René.

"Then he's about due if he's conscientious."

She dialed Morbier's line.

"Commissaire Morbier's attending a refresher training course in Créteil," said the receptionist.

So he'd gone. What about that explosives case he'd mentioned? He'd always said he was too old a dog to learn new tricks.

Didn't he care? Deep down she'd thought maybe he'd . . . what? Give up his caseload and devote himself to her? That wasn't Morbier.

Morbier always struggled with his emotions. Even when her father died. He'd avoided seeing her in the burn hospital after the explosion.

And though she wasn't surprised, it had hurt.

What more could she do?

She wanted to avoid faxing their information about Vaduz to Bellan. Too many prying eyes in the Commissariat. Maybe he wasn't back yet from Brittany? Lieutenant Nord had promised he'd call her.

Right now she had to concentrate on what René wanted to show her.

"Why don't we check Dragos's bag?"

René parked at tree-lined Place Trousseau. Aimée rolled down the window of his Citroen. A police siren reverberated in the distance; the gushing of water and the noise of plastic rakes scraping over the stone sounded in the background.

She inhaled the soft, autumn air tinged by dampness. Sounds of crackling leaves and a dog's faint bark reminded her of why she loved this time of year.

"What does the bag look like, René?"

"Dirty natural canvas, D.I. stitched on the inside of the flap," he said. "Long strap. You know, the ones people drape around themselves on motorcycles."

Common and available everywhere. She pulled the latex gloves on, finger by finger, an arduous process. It reminded her of when she was little and her grandfather insisted she put her winter mittens on by herself. Never mind that she couldn't see where her fingers were going.

"Tell me what you see," she said.

"Better yet," said René. "Open your hands."

"No guessing games."

Too late. Again she felt a long, glass-hard tube. Then another. "Feels like a beaker. From a laboratory. Any markings?"

"Just worn red lines indicating measurements."

She smelled a cloth exuding stale sweat.

"Can you describe this?"

"That's a bandanna, here's some used Métro tickets, a stick of cassis chewing gum," said René, "a roll of black masking tape and a flyer for the Chapel of the hôpital Quinze-Vingts."

"Does the flyer have a map?"

"*Non,* but isn't the Chapel on the right of

the hospital as you enter?"

Now she remembered. She'd seen it, rushing by in the rain, parallel with the disused Opéra exit. The Chapel was tall, medieval-walled. In the centime-sized courtyard before the Chapel, large blue doors led to rue Charenton. A shortcut to Vincent's office.

But the doors had been locked. So, in the pouring rain, she had kept on to the hôpital entrance, the remnant of the Black Musketeers' barracks, surmounted by a surveillance camera.

Her thoughts spun. So easy for someone, if they had a key, to avoid the main portal. Or to jimmy the lock mechanism and avoid the surveillance camera.

"Why would Dragos have this flyer? You wouldn't suppose a thug for hire and dope seller would be religious."

"Says here one of the first French cardinals has a crypt there," he said. "The holy water font was commissioned by the nuns of the Abbaye Royale de Saint-Antoine."

The scratch of the streetcleaner's broom receded in the background. She heard the whirr of the small, green pooper-scooper truck, and exclamations from the pedestrians it dodged on the pavement.

"Could Dragos have killed Josiane? But

346

the man who called spoke without an accent, and he knew her. I'm sure of it," she said. The thoughts spun faster and faster. "If Dragos is newly arrived he'd have a Romanian accent. And the field's specialized. Hired thugs, muscle men, aren't hit men, right? We've been through this before."

"If you say so," said René. "But the Chapel's right there. Dragos could have gone into it on his lunch hour. No, wait, it says here it's only open one Thursday a month for services."

An idea came to her.

"What a perfect place to stash something."

"Stash what?"

"Whatever was in these glass beakers . . . wouldn't it be safer there than on the *péniche?*"

"But how would Dragos get into the Chapel?"

She sat back against the cream-soft leather, let the breeze flutter over her.

"Brault, the architect, knows more than he was telling you, René," she said.

"Shall we pay him a visit?"

"Good idea, partner."

By the time she and René sat in Brault's waiting room, the little light flashes behind her eyes had subsided. The grayish hue had deepened, lightened, fragmented, and then faded out like the snow on a TV screen.

Brault was in a meeting. They waited. Aimée tried Morbier. No answer on his personal line. She left a second message. Then called Bellan. Also, no answer. With her luck they would both be at a retirement party for the Préfet.

She heard René's footsteps. "*Merde,* Brault's crossing the courtyard, I see him from the window. He's trying to avoid us."

"Go ahead, René, I remember the way. I'll catch up."

She felt her hand grabbed, as René ran ahead.

"Trust me, keep up," he said.

She stumbled, awkward and hesitant, to the elevator behind René. Why had she worn her T-strap heels? But the only other pair she had were boots. Just as high-heeled.

On the ground floor, René pulled her along, "Run. We have to stop him before he gets into his car."

Aimée heard a car door slam, an engine start, then a gear whining into first.

"Brault's pointing to his wristwatch," said René, his tone anguished. "I can't believe it, he's driving right by us. He won't stop."

"Oh, yes, he will," she said, waving and stepping off the curb in front of the approaching car. Brakes squealed at the last minute and she felt a bumper dust the hem of her leather skirt. A window rolled down.

"Look, I'm late for a meeting," Brault said irately. The revving of his engine almost drowned out his words.

"Monsieur Brault, you'll be late for a lot more if you don't cooperate," said Aimée. She edged her hands along the car's warm hood. The wind picked up, gusting leaves, a garbage can and what sounded like a clay flower pot striking the stone pavement.

"Threatening me?"

"Where can we talk?"

"I've told him everything I know," Brault said.

"You mean my partner?" she said. Aimée bent down, feeling her way toward Brault's voice. "My partner suspects you withheld information. That's trouble for you, since I feel inclined to name you and your firm in my legal action."

"What legal action?"

"Meet us in the electrical shop in rue Sedaine," she said. "The small one, around the corner from Café de l'industrie, in five minutes."

"Why should I?"

"If I were you, I'd come," she said. "The police want Josiane Dolet's phone. Now that they know Vaduz, the serial killer, had already had a fatal car accident, and couldn't have killed Josiane, they're interested in . . ."

Cars honked behind them.

"That's my boss," said Brault, gunning the engine. "And the administrative staff. Get out of the way."

"Running over a blind woman doesn't look very good," she said. "Any way you put it."

"I know the shop," he admitted, and roared off.

"So I lied," she said, holding René's elbow and trying to keep in step with him over uneven cobblestones.

"Brault's smart," said René.

"Then my lie should get him there."

A buttery lemon smell came from her right where she figured Café de l'industrie stood. She'd frequented the café, enjoyed the unpretentious crowd and simple décor. No *branché* Bastille types here. Turn-of-the-century plates studded the walls. Old wooden tables paired with mismatched chairs. Even a mounted rhinoceros head above the bar.

"Here?" asked René.

"Are we in front of a narrow electrical

shop with fifties irons in the window?"

"Just several old Moulinex vacuums," said René, "like Maman had at home."

"Feels right."

Aimée remembered the shop's worn steps, the iron and rust smell inside, and Medou, Monsieur Fix-it, they called him. His shop was one of the few places left to get an appliance, no matter how old or from what era, repaired. Medou kept cases filled with widgets, wires, and rotary dials. Anything needed to keep one's grandmother's ancient fryer working. Or most anything else.

He'd also been in the Résistance. The rear of his shop connected to an old wallpaper factory, once the meeting site of *La Fiche Rouge* members, a cell of Eastern European Jews active in the Résistance. Two of them had slain a Wehrmacht soldier in the Barbès Métro station. Later they were betrayed, as rumor went, by the Communists in Bastille. The youngest, Maurice Rayman, had been twenty years old.

Now it was a *studio de danse,* replete with buffed ash wood floors, ballet bars, an upright piano, and huge gilt mirrors propped against the walls.

"*Bonsoir,* Monsieur Medou," she said. "Still playing in the *boules* league?"

"I'm too old for bowling, eh, but my

trophy's in the back," he said.

Silence.

"Go ahead, René," she said, gripping his elbow harder, "go where he shows you."

She heard René clear his throat. She'd love to see the look on his face when they entered the dance studio.

"*Merci,* monsieur, our colleague will be joining us."

Her vision field brightened. The skylight must be uncovered. Surprised, she realized how light and dark planes crisscrossed in front of her. Not uncommon, the retinologist had said . . . what was that song . . . a whiter shade of pale?

But worry tugged in back of her mind. Did this, perversely, signal damage? Was this all just a tease?

"How do you know about this place?" asked René.

"Now if I told you, I wouldn't have any secrets, would I?" she said, feeling her way to the wall. "This should convince Brault to unburden himself in total secrecy."

"Says here, hip hop, salsa, tango, and ballet classes offered," said René.

"You might meet someone here at a class, René," she said.

"That's my line to you," said René.

Footsteps, then a muttered curse. Brault

had arrived.

"Blackmail won't work," said Brault. "I'm going to speak with the Commissaire myself . . ."

"Go right ahead," she said, tracking his footsteps and turning that way. "He'll weigh whatever you say against what I tell him. And he's my godfather."

"Who are you?"

"I already told you, the name's Aimée Leduc," she said. "Take a seat, let me explain. There's a chair here somewhere, isn't there?"

She gestured vaguely, heard a chair scrape over the wood.

Then took a deep breath, explained about Josiane, the attack, and her blindness.

Brault stayed silent.

"Tell me," said Aimée, "what's the matter with Dragos?"

"Who knows?"

She detected surprise in his voice.

"Asbestos exposure? Tainted water?" she asked. "Is that it?"

No reply.

"Mirador exposes the workers to unsafe conditions, eh?"

Silence. Then a bird twittered from Medou's shop. And all she could think of was how a caged bird must feel. Caged in darkness.

Back to business. "Look, we need to know," she said, hoping she faced in his direction. She knit her fingers on the ballet barre, to keep her balance. "If Dragos suffers serious health problems, others must be in danger. As a professional, you're obligated to inform those in the area."

"My architecture firm designs for Mirador, that's all."

"Dragos was nabbed selling Ecstasy. He's in Hôtel Dieu, sick as the dog he probably is, with burn marks. Care to comment? And if you don't, I guarantee Commissaire Morbier will be more interested than I am."

"You two don't give up, do you?"

"That's rhetorical, *n'est-ce pas?*" said René. "In fact, we become vicious."

Aimée repressed her smile.

"Whatever I tell you stays off the record. *D'accord?*"

"Of course," said René.

"No asbestos or poison. Nothing toxic at the site, I'm sure. The code's strict and we follow it. After all, the planning commission has to sign off on each job. But I do know that Dragos wanted lead."

"Lead poisoning?"

"Lead." Brault's voice dropped and he sounded tired. "Dragos boasted a lot when he was drunk. He kept saying he could make a profit on lead."

"What did Dragos mean?"

"Beats me."

"How did you know Josiane?"

"Josiane wrote articles for *L'événement* and *Libération,* deploring that all eight Green seats in the European Union had been lost. She wrote pieces on human rights, not popular mainstream themes. I respected her; she wrote what she believed. And she dug for truth. But I don't know what she found, if anything."

"Whatever she found killed her," said René.

"Did Dragos find any lead?"

"No clue," said Brault. "Listen I'm running late . . ."

"But it doesn't make sense to me," said Aimée. "Why would you associate with Josiane if you work for Mirador?"

Brault was full of talk. Good talk. Yet, 10 minutes before he'd been about to run her over.

"I'm an architect. Not a developer," he said. "There is a difference. My goal has been to preserve the *quartier,* however I can, in my own way. Keep the flavor. But in business, sometimes you work with the devil. That's my experience. Mirador's not much worse than the others. At least I thought so at first. Josiane understood she had to protect her sources, that I couldn't be quoted."

Why was he so secretive? Couldn't he just spill it?

"We know about the Romanians evicting old people in the middle of the night . . . What else is there?"

"That's it," he said, seemingly surprised. "Josiane was going to expose this practice of Mirador's. I helped . . . in secret."

Of course. He wanted to have the job, look good, and salve his conscience at the same time. Or was she too hard on him?

"Then what happened? What did Josiane tell you?"

"We were going to meet," he said. "She called me. Sounded excited. But insisted we talk in person."

"Where was that?"

"She never showed up."

"Where and what time was your meeting supposed to be?"

Silence.

"Of course, it's not my business," said Aimée, wishing she could gauge his reaction. "But you were having an affair with her, weren't you? Isn't that what you don't want to admit?"

But she was the one surprised.

"Vincent Csarda was. Not me."

That came off his tongue quickly.

"What do you mean?" asked René.

"Josiane and Vincent were having an affair."

That didn't make sense. If it were true, wouldn't Josiane have spoken with Vincent in the restaurant?

"How do you know this?"

"That's my guess. Somehow in the way he talked, he left me with a sense . . ."

Silence.

"Go on," she said.

"Vincent owed someone," said Brault, his words measured.

"Owed who?"

"I felt from the way Vincent spoke, he was more like a conduit," he said. "And some women like that tortured male type."

"That's news to me," she said. "Weren't you attracted to her? Were you jealous of Vincent?"

A small laugh. "Not me. I go the other way."

Not only had she lost her eyesight, but her touch! Something didn't feel right to her. Didn't "smell" right, as her father used to say.

"You still haven't told us where and when

you were meeting Josiane," said René.

"On rue du Lappe," he said. "Number 24, in a courtyard across from the Balajo."

"Who picked the place?"

"She'd consulted her astrologer," he said. "She always did when she was afraid."

Aimée remembered how she'd chain-smoked and talked nonstop on the cell phone in the restaurant. Like most Parisiens. But Aimée remembered the fear in her eyes.

A gust of air, warmed by the sun, passed by her legs. She heard René clear his throat.

"So let me understand this, Monsieur Brault," said René. "Josiane's writing an exposé about Mirador's practice of hiring Romanian thugs to evict old people from historic buildings. Mirador demolishes them and constructs upmarket buildings. Meanwhile, you sense she's having an affair with Vincent, who's somehow compromised. Dragos shoots his mouth off to you about making a profit on lead and then Josiane calls, saying she has to talk with you in person. But she's a no-show."

"If you put it like that . . . maybe."

"Did she tell you she was having an affair with Vincent?"

"Not in so many words," he said, "but I felt it."

Maybe it was someone else.

"Does Dragos have an accent?" asked Aimée.

"I'm late," said Brault, standing and pushing the chair back. It hit the wall with a dull thud. What sounded like keys jingled in his pocket.

"Does he?" she pressed.

"A thick accent," he said. "Romanian's very close to Latin."

The man calling on Josiane's cell phone had had no accent.

"So what's your connection to Vincent?"

"Vincent organized our ten-year anniversary ad campaign. He's good. The best."

He was. And that always surprised Aimée. Maybe with his clients he sheathed his bristling manner.

"Did Josiane introduce you?"

Silence. "Let me think," he finally said. "Must have been at that party last year. The antique dealer's *hôtel particulier* with the exquisite little theatre."

"Was Dragos there?"

"Why would he be there? As I recall, it was more the limo liberal set we'd mobilized for an Opéra fundraiser."

The set Vincent and Martine reported on in their new magazine.

She tried a hunch.

"Was Malraux there? He's involved with the Opéra."

"But it was his place! He's an Opéra patron," said Brault. "A real aficionado! He donates furniture for the sets. That's funny . . . now I remember. Dragos was moving furniture into the courtyard."

The cell phone vibrated in her skirt pocket.

"Allô?"

"Guess I'm popular, Leduc," said Morbier, "you've tried to reach me several times."

"I found proof."

"Proof of what?"

Footsteps walked by her and Brault muttered something that sounded like goodbye or good riddance, she wasn't sure which.

"Vaduz didn't kill Josiane Dolet," she said.

"Leduc, you still stuck on that?"

"Like glue," she said. "René will leave an envelope containing proof with Bellan, who closed the case too soon."

Silence.

"What's wrong, Morbier?"

"All I want to do is retire. Keep my pension intact. Stay on speaking terms with colleagues I've worked with for most of my life."

"Why wouldn't you, Morbier?" She didn't

like the way the conversation was heading. A bad taste formed in her mouth.

"Leduc, I've been checking into your story. On my own," said Morbier. "But the creek's run dry. No leads. I'm sorry."

Another apology from Morbier? Amazing. At least he'd been trying.

"What if her lover called her," she said, "then killed her, using the Beast of Bastille guise."

"I like that. Shows malice and premeditation. Everything we need for the Judiciare," said Morbier. "The department would look better, the public would forgive us. It's nice." He blew a gust of air into the phone. "But I'm afraid it's too pat. You were hit on the head too many times, Leduc."

"I have Josiane's phone," she told him.

If he was surprised his voice didn't show it. "That's evidence. Why haven't you turned it over?" he said. "Give me a good reason not to nab you for witholding evidence."

"A cheap phone with a phone card?" she said. "The only numbers on her speed dial are an architect, her astrologer, and a doctor at the Nuclear Office in Taverny."

"Taverny?"

"He's away. You'd find more in her apartment overlooking Marché d'Aligre."

"But we didn't," said Morbier.

He'd dole out information to her bit by bit. Make her work for it. Like he always did.

In the background, Aimée heard voices. Phones rang. "BRIF," someone answered.

Her shoulders stiffened. Realization flooded over her. No wonder Morbier moved around. "You're with the explosives division. Terrorism. You never went to Créteil for a seminar."

"I can't say anything, Leduc," he said, with a big sigh. "Go talk to Bellan. Give him your info."

Instead of satisfaction at Morbier's words, her heart sank.

"Look, Morbier —" she said, but he'd hung up.

She shook her head. What was wrong with him?

The phone rang.

"Don't hang up on me like that . . ."

"But I didn't," interrupted Dr. Lambert.

"I'm sorry," she said, surprised.

"Who would hang up on you?" Was that irritation in Lambert's voice?

"My godfather's good at it," she said. "Look, I know I'm not your patient now, but . . ."

"I referred you because Reyaud's an excellent retinologist," Dr. Lambert said. "He can help you more than I'm able to right now." She heard him take a breath over the phone. "The MRI results weren't conclusive. Sorry, I know you were anxious about them. Take the medication, then I'm sure Reynaud will suggest another MRI."

Her hopes were plunged into limbo again. She had better say goodbye: He was in the business of taking care of others.

"Thanks for telling me," she said. "I won't take any more of your time."

"Reyaud's treating you now," he said. "I'm not. So this is a social call."

Right. She'd embarrassed him and he was being polite.

"Dinner . . ." he was saying. "I know you drink. You eat, don't you?"

"Me?"

Was he asking her out for dinner?

"Try to pick a resto. I'll call you later," he said. "After evening rounds, I've got a consultation, so it's hard to predict just when."

Pause.

"Go ahead," he said. "Hang up on me. You'll feel better."

And she did.

SATURDAY

Loïc Bellan trudged up the wide steps, arguing into his cell phone. "No one's there. The boat's shut. Can't the examining magistrate speed up the search permit?"

"All in good time, Bellan," said the *flic* at the other end. "Keep your phone on."

Along the quai, at the end of a row of plane trees, stood a small café. Grass carpeted the slope up to boulevard de la Bastille. Bellan took a seat on the terrace, ordered a café. No booze, he promised himself.

And he watched the navy blue *péniche*. He'd had worse stakeouts than this. The sun beat on his face, a fountain gurgled behind him, and the soft lap of wavelets against the hulls lulled him. The roar of Bastille lay right behind him, but one would never know it.

He'd brought his girls here once. When a very pregnant Marie had a doctor's appointment and she'd begged him to take the afternoon off. A pang of regret hit him. Why hadn't he done that more often? He'd taken his girls to the science museum at Porte de Villette, then for a slow canal ride all the way here. They'd loved it. So had he.

"Monsieur, monsieur!"

Bellan blinked his eyes. He must have dozed in the sun. No one was there. Or at the boat.

"Monsieur!"

He looked around. A small boy stood partly behind a tree, pointing to Bellan's feet, where a soccer ball lay.

"Please throw it, monsieur," said the boy. "We'll get in trouble if we bother café patrons but . . ."

Bellan lifted the ball, stood and stretched, then walked over to the tree. Three young boys, the oldest no more than 10 years of age, a little *bande* from the *quartier,* eyed him.

"Whose ball?"

"Mine," said a red-faced, tow-headed boy.

"*Bon,* I need some help," said Bellan, sending the ball over the grass with a fancy kick. "You boys know about the boats, about the people who live on them?"

They stared. The red-faced boy caught the ball.

"Ever see anyone go onto that dark blue *péniche?*"

They shook their heads in unison.

"André, Marc, Charles! Lunch!"

Good Catholic names.

"Can't you boys help me?"

They backed away.

"Ask Bidi, he's bigger than us. The shop at number 22," said the red-faced boy.

Then they ran past the trees.

He must be losing his edge. After he paid for the coffee, he walked past the hedge and trees.

Number 22, boulevard de la Bastille was a nineteenth-century apartment building. There was a grocery under a striped awning at street level. Bins of bright green peppers, leeks, zucchini, endive spears, and melons lined the façade. From the doorway, Bellan sniffed the detergent smell of a freshly mopped floor.

"*Attention,* monsieur, it's still a bit wet. May I get something for you?" said a bald older man, wiping his hands on his apron, from behind the cash register.

"Bidi, may I speak with him, please?"

"Of course, he's in the back," the man said and smiled. "Bidi!"

Bellan noticed the narrow shop's crammed shelves. Crammed but neat. Organized. Every available space filled: boxes of pasta, flour, tins of cocoa, vacuum packed coffee, biscuits, chocolate or butter, rice, Nutella, and jars of jam and tomato sauces, boxes of brown sugar, slim flaçons of Provençal olive oil and tarragon vinegar, tins of packed sardines and plastic shrink-wrapped eight-packs of bottled mineral water and Orangina. The small refrigerated section was crowded with milk, yogurt, packaged meat and cheeses: goat, sheep, cow, hard, soft, or semi-soft.

This little miracle of convenience was usually known as the *arabe* — because corner shops open late and on weekends, were usually run by North Africans. They existed all over Paris.

"Alors," said the man. "He gets involved in his work, that boy. Bidi!"

Down the aisle, Bellan saw the back of a young man on his knees, stacking cartons of sea salt. His head bobbed; he wore headphones. Bellan tapped him on the shoulder.

"Pardon."

He turned around and Bellan stiffened in surprise.

A smiling Down syndrome-afflicted boy looked up at him.

"Bidi?"

"Ouai?" he said.

Bellan caught his disappointment before he blurted something he'd regret. What could he get out of *this* boy? A big fat nothing.

"I'm sorry, I thought you might help me, but you're busy," said Bellan, hoping to make a tactful exit.

"Are you shouting because of my head-phones?" Bidi said, his words slow but clear. "I took them off. See." He pointed to them around his neck. "I can hear you."

Had he been shouting? Bellan's next words caught in his throat. "I . . . I . . . some children said you might know something."

Bidi got to his feet, dusted off his knees. *"Ouai,"* he said, nodding his head. He had oval close-set eyes, a small mouth, and freckles. "They told me. Said you looked like a serious man."

Bellan felt perspiration beading his brow. Was it that hot? He opened the top button of his shirt.

"You scared André," Bidi said. "But André's scared a lot."

"Do I scare you?"

Bidi grinned. *"Non.* I like your shirt. My brother has one just the same."

"Merci." Bellan shifted on his feet. Marie had picked the shirt out at Printemps for his birthday.

"The boys said you want to know about the boat. The blue one."

"Why yes, actually I wondered if people live on it, you know. But I suppose you're too far away to see from here . . . ."

"Why?"

"These men . . ."

"Are you a *flic?*"

Bellan nodded.

"A real one?"

Bellan pulled out his picture ID and badge. He didn't know if Bidi could read. "It might be hard to read, but there's my photo."

"I can read. Monsieur Tulles says I'm very careful. Handle things just so. And in straight lines," said Bidi. "Look, I put all the items in order: first by type, then by size, and then . . ."

"Bidi, I'm sure the policeman can see how good your work is," interrupted Monsieur Tulles. He came up to Bidi, put his arm on his shoulder, smiled. "I'm so lucky to have you work here every day."

"*Ouai,* after Madame died, you needed help."

Bellan shuffled, felt excluded. And alone. Something radiated from these two. Something warm and caring that he wasn't part of.

"I wondered, since your shop fronts the quai, if you'd seen men going back and forth?"

"They like feta cheese, pickles, and English soda crackers," Bidi said. He pointed to the next aisle. "Over there."

Bidi's watch alarm sounded. He turned abruptly. "I have to finish working. My job ends in five minutes."

"Talk to the policeman, Bidi, it's fine," said Monsieur Tulles.

"But I haven't finished my work . . ." said Bidi. His brow creased.

"The policeman needs information. And you are very observant, haven't I told you so?"

Bidi's face broke out in smiles. He looked with adoration at Monsieur Tulles. "You are a good man." Bidi looked at Bellan. "Are you a good man?"

Bellan put his head down. Ashamed. "Not very often."

"They are bad men. I know that."

Bellan looked up. "How Bidi?"

"They hurt people."

"Did you see them fight?"

"There was blood on their shirts. I said OMO worked best on stains."

Customers came into the shop and Monsieur Tulles left to wait on them.

"One named Dragos has a ponytail and works at the Opéra," said Bellan. "Know him?"

"I like the singing place. He paid me to bring food."

"Aaah," Bellan nodded. "So he wasn't

sick, then?"

Bidi shook his head. He scratched his muscular arm. "No food's allowed backstage, but he showed me a secret way."

Bellan's eyes widened. Would Dragos Iliescu show this simpleminded boy a secret . . . ? But Bidi wasn't so simpleminded, Bellan grudgingly admitted to himself; it was more complicated. He pushed that out of his mind. Bidi seemed loyal, punctual, and a hard worker. That was how someone once referred to him, after his graduation from the police academy. Like a dog who responded to affection.

"Why did Dragos show you a secret way?"

"To bring his lunch. He didn't like his bosses. He laughed at the big one and said he would show him."

Bidi looked at his watch. "It's time to go. Or I'll be late. Can't be late."

"Will you show me?" asked Bellan, hesitant.

"No time. Later."

Bidi stacked his last box, hung up his apron, slipped on his backpack, and was gone.

"Does he have an appointment?"

"He's a bird watcher," Monsieur Tulles nodded. "Every day at this time he watches the falcons nesting behind the Gare de Lyon clockface."

SATURDAY EVENING

"Let's find where Josiane was meeting Brault," said Aimée.

Out on cobbled rue de Lappé, Aimée gripped René's arm.

The early Saturday evening sounds in a quartier thronged with nightlife flowed around them. Laughter and voices spilled over the narrow street. Young voices, those who'd come into the Bastille for a good time. Later, surly and sullen with drink, they'd straggle home. Get sick in the Métro.

Some rollerbladed with gorilla masks, weaving in formation over the garnet-pink bricks outlining the old Bastille prison. They circled the Bastille column, passing the Café des Phares where patrons debated philosophy and solved the world's problems on Sunday mornings.

The Bastille attracted them as it had since the days of the Bal Musette. Sophisticated ones might attend raves outside Paris in abandoned warehouses. But the tradition continued from the 30s, when movie stars and *aristos* had gone slumming on rue de Lappe. Despite the changing face of the *quartier,* working-class types still danced to the accordion, cheek-to-cheek, and everyone drank.

"Brault said it's down from the Balajo," she said. "What do you see?"

"Number twenty-four's next to bar à Nenette," said René. "There's a wooden door covered with graffiti, leading to a courtyard."

"Let's go visit," she said.

"Attention!" said René.

Too late. Her legs hit a metal marker, short and rounded. She crumpled onto the damp, cobbled pavement. Good thing she'd thrown her arms out and landed on her knees and spread palms.

"Where did that come from?" she asked, rubbing her shin. Her legs must be black and blue all over with the way she'd been bumping into things. She wouldn't have a whole pair of stockings left. Better stick to wearing pants.

"I'm sorry," said René. "Bollards dot the walkway, to prevent cars parking."

She knew in the old days they prevented carriages running into the building.

"These resemble chess pieces, pawns," said René.

That was what she felt like. A pawn in life's game. Advancing from square to square but ending in a stalemate.

She heard the unmistakeable crowing of a rooster from inside.

"Let's go," she said.

Uneven cobbles greeted them. The crowing grew louder and the strains of an organ grinder accompanied it. A pocket of life, unchanged and utterly Parisian, part of the passages and courtyards honeycombing the Bastille.

"Lost your way, monsieur *et* mademoiselle?"

"Er . . . you could say that," said René.

"But you might help us," said Aimée. "Do you make organ grinders here?"

"And the sheet music," said the man who'd offered to help them. "With the holes punched in them so the platen can 'read' the notes."

"Do you know Josiane Dolet? I'm asking because she was meeting a friend here on Monday night."

"I'm sorry, I don't."

"Anyone here who might?"

"Hard to say. A few of us live here. The others work in the ateliers in the day. I'm alone here now."

The clucking of hens came from nearby.

"Who owns the chickens, monsieur?"

"They belong to Ravic, the ironsmith."

"He still works in iron?"

"Mais oui," the man said. "The iron forge stands behind the chicken cages. He's closed today. Gone to his niece's wedding."

"Merci for your help, monsieur."

Another dead end. She turned and tugged René's arm.

They walked past the chickens. Strains from the organ grinder's tinny music rose behind them.

And then it clicked. Of course. She turned back, grabbed René's arm.

"May I ask, monsieur, does Ravic work with lead?"

"All kinds of metal. Not just iron. He supplied me with a lead compound for my new handle. My old one wore out."

"Wouldn't that be heavy?"

"Not that heavy."

Her ears perked up.

"Not that heavy?"

"Ravic uses thin leaded sheets," he said. "Mixed with some alloy, for strength."

"Does he supply craftsmen in the area?"

Silence. Did he shrug or shake his head?

"I'm sorry but I can't see you."

"Mais oui," he said, a chuckle in his voice. "He supplies everyone."

"Merci, monsieur."

Buttery smells wafted from somewhere as

they reached rue de Lappé. René told her to wait, then she felt something warm put in her hand.

"What's this?"

"A Bastille *pavé,* a cobblestone," he said. "At least that's what the boulangerie calls them."

"It tastes more like chocolate pastry," she said. "Delicious."

She clutched René's elbow as they walked, cupping crumbs with her other hand.

"What are you getting at, Aimée?" asked René.

"Do you remember what Brault said about Dragos looking for lead?"

"So what does that mean?"

"I'm not sure, but I need to reach Vincent," she said. "To find out. Let's go call from a café. We'll try another number."

"Vincent Csarda," he answered at the first ring.

"We need to talk, Vincent."

"Impossible. Look, sorry," he said. "Let me call you later."

"This can't wait, Vincent."

"Bad time right now," he said.

"Your bad time's just beginning if we don't persuade *la Proc* to ignore your affair,

Vincent," she said, improvising as she went along.

"What do you mean?" His voice lowered.

"Having an affair is your business except . . ."

"Join the planet, Aimée Leduc," he said. "Get back to reality."

"It's who you had the affair with 'Inca,' " she said.

She heard rustling, as if his hand covered the phone. Murmured speech.

"How do you mean?"

"Kinky, threesome or however Inca liked it," she said. "Short for Incandescent."

"Who?"

"Those hot e-mails make it hard to convince the *Proc* you had no involvement with Incandescent."

"Leave my business alone," he said, his voice brittle. "Our contract has ended."

"And to think, a moment before you apologized!" she said. "But in a court of law, as I told you, we're still responsible. Monday's the court date, René expects the subpoena to issue then."

"I can't talk now."

"Vincent, I've got the software to prove it. And I will. It's personal now."

"What do you mean?" he asked.

Why couldn't he understand? Face it, he

didn't want to understand.

He kept talking. "We just settled our negotiations in Bordeaux," said Vincent. "Those vintners take their time. I kept telling them, backing a business isn't like aging wine. One has to move in a flash. Thank God for Martine. She's saved the magazine."

Hadn't Martine spoken with him?

She took a deep breath. "After you stormed out of the resto, when I was en route to the Métro, someone attacked me. Or maybe you know all about that?"

"What do you mean?"

He sounded surprised.

"Josiane, the woman who sat next to us was killed in the adjoining passage. I'm going to find out who attacked me and murdered her. I've got time, since the attacker blinded me."

The words had tumbled from her. She heard him gasp on the other end.

"You? A murder?" His surprise sounded genuine.

Aimée's reply caught in her throat.

And a terrible thought crossed her mind. She remembered Josiane sitting and smoking at the table adjoining theirs. And her glance their way. Had her look been aimed at Vincent?

"You knew Josiane Dolet, didn't you?"

Silence.

Was that planned . . . had there been some code between them? Or had she been about to speak with him, but thought better of it and agreed to meet him later?

"You killed Josiane."

"You're not making sense," he said, his voice hoarse. "All these allegations about an affair and now . . ."

"She investigated your ties to Incandescent. The money laundering for the gun-running . . ."

"This has nothing to do with that," he said, his voice low, filled with emotion. "Look, Aimée I've been keeping this quiet. One of my friends had a relationship with her. But I'm shocked to learn she's dead."

"Your friend? If you knew her, why didn't you speak to her?"

"But I didn't know her, not to talk to anyway. There's a lot more on my mind than a friend's estranged lover."

"Martine was in Bordeaux, didn't you see her?"

Wouldn't Martine have told Vincent about the attack on her?

"*Tiens! I* prepared the groundwork. Then I just missed her. Alain Ducasse had demanded a correction in the nouvelle cuisine review about to print. Another impending catastrophe. So she flew to Lyon, soothed him, and sweet-talked him out of it. She works miracles, does Martine."

She knew Martine. And she believed him.

Metal clanged in the background and what sounded like knocking, then a door opening.

"I have to go," said Vincent.

"Who killed Josiane?"

"Leave me alone," said Vincent. His voice cracked.

"These Russian e-mails weren't part of the Opéra advertising campaign were they?"

"Russian e-mails?"

"Why did you encrypt them?"

"I don't contact the Russian Opéra or encrypt e-mails," said Vincent. "Why would I?" But his voice slowed, as if weighing his words.

"René made backup tapes," she said. "It's all on there."

"You're *folle!* Out of your mind."

And he hung up. One thing she could say for Vincent, he was consistent; tearing up contracts, walking out, and hanging up on her. But he'd sounded genuinely surprised hearing of the attack on her and of Josiane's murder.

Then what was he hiding? And what

friend's affair had he been shielding?

"Where are we going?" asked Aimée, as they got into the Citroen.

"Vincent's office."

"You want to try to make him reconsider in person?"

"Can't hurt," said René. "His office is on rue Charenton. Close by."

She heard René's turn signals beat a pattern. From outside the window came the revving of cars shifting into first gear.

"He's scared, René," she said. "He says his friend was having an affair with Josiane."

"Two ends of the spectrum, aren't they?"

"These e-mails generated a lot of steam," she said.

"But why would Vincent kill her?" asked René.

Aimée shook her head and regretted it. The sparks behind her eyelids moved.

"The *Proc*'s assistant will meet with us before the hearing on Monday if . . ."

"How will we explain the encrypted Russian e-mails?"

"Russian e-mails . . . is that what you were talking about?"

And she described what she'd discovered among Vincent's deleted e-mails as the car sped along.

"I don't like it," she said. "But when I

confronted him now, he sounded surprised. Denied knowledge of them. And somehow, I believe him."

She heard René inhale. "So someone stole his password?"

René had a good point. She hadn't considered that.

"Or used his computer and logged on with their own. A secretary would know who had access to his office," she said. "But first, let's talk with Vincent, make sure he's being straight with us."

But Vincent wasn't in his office. His secretary said he hadn't returned and didn't know when he would.

"Who has access to Monsieur Csarda's office?" asked René.

"Talk to Monsieur Csarda," said the secretary, irritation evident in her voice. "Excuse me, but we're closing now."

Back in Madame Danoux's apartment, Aimée got on her hands and knees and felt each armchair and cabinet until she found the old record player. Right where Madame Danoux had told her it would be. And Madame's records. Her collection of old songs from the Bastille.

The floor grumbled. She clutched the nearest thing. The leg of a coarse horsehair upholstered divan. She had to calm down, remember it was only the Métro passing below in the bowels of Bastille.

René had gone to copy the morgue log and would leave it in an envelope for Bellan at the Commissariat. She didn't want to get Serge in trouble, so they had to disguise her morgue source.

Right now she wanted to hear music. Find the old Bastille songs. The power button stuck out, like the one in her father's old stereo set. Like on all the phonographs from that time. Her hands traveled over the plastic hood.

She pushed what felt like the turntable switch.

The record dropped onto the turntable. The needle joined it with a soft whisper. A slight crackle, then Jacques Brel's voice soared with *When one only has love to give to those whose only fight is to search for daylight.* The guitar and Brel's words, struck her. Moved her.

The French analyzed him. But it was his own Belgians who knew the gray streets of Brussels that he evoked, the wistfulness of old lovers who meet again.

Too much like the way she felt. She ran her fingers over record jackets, so many, dusty and peeling. In the end she put on the next one that smelled old. She put her index finger on the hole and after trial and error, the disk slipped down the tall, thin record holder.

"Nini peau le chien of the Bastille," Aristide Bruant's turn-of-the-century *chanson* of a third-class streetwalker accompanied by accordions and a scratchy voice.

She froze. That was it . . . the song. The one her grandmother used to play, the song she had heard in the background over the cell phone. The funny title, skin of the dog . . . as a little girl she'd wondered if it meant Nini's complexion or her cheap "fur" wrap.

Her mind raced. The same music was in the background . . . *Nini le peau chien* . . . just like that night.

The doorbell rang. Was it René? Should she answer?

"Who's there?"

"Madame Danoux?" asked a familiar voice.

Surprised, Aimée stood, took small steps, then bumped into the door. She felt for the lock, turned the deadbolt, pulled the door ajar with the chain still on it. Cold, stale air came in from the hallway.

"It's me," said Dr. Guy Lambert. "Can I come in?"

She slid the chain back and let him in.

A warm hand cupped her shoulder. *"Ça va?"*

"Never better," she said, giving him what she hoped was a huge smile. "Madame Danoux's not here."

"But you're the purpose of my visit," he said, taking her hand. "We were talking about dinner, remember?"

She liked his hands; the warmth and the way his fingers tapered. Slender yet strong.

How could she have forgotten?

"Notice any changes in your vision?"

"More of the same: swirling dots and pebble patterns or a grayish net. Is this what it will be like?" she said. "It makes me dizzy like a whirlpool that never ends. Nauseous."

"That could persist for a long time," he said. "Nothing happens quickly, I'm afraid."

His voice moved. Where was he?

"Except for how I feel about you."

Had he said what she thought she heard?

"What do you mean?"

"You're always getting into trouble," he said.

"Everyone needs a trademark."

But he didn't laugh. She sensed him standing next to her. And all her consciousness settled on his hands enveloping hers.

"You're different from anyone I've ever met." His hands traveled up her arm, to the place where her shoulder met her neck. "I'm getting to like keeping you out of broom closets and safe from attackers."

Was this some rescue fantasy he had? His words didn't feel as welcome as she thought they would. But his warmth and the faint scent of Vetiver did.

From somewhere in the street came the muted clash of cymbals, the thunder of a kettle drum, and the clear peal of a tenor's voice.

"Opéra tonight," he said. "*Don Giovanni.*"

"Believe it or not," she said. "I've taken care of myself since I was eight."

"You're boasting."

Maybe she was. "Boastful or not, it's the way my life's played out. No one's ever wanted to take care of me except my father."

Her hand brushed a stiff plastic rectangle of his badge, then the cold metal of his stethoscope.

"On duty, Doctor?"

"Just on call, until morning."

"So that means?"

"I'm at the mercy of my beeper, but we can have dinner," he said.

"Hungry?" She felt for his warm hand.

And she wanted to be close to him. Right now.

"Famished."

"Feel like appetizers in my room?" she said, turning and pulling his stethoscope. "That's if I can find it."

His footsteps stopped.

What was wrong?

"Attends," he said. "This isn't right."

"What do you mean?" She let go of the stethoscope.

"I know about people in your condition," he said. "You feel grateful but . . ."

"I'm not people. I'm me."

Pause.

"There's the doctor and patient relationship to consider . . ." he said.

"But you're no longer my doctor," she said. "You referred me to a retinologist. Remember?"

Another pause.

"Is that it? A quick jump under the duvet?" he said, his voice low.

Was that anger in his voice?

She sensed him moving away.

Great. She wanted to curl up and disappear. What in the world had she done? Thrown herself at this man who smelled delicious, whose touch thrilled her?

Merde! She deserved some kind of medal, ruining her chances with a man in record time. Talk about faux pas. Why had she done that? Acted so desperate with her doctor!

Better salvage a scrap of dignity and see him to the door.

"Bet you thought I meant it, didn't you?" she said. "I was testing you."

"Liar." His scent wafted in front of her. He pulled her close. "But you're beautiful. Banged up knees, spikey hair, and all."

She didn't expect that.

"You've as much as said I'll never see again."

"What does that matter?"

"A lot."

"To you," he said. "But you have to get over that hurdle. Move on. Try. You'll be happier when you do."

Could she be happy without seeing?

This felt all mixed up and strange. She couldn't remember the last time a man *refused* to sleep with her. Time to take her wounded vanity and climb into a hole.

"You don't get it, do you?" he said.

"Enlighten me."

"Before medicine, I studied literature," he said. "Scribbled poetry. You make me think of Byron's lines . . . 'She walks in beauty like the night.' "

Out in the night, a police siren wailed.

"I wish I wasn't so attracted to you," he said.

Now she was more confused than ever.

And then suddenly he was kissing her like last time. Her leg wrapped around his and she held him tight. He pulled her down onto the horsehair sofa.

His scent was in her hair, his lips brushing her neck. She gripped his back. And that's when his pager went off, beeping near her elbow.

"Merde!" he said.

Non. Non, non, she almost shouted.

"You couldn't pretend you didn't hear it, could you?" she asked, feeling his elbow and warm breath in between kisses on her arm.

She heard clicking as he read his message. Felt his body stiffen. "Not when a three-year-old's spilled acid base photograph developing emulsion and rubbed it in his eyes." She felt him pulling away, his hands helping her up. "If I hurry I'll get there when the ambulance does."

And in two minutes he was gone. Only his Vetiver scent lingered.

She woke up to the rain spattering on the skylight above.

And she felt safe, cocooned in the big warmth of the duvet.

Her senses were heightened. Every part of her tingled remembering his kiss, the way he hadn't stopped. . . .

And then she heard the accordion strains of *Nini le peau de chien* . . .

Again . . . like the background of the phone call on the stranger's cell phone.

She froze.

Was the killer here? In the apartment?

But how?

Doubt invaded her. And for a moment she wondered if she'd gotten it all wrong. Made a mistake. The serial killer was alive and still . . . *non,* that made no sense.

Yet her blood ran cold.

She pulled the duvet off, crawled her way to the door. Listened.

Madame Danoux's voice joined the chorus of *Nini* on the record. Footsteps beat a pattern on the floor as if she were dancing. The old folkdance, *la bourrée.* So Madame Danoux danced by herself on Saturday nights.

But Aimée couldn't sleep any more. She felt for the bed, then sat down on the floor and combed her fingers through her short hair.

She'd set the talking alarm clock to wake her up, but there was no reason to wait. She called Le Drugstore, followed the procedure, and within four minutes spoke to Martin.

"It's like this, *ma petite* mademoiselle,"

said Martin, as if imparting a confirmation gift. "No news at all, nothing really."

She figured his usual police informants had clammed up. "But Martin, you of all people have impeccable connections."

"So some say," he replied. She heard a pleased chuckle in his voice.

"There's a whisper. Something to do with *Don Giovanni*," he said. "Know him?"

"Not personally. It's an opera."

"My source says a Romanian caught in the 11ième for selling Ecstasy died."

"Dragos Iliescu?"

She heard Martin expel a deep breath. Tinged with smoke, no doubt. "Why do you need me? You know already."

"Was it bad dope?"

"The BRIF got involved immediately."

That meant heavy duty. And Morbier was with them.

"If it's not dope, Martin, what is it?"

"Not known by my usual channels. A mystery, they say. Probably the Romanians had a sweet deal. But they got careless, were at the wrong place at the wrong time. People got burned."

Her excitement mounted. Where had she heard that before?

"Burned?"

"And I don't mean figuratively."

■ ■ ■ ■

From the the hallway, she heard water running in Madame Danoux's kitchen.

She pushed the talking clock, which said 1:00 a.m., then pulled on the nearest things she could reach. Her leather skirt, the tight zip-up sweatshirt. She struggled into her ankle boots and felt her way into kitchen.

"Madame Danoux, are you dressed?"

"What a question! Of course, I haven't even taken my makeup off yet . . ."

"Bon," she interrupted. "Be an angel."

"And do what?"

"Come for a drink with me," she said, reaching for Madame Danoux's arm. "Let's go down the street. To the corner."

In the *bar-tabac* on rue Moreau, a block away, Aimée's hand trembled. She couldn't lift the *panache* to her lips without spilling.

"Why so nervous?" asked Madame Danoux, beside her at the counter, yawning. She sounded petulant. "You wanted to come here!"

She gripped Madame Danoux's warm hand. What if the killer was here tonight? But she hadn't confided in her, she had to see if her hunch was right.

"I need to talk with Clothilde, the owner, Mimi's friend," said Aimée.

"Aaah, I know the one."

"Did you see her tonight?"

"By the door," she said. "The accordion player comes, she lets in those she likes. Then locks the door. Only a natural disaster will get you out before dawn."

"Please, can you ask her to join us," she said.

"Let me try and get her attention."

Around her, glasses tinkled, the milk steamer hissed and grumbled, and a woman's shrill laughter came from somewhere farther down the counter. Aimée smelled the thick tang from a cigarette burning somewhere in an ashtray. Here she stood in a smoke-filled café and didn't have one.

She turned toward a conversation. The barman?

"Sorry to interrupt, a pack of Gauloise light please."

"Too bright in here for you?"

"I wish." She'd worn dark glasses, a pair Martine had sent.

"But, I see," he said, his voice hesitant. "I mean, sorry . . ."

"Don't worry," she said. "Everyone stumbles over those phrases. Me, too. How much?"

"Won't your doctor get upset?" he asked.

"I'm a big girl," she said, sliding a twenty franc note along the zinc counter.

She felt Madame Danoux's breath in her hair. "Clothilde's busy. That drink hit me, I'm tired. Let me take you back."

Part of her wanted that. The other part refused. She *had* to find out who had called.

"You go ahead," she said. A frisson of fear passed through her.

"You seem nervous." Madame Danoux squeezed her arm. "Sure?"

"Bien sûr," she said. "I'll get help to go back."

Her landlady left.

"Monsieur, where's the phone?"

"End of the counter."

"Remember a person who used the phone on Monday night?"

"Could have been anyone."

"Someone called me, then they hung up," she said, keeping her voice calm with effort. "I heard the accordion in the background."

"You're lucky," he said. "When they start singing, it's impossible to hear."

Someone pressed a paper into her hand. "That's sheet music."

Sheet music? As though she could read.

"Sorry, my bus broke down. I got here late Monday," the bartender said. "Anyone see who used the phone on Monday? Help this lady?"

"How about Lucas?" said someone at the counter. "He sees everything!"

The remark, greeted with laughter, made her want to slink away, fly a million miles off. Blindness felt like being naked in a world of clothed people. All her expressions were read, but she could decipher none.

"Give me a break, eh!"

She recognized Lucas's voice. But he was laughing.

"Aimée Leduc? Pay no attention to these old men," he said, clutching her elbow. "I know all the songs by heart. You don't need to read. They're jealous."

"Lucas, do you know if Clothilde's still busy?" she said, glad the dark glasses masked her eyes. Milky opaqueness crackled in the corners of her vision. Veins of shooting dull lights throbbed at the edges. Like slowly flowing lava.

Merde. It was if the earth shifted and gravity pulled her sideways.

She clutched the rounded zinc counter, her fingers on the filature, trying to concentrate.

"Clothilde?" Lucas said, stools scraping beside him. "You give me too much credit;

peripheral vision isn't all it's made out to be."

This time his voice boomed over the accordion, tinkling glasses and conversation. "Clothilde!"

"J'arrive!"

The eruptions taking place in her eyes made her dizzy. Blinks of light, a lessening of the pressure on the optic nerve . . . hadn't the retinologist said that? Maybe those pills had already reduced the swelling.

It made her yearn to see more. But deep down she feared it wouldn't happen. Face it. She was afraid to hope.

"Lucas, your women get younger and younger!" said Clothilde.

Aimée heard what sounded like a slap on his rear. And felt the presence of a towering, perfumed woman.

"Clothilde, you broke my heart," he said, "Now I have to go for the young ones."

"*Bonsoir,* Clothilde, I know you're busy," Aimée said. "But Mimi is my neighbor."

"Mimi . . . of course!" she said.

"She mentioned you might help. Someone using your phone called me Monday night about eleven. Remember?"

"Monday, *never,*" she said. "I opened at midnight."

Aimée's heart sank. The counter jumped

as a bottle landed by her.

"*Mais non* . . . what am I saying? Monday night my accordionist started at ten p.m. He left early for an accordion slam . . . whatever that is!"

"Do you remember who was here at the counter?"

"My *habitués,* the regulars."

"Do you know who used the phone?"

"*Chérie,* for one franc, anyone uses the phone," she said.

Aimée expected that. And it could be true. But she suspected Clothilde ran a tight ship and had eyes in the back of her head, like any good owner would. She'd know who drank what, how to keep the regulars happy, when to talk and when to listen.

It was hard to trawl for information and remain casual. Clothilde had been around before Aimée was born. How could she get her to reveal the truth or to let something slip?

"Clothilde, you're right. But today so many use cell phones. Mimi said your memory's sharper than a razor. You see," she leaned toward where she suspected Clotilde to be. "It's a bit private. Wouldn't want the world to know. Or the doctor."

"My ear's right here, *cherie,*" she said. "Turn away, Lucas!"

Aimée had to think fast. Faster than she ever had. And make it work.

"*Alors,* he invested in a project. But he thinks I owe him money . . ." she said, her voice low. Then she paused for dramatic effect. "Call it an investment, I told him. No guarantees, eh? At first it was a gift, then he called it a loan. I don't want to bring it all up again if he's let it pass! But I have to know if he called. Then we'll settle this. Do you understand, Clothilde?"

"What's his name?"

Great . . . how could she get out of this now?

"I can't say, it's not right, if . . . well you know, he's not the one or doesn't . . ."

"But why . . ."

"He called me from here. I remember *Nini peau de chien* in the background."

A perfumed sigh tinged by garlic wafted toward her.

"No wonder. One comes to mind."

Say his name, she prayed.

"*Alors,* he's a bit old for you. Dull, too. But it wouldn't be him, eh?"

Say it, she wanted to yell. *Say it.*

"Age doesn't matter."

Clothilde sighed. "Men continue to surprise me."

Aimée took a deep drag. Clenched her fist,

398

willing her to talk. "He certainly surprised me."

"Mathieu uses the phone. Doesn't believe in cell phones, he tells me. He was here tonight," she said. "Maybe half an hour ago. Hard to believe it was him."

Mathieu?

How could it be Mathieu? Yet thinking back, Chantal had told her the *flics* brought him in for questioning. But attacking her and killing Josiane . . . ?

Aimée felt a garlic-scented breath on her face. "But everyone's taste is different."

"Well, I thought . . ."

"Now that I think about it, Mathieu's father," said Clothilde, "invested in girls. He made everyone turn a blind eye to the women he supplied from our place. In turn, he got favors."

"Mathieu's father? Wasn't he a craftsman?"

"Ask Mimi. The high-ranking SS loved it . . . earthy Parisian girls from Marché d'Aligre. They liked peasant costumes." Clothilde blew a breath of smoke in the air. "Go figure."

"But I thought Mathieu's family were respected *ébénistes.*"

"Eh *chérie,* who was acquiring works of art during the Occupation? 'Buying' is a polite term. 'Appropriating' says it better. Who better to take a wealthy deportee's furniture and make money from it?"

Did that have anything to do with the old woman she'd seen coming out of Mathieu's with the silvery hair?

"Clothilde!"

Voices had risen, singing along with the accordion. Old songs, like her grandmother had played.

"Excuse me, time to close the doors."

"Lucas, mind helping me back?" asked Aimée.

She heard him gulp his wine.

"We'll never get out if we don't leave now."

"D'accord," he agreed.

Out on the street, the only sounds were their footsteps and the click of Lucas's cane on the rain-dampened cobbles. The music had faded into the night. Rain-freshened air scented the stone-walled street.

"How well do you know Mathieu?"

"Listen, that Clothilde talks a blue streak," said Lucas. "She wasn't so clean herself in the war. I heard stories. But people did what they had to. And it's over."

"Do you think Mathieu's hiding something?" she said. "Was he afraid Josiane would find out?"

"Zut!" he said. "We all hide things."

400

"I have to talk with Mathieu," she said. "Take me there."

"Why would I do that?" he said. "I'm tired. Leave all this alone."

She felt inside her bag, found the Beretta.

"Here," she said, taking the cane from him and putting the Beretta in his hand. "Didn't you want to try this?"

"You've got a deal," said Lucas, his voice changed. "I hope you left the safety on or I'll cause some serious damage."

"At least you'll aim better, with your peripheral vision, than I would," she said.

"That's a joke right?"

"But if Mathieu's forgotten, you can remind him."

She felt their way down rue Charenton with the cane. Tap, tap, tap. At the gurgling fountain she remembered and turned right into what she figured was the entrance to the courtyard of Mathieu's shop. The tall doors were closed. She felt all over with the cane, found the digicode, and hit some buttons.

"Who's there?" came an irate reply.

"Pardon, I forgot my uncle Mathieu's digicode. He's asleep. Please let me in," she said.

"Write it down next time."

A loud buzzing came from their right.

She and Lucas pushed the heavy door open.

"How did you know about this entrance through this building?"

"Well, it's opposite the old part of the Résidence built in the Musketeers' time. They all connected at one time. Feel the wall's thickness. Like the Résidence."

"Saves us from going up to rue Faubourg St. Antoine and entering Cour du Bel Air that way."

Or through the back of Passage de la Boule Blanche. She wouldn't do that again.

"Sounds funny to ask this Lucas, but can you see *anything?*"

"I didn't want to admit it, but the little peripheral vision I have crashes at night."

"Crashes?"

"Grays and shadows are subtle at the best of times. Darkness blacks it all out."

Pills. She had to take her pills. *Merde!*

She found them, swallowed, and tapped her way over the cobbles to the gurgling fountain. She stuck her head under, lapped up the water, welcoming the coldness. The clean mineral taste slid down her throat. It must tap into the old artesian source from the Trogneux fountain across the street.

Late-night starlings twittered in the court-yard. The honeysuckle scent she remembered seemed stronger in the night air. By the time they reached the atelier's glass door, she'd tripped several times on the worn stones.

She felt the glass. Tapped it lightly. "Mathieu?"

"Door's open," said Lucas.

She grabbed Lucas's elbow, followed him. Followed the strong smells of paint thinner emanating from Mathieu's atelier.

"Mathieu?"

No answer. From somewhere a Mozart sonata played, low and soothing. A tape, the radio?

She heard Lucas feeling around ahead of her. Wood scraped and was pushed aside. They hadn't gone far. Then a loud *ouff* as Lucas sat down.

"Look, I don't feel good prowling in his atelier. He's probably upstairs asleep. We're blind, so our sleep patterns are off. Night or day means nothing to us, but to the rest of the world it does."

"I'll be right back."

She tapped with the cane, feeling her way ahead. Sensed the legs of work tables, rectangles of picture frames, hollow panels, the thick metal block of what must be the heater emitting sputtering bursts of warmth. Then the stone wall, thick and damp.

And she heard the gun fall on the floor, skidding over the wood. Her reflex was automatic. "Lucas! Duck and cover your head!"

She ducked down under a thick-legged work table. No shot.

"Lucas?"

No answer. Silence.

Then she heard the door close. The metallic ratchet fell as it locked.

Saturday Night

"This came for you, Sergeant Bellan," said the night duty desk officer. "And these messages."

All from Aimée Leduc.

Bellan took them, with his espresso, and sat down at the desk. He'd closed the Beast of Bastille file, sent it to the *frigo.* He wanted to throw Aimée's things in the trash bin to join the cigarette butts, coffee-stained memos, and wilted violets.

But he set Officer Nord's report down to read first. Then he opened the thick envelope, scanned the morgue log, and read the note Aimée's partner, René, had written.

He gulped the espresso.

"I need a driver, officer," he said, stuffing the report in his case.

"No one left in the driving pool tonight, sir," he was told. "We're short on officers if you need a backup."

"No problem, no backup. I'm on special detail. Get me a car."

Loïc Bellan sped over the pont Notre-Dame, the dark Seine illumined by pin-pricks of blue light from the *bateaux-mouches* below. He pulled into the Place Lepine, on the Île de la Cité, where vendors were setting up stalls for the Sunday flower market.

He ran into Hôtel Dieu, flashed his badge, and was pointed in a direction by the sleepy-eyed security guard. Several long hallways and wrong turns later, he found Intensive Care.

"Nurse, I need to speak with a patient in custody, Dragos Iliescu."

From around the night desk came the beeping of machines, and the sound of a floor waxer in the cavernous hallway. The ancient stone had been sandblasted, giving it a butterscotch hue in the dim lighting.

"Let me check, I just came on shift," she said, consulting a computer. He saw the other nurse in the station nudge her, point to a file. A dark blue folder.

"Too late, I'm afraid, Sergeant," she said. "He passed away."

Frustrated, Bellan wanted to kick himself. Why hadn't he come earlier?

"What was the cause of death?"

"The doctors are doing a preliminary now, taking a toxicology screening to determine if it was drugs."

"Here's my card. My number's there. Have the doctor call me the minute he knows."

If he hadn't been so stubborn . . . so rigid in the way he thought. Wasn't that what Marie told him, "Loïc listen to someone else sometime, *then* make up your mind."

Merde!

All the way in the car, he berated himself. There was only one other way. He parked on the curb of 22, boulevard de la Bastille. He turned off the ignition and sat in the car. The small shop was lighted. A minute later he got out.

"*Bonsoir,* Monsieur Tulles," he said. "Is Bidi here?"

"We're just closing up," smiled Monsieur Tulles. "Bidi! Guess you want to ask him more questions."

No answer.

"I'm sorry, that boy with those headphones is . . . Bidi!"

Bellan looked down at his feet. Something about this place, Monsieur Tulles, and Bidi made him tongue-tied. He hesitated, swallowed hard.

"Actually, Monsieur Tulles, if you don't mind, I need Bidi's help."

SATURDAY NIGHT

Aimée shuddered and called out, "Tell me . . . Lucas, are you all right."

Mozart's piano music trilled faintly in the atelier's background.

Had Lucas been knocked out . . . by Mathieu?

"Mathieu . . . who's that?"

A sound like a deadbolt slipping into place.

"Who's there?" Her words caught in her throat.

What was going on?

She couldn't wait to find out, she had to do something. Quickly.

She groped ahead of her along the floor. Felt a sheet of dense, smooth metal. Hard and thick. She figured it was lead.

Something rustled from the far corner.

Her breath caught. She reached her hands out. Felt a shoe . . . no the curved wooden heel of a clog. She kept on. Her fingers came back sticky and metallic smelling. Blood.

Mathieu.

Now she knew why his door was open but he didn't answer. Her fingers brushed a smooth round dome. His head. Then she froze.

He was bald.

Why hadn't she thought to ask before. He was *bald*. No need for that shampoo.

Too late. She'd been about to accuse him of attacking her, killing Josiane, but he couldn't have. So dumb. Why hadn't she realized? If she had, he might still be alive.

And it all fell into place. The tar smell, the burns on Dragos, the lead, and the odd thing she'd knocked over, then touched. She realized that Morbier had been on a wild goose chase looking all over Paris for the "explosives" when they were here.

Right here.

She felt around Mathieu's body. Next to the sheet of lead were glass bulbs and beakers. Like the ones René had found. But these had raised letters on them. On the bottom.

РАДПИОАКГИВНЬIЙ

The script must be Cyrillic. But she traced an upside down U, then numbers. Her stomach jolted.

The symbol for enriched uranium.

U-235.

Weapons grade enriched uranium.

Probably five or ten gram samples from the size of the beaker. Dangerous enough. More than lethal if enough samples were put together. Enough for a dirty bomb.

And the killer had the perfect cover for customs checks.

Of course he must have been here, unpacking a shipment. They'd interrupted him. She prayed he'd knocked Lucas out, not killed him. All she could do was to try to get him talking. Get him near her.

"I know how you did it," she said, her voice steady. "Ingenious. And I have to say, I admire your plan. But why?"

The Mozart piano concerto rose in the background.

"You," he breathed. "You're the one."

Her breath caught again as she recognized the voice. Shivers ran down her spine. The uranium . . . where was it? Had she touched it?

"I don't understand. Why?"

"It's my business," said Malraux. "I sell and trade."

"This isn't smuggling Fabergé eggs, antique icons, or fake Lee jeans," she said.

"Uranium and radiation kill people. Horribly."

"Commodities," he said. "They're called commodities."

"So you know the price of everything and the value of nothing."

"I like that."

"Oscar Wilde said it first."

"But you're wrong," said Malraux. "I know the price and the value."

Malraux's tone, chillingly matter-of-fact, filled her with disgust and fear.

"It's a business," he said. "Like any other."

"But Josiane found out, didn't she? Somehow Vincent owed you. In return he let you use his e-mail account."

She heard him sigh. "That part I'm sorry for," he said, his voice softening, "I never wanted to hurt her. And if you hadn't got in the way . . ."

"Me?" As if it were her fault?

"I was trying to talk Josiane out of writing her story. Make her listen to reason. This was the last shipment."

It was always the last shipment, the last time, the last throw of the dice.

"Years ago, we were lovers," he said. "But we were married to other people at the time. You know, regret lodged in my heart. Buried deep. Then when we met again after all those years at an Opéra benefit . . . it was like we'd never been apart."

Startled, Aimée listened. Had he been at least a little in love with Josiane? Had she fallen for him again, then discovered what he'd done? And paid with her life?

"I'm not a killer."

"So how do you explain Mathieu?"

"He tried to stop me tonight; he'd grown a conscience."

"Maybe over something else," she said. "But I don't believe he knew what you really were doing. You'd planned it all. From someone in your set you heard of the Beast of Bastille's release."

"My cousin's married to his lawyer, Verges."

Of course.

"So you staged a copycat murder and Vaduz conveniently died before he could deny murdering Josiane. All to conceal the fact that you had the uranium, sheathed in lead, hidden in the drawers of furniture."

"Mademoiselle, you've got something under that messy head of hair after all."

Now she wanted to punch him. But she had to get close enough first. Stay patient, keep him talking. Keep him talking until she could figure a way out.

She kept feeling around with her hands,

away from Mathieu. Poor, sad Mathieu.

"I didn't understand why Mathieu dealt with you," she said. "But he had to. You had the sales connections."

"And now I have the pieta dura. Mathieu tried to keep the real estate developers at bay so he could keep his atelier open," said Malraux. "It's over. He fought a losing battle. The smart choice would have been for him to join the winner."

Her hands touched a large, cold, ceramic jug . . . beaded with chill liquid. Drinking water.

"But it's so ingenious," she said. "These antique pieces all have secret compartments, hidden places and false fronts, pillars that pull out. They're so heavy anyway, adding sheets of lead wouldn't matter."

"Please know, that night, when I had you round the neck," he said. "I couldn't do it. You're attractive, you know . . ."

She doubted that he had spared her deliberately. He made her sick.

"Then people came," he said. "I heard Josiane run towards the atelier."

The big work table crashed against her. Tools clattered onto the floor. Over Mathieu's body?

She wondered if the lights were on? Malraux must have covered the windows. The

412

atelier would have shades or wooden shutters. Mozart's piano étude soared now. He must have turned up the volume . . . easier to kill her that way.

Where was her Beretta?

"I've dealt with this scientist for years," said Malraux, his voice patient now. She heard him moving, hammering things. Shoving things across the floor. "We met when he wanted to sell some of his family icons. Later, his friends' families' icons. Then the country's power shifted. This scientist liked heading a nuclear submarine plant, having a country *dacha* and driving a Lada. But the Soviet Union fell and there was no more gas for the Lada or food on the table. But he still has access to the top grade stuff . . . not orphaned uranium that was lost, stolen or abandoned, or spent nuclear fuel. *He* suggested it to me, he has the contacts here. All I did was arrange for transport. That fool Dragos thought he could double-cross me. Greedy. Look what happened."

"Dead from radiation sickness." She shook her head.

"People want my product. Finding buyers presents no problem," he said. "It's like in the war. My mother had paintings and art for sale to the highest bidder. Who didn't?

That was, anyone who wanted to survive. The *Oberstampführer* dabbled in art. And in Maman. How else could she have kept the business? While Papa dabbled in everyone and everything. Clothilde was his mistress once."

Perhaps that was why she'd pointed Aimée at the wrong person.

"Where's Lucas?"

No answer. She heard rubbing and scraping. Tried to visualize where she was. Not far away from the heater. But were the lights on . . . was he watching her closely? Or was he more attentive to his uranium? Then her hand hit a pole . . . a lamp? It felt hot.

Now she had a plan. She had to keep him talking and get him to touch her.

"No one deals in the art world wearing white gloves." A snicker. "Only the wealthy own art. The ones with power. They used to say if there were no Jews, there'd be no art collectors. *Alors,* before the war, it was true. In art, one trades with those in power. Let's face it. You need bread you go to the boulangerie. To pass something down in the family, you go first to the art dealer, then the stockbroker. Nowadays they buy cars, computers, bigger houses — but the best investment, besides diamonds, is art. Look how it endures."

She shuddered at his tone. He sounded as if he spoke about differences of investment opinion, not weapons grade enriched uranium capable of killing and irradiating a whole chunk of some city.

Lights blipped across her eyes . . . crinkled then waved. She steadied herself against the table.

"Don't get any ideas," he said.

"It's my eyes . . . they make me dizzy."

"Don't worry, that won't matter soon."

"What are you doing?"

Of course, he'd kill her.

"None of your business."

She heard him swearing, slamming drawers.

"So Dragos skimmed some uranium off the top?"

She felt the hard rungs of a chair whack her ribs. A cracking, searing pain shot up her side. Then again.

Try to stay upright. Keep him talking, keep his attention away from her.

"But Mathieu's a craftsman . . ."

"Mathieu's father participated, too. And his father. Half the art world steals from the other half. Over and over. Skip a generation or two and the original owner steals it back. You think Leonardo da Vinci's work stays in one family? Look at the Comte de Breuve."

The water cooler jug was on the stand. Heavy.

"I thought you dealt in art because . . ."

"I'm passionate about it?" he interrupted, his educated formal French gone. "I hate old things. They smell. Ever since I could crawl, we've had decaying, musty pieces built or painted by dead people *everywhere.* I'm alive. I don't want to be chained to the expressions of someone who died four hundred years ago."

"So it's all a front?"

"Front? People see what they want to see. The *hôtel particulier* . . . no real choice there. If I sold it, taxes would cost me eighty percent of the profit on the sale of the building."

She clung to the lamp pole for support. Gasped. Her ribs felt as if they were broken.

"Everything's protected by historical decree. The furniture goes with the place, I can't even sell it. The oil paintings are blistered, the lacquered furniture peeling, and I don't have the money for repairs. It costs next to nothing to stay there if I use it for a gallery/showroom like my parents did. But in my wing, everything comes from Ikea and Conran. Plastic — that hated word — I love it."

She felt the base of the lamp.

416

"You know you're wrong about Vaduz," he volunteered

His footsteps were closer. She heard him grunting and pushing. Something inching along on the floor. And that tar smell. His shampoo. He couldn't be much more than an arm's length away.

"But I knew Vaduz didn't attack me," she said.

She lurched against the porcelain water cooler. It cracked and shattered. Water sprayed and flooded over the sloped floor, pooling toward the heater.

"*Salope* . . . you've got my tuxedo sopping wet!"

She whammed the lamp full force in the direction of his voice. Her ribs jabbed like knives against her skin. As the glass bulb shattered, she felt him recoil. But she didn't want that.

She thrust the lamp pole forward, whacking him again, keeping the exposed socket toward him. She felt him trying to get it away. But it connected with something metallic on his wrist. A bracelet? Or his cufflinks? He yelled as the alternating current traveled up his right hand. Shook and tried to get free. She held the pole as long as she could. He went rigid. She heard a faint low buzz, barely audible over the music.

And then water dripped on her and she let go of the pole.

Something beeped. Layers of unconsciousness peeled away, slowly, like veils of fog. She felt around for the phone in her pocket. *"Allô?"*

"You're a Catholic, aren't you Leduc?" said Bellan.

Echoing sounds came from the background.

Her brain felt fuzzy, her mouth even more. Little twitches of light ran across her eyelids.

"Made my First Communion," she said.

"*Bon* . . . where would you hide something in a chapel?"

"Under the holy water font." It was the first thing that came into her mind. "Sometimes they have a donation box in the bottom. But if it's uranium you're looking for, there's some right here. Bodies, too."

"Where?"

"Mathieu's atelier. Easy to find. We probably glow in the dark."

She heard moaning and someone stirring.

"Better hurry, someone's waking up," she said. "I wish I could tell you who it is."

Bellan emptied the whiskey flask down the toilet, pulled his jacket off the hook in the dormitory, and left. In the Métro, he fingered the folded pamphlet for parents he'd picked up at the Mairie. He climbed the Montgallet Métro stairs and almost turned back. *Non,* keep going, he told himself.

Place de Fontenay, in the shadowed twilight, was crowded with children returning home from lessons and couples going out. Clusters of discount computer shops in nineteenth-century storefronts lined the street. The old, faded lettering *tapisserie* was visible under a sign reading TEKNOWARE. Bells pealed from a distant church.

Bellan saw the Jardin de Reuilly, a vast open green space with its state-of-the-art covered indoor pool. The girls would love it; Monique could start swimming lessons.

Bellan paused at the door of 11, rue Montgallet, under the sign *Services Sociaux Assoc de parents d'enfants déficients mentaux.* Three cigarettes later, he still paced in the doorway.

Would it matter to Marie if he went in? Would she believe him? And what would a meeting of blathering, self-involved parents with Down syndrome children tell him that he didn't know? That he didn't feel already? Who needed a moan and groan session . . . he got enough of that at the Commissairiat with all the staff cuts.

He turned to leave and bumped into a middle-aged man, out of breath, who held the hand of a young girl. A Down syndrome girl who was laughing.

"Excuse us, we're late," he said. "The soccer game ran into overtime."

Bellan noticed the girl's striped jersey, black shorts, muddy soccer cleats, and socks. And her flushed face, wreathed in smiles.

"Who won?"

"My daughter Arlette's team. She's the goalie," he said, beaming. "On to the quarterfinals!'

Arlette hugged her father, then reached out her mud-spattered palm to Bellan.

"Well done," he said, shaking her hand.

"After you, monsieur," the man said, reaching for the door. "We don't want to make you late, too."

Bellan's hand twisted in his pocket. He couldn't do what Marie or anyone wanted him to. Only what his heart told him to. And for that he had to take the first step.

"I'm already late. *Merci,*" Bellan said. "But

I'm here." He took a deep breath and went in.

SUNDAY EVENING

Aimée stroked Miles Davis. His wet nose nudged her neck and his dogtags tinkled over the hospital bed.

"I think you have a princess complex," said René, a shadowy figure beside her.

"Why?" She felt her taped-up ribs. Smelled roses somewhere near her. A glowing rectangular blur of white passed in the distance. A nurse?

"In pre-op you said some funny things under anesthesia."

She froze. "*Mon dieu,* what did I say?"

She heard him laughing.

"Of course, it's all the opposite," she said, on the defensive. Had she mentioned Guy? Stupid, that would go nowhere. "Everyone babbles the opposite of what they really think. Thanks for the roses," she said, hoping to cover her embarrassment.

"Don't thank me, the card is signed *Guy,*" he said. "You said something about losing your crown."

Crown? Oh no. Her father had always called her his princess.

"But I couldn't find a crown so I brought

421

you this instead."

She felt something long and slim pressed in her hand. It shone and gleamed, like a dancing flicker of stars. Distorted but steady. She began to focus. Her dizziness had disappeared. "A wand . . . to make your dreams come true."

She could see it now. She grinned. "They already have." In more ways than one, she thought. "You sent Vincent's file to the *Proc.*"

Miles Davis responded with a resounding bark.

And a gust from the Seine blew in the hospital window, shifting the sheets, freshening the air, a foretaste of a mild winter.

ABOUT THE AUTHOR

Cara Black lives with her husband, a bookseller, and their son in San Francisco, and frequently travels to Paris.

We hope you have enjoyed this Large Print book. Other Thorndike, Wheeler, and Chivers Press Large Print books are available at your library or directly from the publishers.

For information about current and upcoming titles, please call or write, without obligation, to:

Publisher
Thorndike Press
295 Kennedy Memorial Drive
Waterville, ME 04901
Tel. (800) 223-1244

or visit our Web site at:

www.gale.com/thorndike
www.gale.com/wheeler

OR

Chivers Large Print
published by BBC Audiobooks Ltd
St James House, The Square
Lower Bristol Road
Bath BA2 3SB
England
Tel. +44(0) 800 136919
email: bbcaudiobooks@bbc.co.uk
www.bbcaudiobooks.co.uk

All our Large Print titles are designed for easy reading, and all our books are made to last.